PAUL AUSTER

Leviathan

faber and faber

First published in the UK in 1992
by Faber and Faber Ltd
Bloomsbury House
74–77 Great Russell Street
London WC1B 3DA
Open market paperback edition first published in 1993
UK paperback edition first published in 1993
This paperback edition first published in 2011

Printed in England by CPI Bookmarque, Croydon

The right of Paul Auster to be identified as author of this work has
been asserted in accordance with Section 77 of the
Copyright, Designs and Patents Act 1988

A CIP record for this book
is available from the British Library

ISBN 978-0-571-27661-5

2 4 6 8 10 9 7 5 3 1

for Don DeLillo

Every actual State is corrupt.

Ralph Waldo Emerson

Six days ago, a man blew himself up by the side of a road in northern Wisconsin. There were no witnesses, but it appears that he was sitting on the grass next to his parked car when the bomb he was building accidentally went off. According to the forensic reports that have just been published, the man was killed instantly. His body burst into dozens of small pieces, and fragments of his corpse were found as far as fifty feet away from the site of the explosion. As of today (July 4, 1990), no one seems to have any idea who the dead man was. The FBI, working along with the local police and agents from the Bureau of Alcohol, Tobacco and Firearms, began their investigation by looking into the car, a seven-year-old blue Dodge with Illinois license plates, but they quickly learned that it had been stolen – filched in broad daylight from a Joliet parking lot on June 12. The same thing happened when they examined the contents of the man's wallet, which by some miracle had come through the explosion more or less unscathed. They thought they had stumbled onto a wealth of clues – driver's license, Social Security number, credit cards – but once they fed these documents into the computer, each one turned out to have been either forged or stolen. Fingerprints would have been the next step, but in this case there were no fingerprints, since the man's hands had been obliterated by the bomb. Nor was the car of any help to them. The Dodge had been turned into a mass of charred steel and melted plastic, and in spite of their efforts, not a single print could be found on it. Perhaps they'll have more luck with his teeth, assuming there are enough teeth to work with, but that's bound to take some time, perhaps as long as several months. In the end, there's no doubt they'll think of something, but until they can establish the identity of their mangled victim, their case has little chance of getting off the ground.

As far as I'm concerned, the longer it takes them the better. The story I have to tell is rather complicated, and unless I finish it before they come up with their answer, the words I'm about to write will mean nothing. Once the secret is out, all sorts of lies are going to be told, ugly distortions will circulate in the newspapers and magazines, and within a matter of days a man's reputation will be destroyed. It's not that I want to defend what he did, but since he's no longer in a position to defend himself, the least I can do is explain who he was and give the true story of how he happened to be on that road in northern Wisconsin. That's why I have to work fast: to be ready for them when the moment comes. If by some chance the mystery remains unsolved, I'll simply hold on to what I have written, and no one will need to know a thing about it. That would be the best possible outcome: a perfect standstill, not one word spoken by either side. But I mustn't count on that. In order to do what I have to do, I have to assume they're already closing in on him, that sooner or later they're going to find out who he was. And not just when I've had enough time to finish this – but at any moment, at any moment beginning now.

The day after the explosion, the wire services ran a brief article about the case. It was one of those cryptic, two-paragraph stories they bury in the middle of the paper, but I happened to catch it in *The New York Times* while I was eating lunch that afternoon. Almost inevitably, I began to think about Benjamin Sachs. There was nothing in the article that pointed to him in any definite way, and yet at the same time everything seemed to fit. We hadn't talked in close to a year, but he had said enough during our last conversation to convince me that he was in deep trouble, rushing headlong toward some dark, unnameable disaster. If that's too vague, I should add that he mentioned bombs as well, that he talked about them endlessly during his visit, and for the next eleven months I had walked around with just such a fear inside

2

me – that he was going to kill himself, that one day I would open the newspaper and read that my friend had blown himself up. It was no more than a wild intuition at that point, one of those insane leaps into the void, and yet once the thought entered my head, I couldn't get rid of it. Then, two days after I ran across the article, a pair of FBI agents came knocking at my door. The moment they announced who they were, I understood that I was right. Sachs was the man who had blown himself up. There couldn't be any question about it. Sachs was dead, and the only way I could help him now was to keep his death to myself.

It was probably fortunate that I read the article when I did, although I remember wishing at the time that I hadn't even seen it. If nothing else, it gave me a couple of days to absorb the shock. When the FBI men showed up here to ask their questions, I was already prepared for them, and that helped me to keep myself under control. It also didn't hurt that an extra forty-eight hours had gone by before they managed to track me down. Among the objects recovered from Sachs's wallet, it seems there was a slip of paper bearing my initials and telephone number. That was how they came to be looking for me, but as luck would have it, the number was for my telephone back home in New York, and for the past ten days I've been in Vermont, living with my family in a rented house where we plan to spend the rest of the summer. God knows how many people they had to talk to before they discovered I was here. If I mention in passing that this house is owned by Sachs's ex-wife, it is only to give one example of how tangled and complicated this story finally is.

I did my best to play dumb for them, to give away as little as I could. No, I said, I hadn't read the article in the paper. I didn't know anything about the bombs or stolen cars or back-country roads in Wisconsin. I was a writer, I said, a man who wrote novels for a living, and if they wanted to check into who I was, they could go right ahead – but it wasn't going to help them with their case, they'd only be wasting their time. Probably so, they said, but what about the slip of paper in the dead man's wallet? They weren't trying to accuse me of anything, but the fact that he'd been carrying around my telephone number seemed to prove there was a connection between us. I had to admit that, didn't I? Yes, I said, of course I did, but just because it looked like that didn't mean it was true. There were a thousand ways that man could have gotten hold of my number. I had friends scattered all over the world, and any one of them could have passed it on to a stranger. Perhaps that stranger had passed it on to another stranger, who in turn had passed it on to yet another stranger. Perhaps, they said, but why would anyone carry around the telephone number of a person he didn't know? Because I'm a writer, I said. Oh? they said, and what difference does that make? Because my books are published, I said. People read them, and I don't have any idea who they are. Without even knowing it, I enter the lives of strangers, and for as long as they have my book in their hands, my words are the only reality that exists for them. That's normal, they said, that's the way it is with books. Yes, I said, that's the way it is, but sometimes these people turn out to be crazy. They read your book, and something about it strikes a chord deep in their soul. All of a sudden, they imagine that you belong to them, that you're the only friend they have in the world. To illustrate my point, I gave them several examples – all of them true, all of them taken directly from my own experience. The unbalanced letters, the telephone calls at three o'clock in the morning, the anonymous threats. Just last year, I continued, I discovered that someone had been impersonating me – answering letters in my name, walking into bookstores and autographing my books, hovering like some malignant shadow around the edges of my life. A book is a mysterious object, I said, and once it floats out into the world, anything can happen. All kinds of mischief can be caused, and there's not a damned thing you can do about it. For better or worse, it's completely out of your control.

I don't know if they found my denials convincing or not. I tend to think not, but even if they didn't believe a word I said, it's possible that my strategy bought me some time. Considering that I had never spoken to an FBI agent before, I don't feel too bad

4

about the way I handled myself during the interview. I was calm, I was polite, I managed to project the proper combination of helpfulness and bafflement. That alone was something of a triumph for me. Generally speaking, I don't have much talent for deception, and in spite of my efforts over the years, I've rarely fooled anyone about anything. If I managed to turn in a creditable performance the day before yesterday, the FBI men were at least partially responsible for it. It wasn't anything they said so much as how they looked, the way they dressed for their roles with such perfection, confirming in every detail the way I had always imagined FBI men should look: the lightweight summer suits, the sturdy brogans, the wash-and-wear shirts, the aviator sunglasses. These were the obligatory sunglasses, so to speak, and they lent an artificial quality to the scene, as if the men who wore them were merely actors, walk-ons hired to play a bit part in some low-budget movie. All this was oddly comforting to me, and when I look back on it now, I understand how this sense of unreality worked to my advantage. It allowed me to think of myself as an actor as well, and because I had become someone else, I suddenly had the right to deceive them, to lie without the slightest twinge of conscience.

They weren't stupid, however. One was in his early forties, and the other was a good deal younger, perhaps as young as twenty-five or twenty-six, but they both had a certain look in their eyes that kept me on my guard the whole time they were here. It's difficult to pinpoint exactly what was so menacing about that look, but I think it had something to do with its blankness, its refusal to commit itself, as if it were watching everything and nothing at the same time. So little was divulged by that look, I could never be sure what either of those men was thinking. Their eyes were too patient, somehow, too skilled at suggesting indifference, but for all that they were alert, relentlessly alert in fact, as if they had been trained to make you feel uncomfortable, to make you conscious of your flaws and transgressions, to make you squirm in your skin. Their names were Worthy and Harris, but I forget which one was which. As physical specimens, they were

5

disturbingly alike, almost as if they were younger and older versions of the same person: tall, but not too tall; well built, but not too well built; sandy hair, blue eyes, thick hands with impeccably clean fingernails. It's true that their conversational styles were different, but I don't want to make too much of first impressions. For all I know they take turns, switching roles back and forth whenever they feel like it. For my visit two days ago, the young one played the heavy. His questions were very blunt, and he seemed to take his job too much to heart, rarely cracking a smile, for example, and treating me with a formality that sometimes verged on sarcasm and irritation. The old one was more relaxed and amiable, readier to let the conversation take its natural course. He's no doubt more dangerous because of that, but I have to admit that talking to him wasn't entirely unpleasant. When I began to tell him about some of the crackpot responses to my books, I could see that the subject interested him, and he let me go on with my digression longer than I would have expected. I suppose he was feeling me out, encouraging me to ramble on so he could get some sense of who I was and how my mind worked, but when I came to the business about the impostor, he actually offered to start an investigation into the problem for me. That might have been a trick, of course, but I somehow doubt it. I don't need to add that I turned him down, but if the circumstances had been any different, I probably would have thought twice about accepting his help. It's something that has plagued me for a long time now, and I would dearly love to get to the bottom of it.

'I don't read many novels,' the agent said. 'I never seem to have time for them.'

'No, not many people do,' I said.

'But yours must be pretty good. If they weren't, I doubt you'd be bothered so much.'

'Maybe I get bothered because they're bad. Everyone is a literary critic these days. If you don't like a book, threaten the author. There's a certain logic to that approach. Make the bastard pay for what he's done to you.'

'I suppose I should sit down and read one of them myself,' he said. 'To see what all the fuss is about. You wouldn't mind, would you?'

'Of course I wouldn't mind. That's why they're in the bookstores. So people can read them.'

It was a curious way for the visit to end – writing down the titles of my books for an FBI agent. Even now, I'm hard-pressed to know what he was after. Perhaps he thinks he'll find some clues in them, or perhaps it was just a subtle way of telling me that he'll be back, that he hasn't finished with me yet. I'm still their only lead, after all, and if they go on the assumption that I lied to them, then they're not about to forget me. Beyond that, I haven't the vaguest notion of what they're thinking. It seems unlikely that they consider me a terrorist, but I say that only because I know I'm not. They know nothing, and therefore they could be working on that premise, furiously searching for something that would link me to the bomb that went off in Wisconsin last week. And even if they aren't, I have to accept the fact that they'll be on my case for a long time to come. They'll ask questions, they'll dig into my life, they'll find out who my friends are, and sooner or later Sachs's name will come up. In other words, the whole time I'm here in Vermont writing this story, they'll be busy writing their own story. It will be my story, and once they've finished it, they'll know as much about me as I do myself.

My wife and daughter returned home about two hours after the FBI men left. They had gone off early that morning to spend the day with friends, and I was glad they hadn't been around for Harris's and Worthy's visit. My wife and I share almost everything with each other, but in this case I don't think I should tell her what happened. Iris has always been very fond of Sachs, but I come first for her, and if she discovered that I was about to get into trouble with the FBI because of him, she would do everything in her power to make me stop. I can't run that risk now. Even if I managed to convince her that I was doing the right thing, it would take a long time to wear her down, and I don't have that luxury, I have to spend every minute on the job I've set for myself. Besides, even if she gave in, she would only worry herself sick about it, and I don't see how any good could come of that. Eventually, she's going to learn the truth anyway; when the time comes, everything will be dragged out into the open. It's not that I want to deceive her, I simply want to spare her for as long as possible. As it happens, I don't think that will be terribly difficult. I'm here to write, after all, and if Iris thinks I'm up to my old tricks out in my little shack every day, what harm can come of that? She'll assume I'm scribbling away on my new novel, and when she sees how much time I'm devoting to it, how much progress is being made from my long hours of work, she'll feel happy. Iris is a part of the equation, too, and without her happiness I don't think I would have the courage to begin.

This is the second summer we've spent in this place. Back in the old days, when Sachs and his wife used to come here every July and August, they would sometimes invite me up to visit, but those were always brief excursions, and I rarely stayed for more than three or four nights. After Iris and I were married nine years ago, we made the trip together several times, and once we even helped Fanny and Ben paint the outside of the house. Fanny's parents bought the property during the Depression, at a time when farms like this one could be had for next to nothing. It came with more than a hundred acres and its own private pond, and although the house was run down, it was spacious and airy inside, and only minor improvements were needed to make it habitable. The Goodmans were New York City school teachers, and they could never afford to do much with the place after they bought it, so for all these years the house has kept its primitive, bare-bones look: the iron bedsteads, the potbellied stove in the kitchen, the cracked ceilings and walls, the gray painted floors. Still, there's something solid in this dilapidation, and it would be difficult for anyone not to feel at home here. For me, the great lure of the house is its remoteness. It sits on top of a small mountain, four miles from the nearest village by way of a narrow dirt road. The winters must be ferocious on this mountain, but during the summer everything is green, with birds singing all around you, and the meadows are filled with countless wildflowers: orange hawkweed, red clover, maiden pink, buttercup. About a hundred feet from the main house, there's a simple outbuilding that Sachs used as his work studio whenever he was here. It's hardly more than a cabin, with three small rooms, a kitchenette, and a bathroom, and ever since it was vandalized twelve or thirteen winters ago, it has fallen into disrepair. The pipes have cracked, the electricity has been turned off, the linoleum is peeling up from the floor. I mention these things because that is where I am now – sitting at a green table in the middle of the largest room, holding a pen in my hand. For as long as I knew him, Sachs spent every summer writing at this same table, and this is the room where I saw him for the last time, where he poured out his heart to me and let me in on his terrible secret. If I concentrate hard enough on the memory of that night, I can almost delude myself into thinking that he's still here. It's as if his words were still hanging in the air around me, as if I could still reach out my hand and touch him. It was a long and grueling conversation, and when we finally came to the end of it (at five or six in the morning), he made me promise not to let his secret go beyond the walls of this room. Those were his exact words: that nothing he said should escape this room. For the time being, I'll be able to keep my promise. Until the moment comes for me to show what I've written here, I can comfort myself with the thought that I won't be breaking my word.

The first time we met, it was snowing. More than fifteen years have gone by since that day, but I can still bring it back whenever I wish. So many other things have been lost for me, but I remember that meeting with Sachs as clearly as any event in my life.

It was a Saturday afternoon in February or March, and the two of us had been invited to give a joint reading of our work at a bar in the West Village. I had never heard of Sachs, but the person who called me was too rushed to answer my questions over the phone. 'He's a novelist,' she said. 'His first book was published a couple of years ago.' Her call came on a Wednesday night, just three days before the reading was supposed to take place, and there was something close to panic in her voice. Michael Palmer, the poet who was supposed to appear on Saturday, had just canceled his trip to New York, and she wondered if I would be willing to stand in for him. It was a somewhat backhanded request, but I told her I would do it anyway. I hadn't published much work at that point in my life – six or seven stories in little magazines, a handful of articles and book reviews – and it wasn't as though people were clamoring for the privilege of hearing me read out loud to them. So I accepted the frazzled woman's offer, and for the next two days I fell into a panic of my own, frantically searching through the midget world of my collected stories for something that wouldn't embarrass me, for one scrap of writing that would be good enough to expose to a roomful of strangers. On Friday afternoon, I stopped in at several bookstores and asked for Sachs's novel. It seemed only right that I should know something about his work before I met him, but the book was already two years old, and no one had it in stock.

As chance would have it, an immense storm blew in from the Midwest on Friday night, and by Saturday morning a foot and a half of snow had fallen on the city. The reasonable thing would have been to get in touch with the woman who had called me, but I had stupidly forgotten to ask for her number, and when I still hadn't heard from her by one o'clock, I figured I should get myself downtown as quickly as possible. I bundled up in my overcoat and galoshes, stuck the manuscript of my most recent story into one of the coat pockets, and then tramped out onto Riverside Drive, heading toward the subway station at 116th Street and Broadway. The sky was beginning to clear by then, but the streets and sidewalks were still clogged with snow, and there was scarcely any traffic. A few cars and trucks had been abandoned in tall drifts by the curb, and every now and then a lone vehicle would come inching down the street, skidding out of control whenever the driver tried to stop for a red light. I normally would have enjoyed this mayhem, but the weather was too fierce that day for me to lift my nose out of my scarf. The temperature had been falling steadily since sunrise, and by now the air was bitter, with wild surges of wind blowing off the Hudson, enormous gusts that literally pushed my body up the street. I was half-numb by the time I reached the subway station, but in spite of everything, it appeared that the trains were still running. This surprised me, and as I walked down the stairs and bought my token, I assumed that meant the reading was on after all.

I made it to Nashe's Tavern at ten past two. The place was open, but once my eyes adjusted to the darkness inside, I saw that no one was there. A bartender in a white apron stood behind the bar, methodically drying shot-glasses with a red towel. He was a hefty man of about forty, and he studied me carefully as I approached, almost as if he regretted this interruption of his solitude.

'Isn't there supposed to be a reading here in about twenty minutes?' I asked. The moment the words left my mouth, I felt like a fool for saying them.

'It was canceled,' the bartender said. 'With all that slop out there today, there wouldn't have been much point to it. Poetry's a beautiful thing, but it's hardly worth freezing your ass off for.'

I sat down on one of the barstools and ordered a bourbon. I was still shivering from my walk in the snow, and I wanted to warm my innards before I ventured outside again. I polished off the drink in two swallows, then ordered a refill because the first one had tasted so good. Midway through that second bourbon, another customer walked into the bar. He was a tall, exceedingly thin young man with a narrow face and a full brown beard. I watched him as he stamped his boots on the floor a couple of times, smacked his gloved hands together, and exhaled loudly from the effects of the cold. There was no question that he cut an odd figure – towering there in his moth-eaten coat with a New York Knicks baseball cap perched on his head and a navy blue scarf wrapped around the cap to protect his ears. He looked like someone with a bad toothache, I thought, or else like some half-starved Russian soldier stranded on the outskirts of Stalingrad. These two images came to me in rapid succession, the first one

11

comic, the second one forlorn. In spite of his ridiculous get-up, there was something fierce in his eyes, an intensity that quelled any desire to laugh at him. He resembled Ichabod Crane, perhaps, but he was also John Brown, and once you got past his costume and his gangly basketball forward's body, you began to see an entirely different sort of person: a man who missed nothing, a man with a thousand wheels turning in his head.

He stood in the doorway for a few moments scanning the empty room, then walked up to the bartender and asked more or less the same question that I had asked ten minutes earlier. The bartender gave more or less the same answer he had given me, but in this case he also gestured with a thumb in my direction, pointing to where I was sitting at the end of the bar. 'That one came for the reading, too,' he said. 'You're probably the only two guys in New York who were crazy enough to leave the house today.'

'Not quite,' said the man with the scarf wrapped around his head. 'You forgot to count yourself.'

'I didn't forget,' the bartender said. 'It's just that I don't count. I've got to be here, you see, and you don't. That's what I'm talking about. If I don't show up, I lose my job.'

'But I came here to do a job, too,' the other one said. 'They told me I was going to earn fifty dollars. Now they've called off the reading, and I've lost the subway fare to boot.'

'Well, that's different, then,' the bartender said. 'If you were supposed to read, then I guess you don't count either.'

'That leaves just one person in the whole city who went out when he didn't have to.'

'If you're talking about me,' I said, finally entering the conversation, 'then your list is down to zero.'

The man with the scarf wrapped around his head turned to me and smiled. 'Ah, then that means you're Peter Aaron, doesn't it?'

'I suppose it does,' I said. 'But if I'm Peter Aaron, then you must be Benjamin Sachs.'

'The one and only,' Sachs answered, letting out a short, self-deprecatory laugh. He walked over to where I was sitting and extended his right hand. 'I'm very happy you're here,' he said. 'I've been reading some of your stuff lately and was looking forward to meeting you.'

That was how our friendship began – sitting in that deserted bar fifteen years ago, each one buying drinks for the other until we both ran out of money. It must have lasted three or four hours, for I distinctly remember that when we finally staggered out into the cold again, night had already fallen. Now that Sachs is dead, I find it unbearable to think back to what he was like then, to remember all the generosity and humor and intelligence that poured out of him that first time we met. In spite of the facts, it's difficult for me to imagine that the person who sat with me in the bar that day was the same person who wound up destroying himself last week. The journey must have been so long for him, so horrible, so fraught with suffering, I can scarcely think about it without wanting to cry. In fifteen years, Sachs traveled from one end of himself to the other, and by the time he came to that last place, I doubt he even knew who he was anymore. So much distance had been covered by then, it wouldn't have been possible for him to remember where he had begun.

'I generally manage to keep up with what's going on,' he said, untying the scarf from under his chin and removing it along with the baseball cap and his long brown overcoat. He flung the whole pile onto the barstool next to him and sat down. 'Until two weeks ago, I'd never even heard of you. Now, all of a sudden, you seem to be popping up everywhere. To begin with, I ran across your piece on Hugo Ball's diaries. An excellent little article, I thought, deft and nicely argued, an admirable response to the issues at stake. I didn't agree with all your points, but you made your case well, and I respected the seriousness of your position. This guy believes in art too much, I said to myself, but at least he knows where he stands and has the wit to recognize that other views are possible. Then, three or four days after that, a magazine arrived in the mail, and the first thing I opened to was a story with your name on it. *The Secret Alphabet*, the one about the student who keeps finding messages written on the walls of buildings. I loved

13

it. I loved it so much that I read it three times. Who is this Peter Aaron? I wondered, and where has he been hiding himself? When Kathy what's-her-name called to tell me that Palmer had bagged out of the reading, I suggested that she get in touch with you.'

'So you're the one responsible for dragging me down here,' I said, too stunned by his lavish compliments to think of anything but that feeble reply.

'Well, admittedly it didn't work out the way we thought it would.'

'Maybe that's not such a bad thing,' I said. 'At least I won't have to stand up in the dark and listen to my knees knock together. There's something to be said for that.'

'Mother Nature to the rescue.'

'Exactly. Lady Luck saves my skin.'

'I'm glad you were spared the torment. I wouldn't want to be walking around with that on my conscience.'

'But thank you for getting me invited. It meant a lot to me, and the truth is I'm very grateful to you.'

'I didn't do it because I wanted your gratitude. I was curious, and sooner or later I would have been in touch with you myself. But then the opportunity came along, and I figured this would be a more elegant way of going about it.'

'And here I am, sitting at the North Pole with Admiral Peary himself. The least I can do is buy you a drink.'

'I accept your offer, but only on one condition. You have to answer my question first.'

'I'll be glad to, as long as you tell me what the question is. I don't seem to remember that you asked me one.'

'Of course I did. I asked you where you've been hiding yourself. I could be mistaken, but my guess is that you haven't been in New York very long.'

'I used to be here, but then I went away. I just got back five or six months ago.'

'And where were you?'

'France. I lived there for close to five years.'

'That explains it, then. But why on earth would you want to live in France?'

'No particular reason. I just wanted to be somewhere that wasn't here.'

'You didn't go to study? You weren't working for UNESCO or some hot-shot international law firm?'

'No, nothing like that. I was pretty much living hand to mouth.'

'The old expatriate adventure, was that it? Young American writer goes off to Paris to discover culture and beautiful women, to experience the pleasures of sitting in cafés and smoking strong cigarettes.'

'I don't think it was that either. I felt I needed some breathing room, that's all. I picked France because I was able to speak French. If I spoke Serbo-Croat, I probably would have gone to Yugoslavia.'

'So you went away. For no particular reason, as you put it. Was there any particular reason why you came back?'

'I woke up one morning last summer and told myself it was time to come home. Just like that. I suddenly felt I'd been there long enough. Too many years without baseball, I suppose. If you don't get your ration of double plays and home runs, it can begin to dry up your spirit.'

'And you're not planning to leave again?'

'No, I don't think so. Whatever I was trying to prove by going there doesn't feel important to me anymore.'

'Maybe you've proved it already.'

'That's possible. Or maybe the question has to be stated in different terms. Maybe I was using the wrong terms all along.'

'All right,' Sachs said, suddenly slapping his hand on the bar. 'I'll take that drink now. I'm beginning to feel satisfied, and that always makes me thirsty.'

'What will you have?'

'The same thing you're having,' he said, not bothering to ask me what it was. 'And since the bartender has to come over here anyway, tell him to pour you another. A toast is in order. It's your

15

homecoming, after all, and we have to welcome you back to America in style.'

I don't think anyone has ever disarmed me as thoroughly as Sachs did that afternoon. He came on like gangbusters from the first moment, storming through my most secret dungeons and hiding places, opening one locked door after another. As I later learned, it was a typical performance for him, an almost classic example of how he steered himself through the world. No beating about the bush, no standing on ceremony – just roll up your sleeves and start talking. It was nothing for him to strike up conversations with absolute strangers, to plunge in and ask questions no one else would have dared to ask, and more often than not to get away with it. You felt that he had never learned the rules, that because he was so utterly lacking in self-consciousness, he expected everyone else to be as open-hearted as he was. And yet there was always something impersonal about his probing, as if he weren't trying to make a human connection with you so much as to solve some intellectual problem for himself. It gave his remarks a certain abstract coloration, and this inspired trust, made you willing to tell him things that in some cases you hadn't even told yourself. He never judged anyone he met, never treated anyone as an inferior, never made distinctions between people because of their social rank. A bartender interested him just as much as a writer, and if I hadn't shown up that day, he probably would have spent two hours talking to that same man I hadn't bothered to exchange ten words with. Sachs automatically assumed great intelligence on the part of the person he was talking to, thereby investing that person with a sense of his own dignity and importance. I think it was that quality I admired most about him, that innate skill at drawing out the best in others. He often came across as an oddball, a gawky stick of a man with his head in the clouds, permanently distracted by obscure thoughts and preoccupations, and yet again and again he would surprise you with a hundred little signs of his attentiveness. Like everyone else in the world, but only more so perhaps, he managed to combine a multitude of contradictions into a single, unbroken

16

presence. No matter where he was, he always seemed to be at home in his surroundings, and yet I've rarely met anyone who was so clumsy, so physically inept, so helpless at negotiating the simplest operations. All during our conversation that afternoon, he kept knocking his coat off the barstool onto the floor. It must have happened six or seven times, and once, when he bent down to pick it up, he even managed to bang his head against the bar. As I later discovered, however, Sachs was an excellent athlete. He had been the leading scorer on his high school basketball team, and in all the games of one-on-one we played against each other over the years, I don't think I beat him more than once or twice. He was garrulous and often sloppy in the way he spoke, and yet his writing was marked by great precision and economy, a genuine gift for the apt phrase. That he wrote at all, for that matter, often struck me as something of a puzzle. He was too out there, too fascinated by other people, too happy mixing with crowds for such a lonely occupation, I thought. But solitude scarcely disturbed him, and he always worked with tremendous discipline and fervor, sometimes holing up for weeks at a stretch in order to complete a project. Given who he was, and the singular way in which he kept these various sides of himself in motion, Sachs was not someone you would have expected to be married. He seemed too ungrounded for domestic life, too democratic in his affections to be capable of sustaining intimate relations with any one person. But Sachs married young, much younger than anyone else I knew, and he kept that marriage alive for close to twenty years. Nor was Fanny the kind of wife who seemed particularly well suited to him. In a pinch, I could have imagined him with a docile, mothering sort of woman, one of those wives who stands contentedly in her husband's shadow, devoted to protecting her boy-man from the harsh practicalities of the everyday world. But Fanny was nothing like that. Sachs's partner was every bit his equal, a complex and highly intelligent woman who led her own independent life, and if he managed to hold onto her for all those years, it was only because he worked hard at it, because he had an enormous talent for understanding

17

her and keeping her in balance with herself. His sweet temper no doubt helped the marriage, but I wouldn't want to over-emphasize that aspect of his character. In spite of his gentleness, Sachs could be rigidly dogmatic in his thinking, and there were times when he let loose in savage fits of anger, truly terrifying outbursts of rage. These were not directed at the people he cared about so much as at the world at large. The stupidities of the world appalled him, and underneath his jauntiness and good humor, you sometimes felt a deep reservoir of intolerance and scorn. Nearly everything he wrote had a peevish, embattled edge to it, and over the years he developed a reputation as a trouble-maker. I suppose he deserved it, but in the end that was only one small part of who he was. The difficulty comes from trying to pin him down in any conclusive way. Sachs was too unpredictable for that, too large-spirited and cunning, too full of new ideas to stand in one place for very long. I sometimes found it exhausting to be with him, but I can't say it was ever dull. Sachs kept me on my toes for fifteen years, constantly challenging and provoking me, and as I sit here now trying to make sense of who he was, I can hardly imagine my life without him.

'You've put me at a disadvantage,' I said, taking a sip of bourbon from my replenished glass. 'You've read nearly every word I've written, and I haven't seen a single line of yours. Living in France had its benefits, but keeping up with new American books wasn't one of them.'

'You haven't missed much,' Sachs said. 'I promise you.'

'Still, I find it a little embarrassing. Other than the title, I don't know a thing about your book.'

'I'll give you a copy. Then you won't have any more excuses for not reading it.'

'I looked for it in a few stores yesterday ... '

'That's all right, save your money. I have about a hundred copies, and I'm happy to get rid of them.'

'If I'm not too drunk, I'll start reading it tonight.'

'There's no rush. It's only a novel, after all, and you shouldn't take it too seriously.'

'I always take novels seriously. Especially when they're given to me by the author.'

'Well, this author was very young when he wrote his book. Maybe too young, in fact. Sometimes he feels sorry it was ever published.'

'But you were planning to read from it this afternoon. You can't think it's that bad, then.'

'I'm not saying it's bad. It's just young, that's all. Too literary, too full of its own cleverness. I wouldn't even dream of writing something like that today. If I have any interest in it now, it's only because of where it was written. The book itself doesn't mean much, but I suppose I'm still attached to the place where it was born.'

'And what place was that?'

'Prison. I started writing the book in prison.'

'You mean an actual prison? With locked cells and bars? With numbers stenciled on the front of your shirt?'

'Yes, a real prison. The federal penitentiary in Danbury, Connecticut. I was a guest in that hotel for seventeen months.'

'Good lord. And how did you happen to wind up there?'

'It was very simple, really. I refused to go into the army when they called me up.'

'Were you a conscientious objector?'

'I wanted to be, but they turned down my application. I'm sure you know the story. If you belong to a religion that preaches pacifism and is opposed to all wars, then there's a chance they'll consider your case. But I'm not a Quaker or a Seventh-Day Adventist, and the fact is I'm not opposed to all wars. Only to that war. Unfortunately, that was the one they were asking me to fight in.'

'But why go to jail? There were other choices. Canada, Sweden, even France. Thousands of people took off to those places.'

'Because I'm a stubborn son-of-a-bitch, that's why. I didn't want to run away. I felt I had a responsibility to stand up and tell them what I thought. And I couldn't do that unless I was willing to put myself on the line.'

'So they listened to your noble statement, and then they locked you up anyway.'

'Of course. But it was worth it.'

'I suppose. But those seventeen months must have been awful.'

'They weren't as bad as you'd think. You don't have to worry about anything in there. You're given three meals a day, you don't have to do your laundry, your whole life is mapped out for you in advance. You'd be surprised how much freedom that gives you.'

'I'm glad you're able to joke about it.'

'I'm not joking. Well, maybe just a little. But I didn't suffer in any of the ways you're probably imagining. Danbury isn't some nightmare prison like Attica or San Quentin. Most of the inmates are there for white-collar crimes – embezzlement, tax fraud, writing bad checks, that kind of thing. I was lucky to be sent there, but the main advantage was that I was prepared. My case dragged on for months, and since I always knew that I was going to lose, I had time to adjust myself to the idea of prison. I wasn't one of those sad-sacks who moped around counting the days, crossing out another box on the calendar every time I went to bed. When I went in there, I told myself this is it, this is where you live now, old man. The boundaries of my world had shrunk, but I was still alive, and as long as I could go on breathing and farting and thinking my thoughts, what difference did it make where I was?'

'Strange.'

'No, not strange. It's like the old Henny Youngman joke. The husband comes home, walks into the living room, and sees a cigar burning in an ashtray. He asks his wife what's going on, but she pretends not to know. Still suspicious, the husband starts looking through the house. When he gets to the bedroom, he opens the closet and finds a stranger in there. "What are you doing in my closet?" the husband asks. "I don't know," the man stutters, shaking and sweating all over. "Everybody has to be somewhere." '

'All right, I get the point. But still, there must have been some rough characters in that closet with you. It couldn't always have been very pleasant.'

'There were a few dicey moments, I'll admit that. But I learned how to handle myself pretty well. It was the one time in my life when my funny looks proved to be helpful. No one knew what to make of me, and after a while I managed to convince most of the other inmates that I was crazy. You'd be astounded at how thoroughly people leave you alone when they think you're nuts. Once you get that look in your eye, it inoculates you against trouble.'

'And all because you wanted to stand up for your principles.'

'It wasn't so hard. At least I always knew why I was there. I didn't have to torture myself with regrets.'

'I was lucky compared to you. I flunked the physical because of asthma, and I never had to think about it again.'

'So you went to France, and I went to jail. We both went somewhere, and we both came back. As far as I can tell, we're both sitting in the same place now.'

'That's one way of looking at it.'

'It's the only way of looking at it. Our methods were different, but the results were exactly the same.'

We ordered another round of drinks. That led to another round, and then another, and then another one after that. In between, the bartender stood us to a couple of glasses on the house, an act of kindness that we promptly repaid by encouraging him to pour one for himself. Then the tavern began to fill up with customers, and we went off to sit at a table in the far corner of the room. I can't remember everything we talked about, but the beginning of that conversation is a lot clearer to me than the end. By the time we came to the last half hour or forty-five minutes, there was so much bourbon in my system that I was actually seeing double. This had never happened to me before, and I had no idea how to bring the world back into focus.

Whenever I looked at Sachs, there were two of him. Blinking my eyes didn't help, and shaking my head only made me dizzy. Sachs had turned into a man with two heads and two mouths, and when I finally stood up to leave, I can remember how he caught me in his four arms just as I was about to fall. It was probably a good thing that there were so many of him that afternoon. I was nearly a dead weight by then, and I doubt that one man could have carried me.

I can only speak about the things I know, the things I have seen with my own eyes and heard with my own ears. Except for Fanny, it's possible that I was closer to Sachs than anyone else, but that doesn't make me an expert on the details of his life. He was already pushing thirty when I met him, and neither one of us spent much time talking about our pasts. His childhood is largely a mystery to me, and beyond a few casual remarks he made about his parents and sisters over the years, I know next to nothing about his family. If the circumstances were different, I would try to talk to some of these people now, I would make an effort to fill in as many blanks as I could. But I'm not in a position to start hunting for Sachs's grade school teachers and high school friends, to set up interviews with his cousins and college class-mates and the men he was in prison with. There isn't enough time for that, and because I'm forced to work quickly, I have nothing to rely on but my own memories. I'm not saying that these memories should be doubted, that there is anything false or tainted about the things I do know about Sachs, but I don't want to present this book as something it's not. There is nothing definitive about it. It's not a biography or an exhaustive psycho-logical portrait, and even though Sachs confided a great deal to me over the years of our friendship, I don't claim to have more than a partial understanding of who he was. I want to tell the truth about him, to set down these memories as honestly as I can, but I can't dismiss the possibility that I'm wrong, that the truth is quite different from what I imagine it to be.

He was born on August 6, 1945. I remember the date because

he always made a point of mentioning it, referring to himself in various conversations as 'America's first Hiroshima baby,' 'the original bomb child,' 'the first white man to draw breath in the nuclear age.' He used to claim that the doctor had delivered him at the precise moment Fat Man was released from the bowels of the *Enola Gay*, but that always struck me as an exaggeration. The one time I met Sachs's mother, she wasn't able to recall when the birth had taken place (she'd had four children, she said, and their births were all mixed up in her mind), but at least she confirmed the date, adding that she distinctly remembered that she was told about Hiroshima *after* her son was born. If Sachs invented the rest, it was no more than a bit of innocent mythologizing on his part. He was a great one for turning facts into metaphors, and since he always had an abundance of facts at his disposal, he could bombard you with a never-ending supply of strange historical connections, yoking together the most far-flung people and events. Once, for example, he told me that during Peter Kropotkin's first visit to the United States in the 1890s, Mrs Jefferson Davis, the widow of the Confederate president, requested a meeting with the famous anarchist prince. That was bizarre enough, Sachs said, but then, just minutes after Kropotkin arrived at Mrs Davis's house, who else should turn up but Booker T. Washington? Washington announced that he was looking for the man who had accompanied Kropotkin (a mutual friend), and when Mrs Davis learned that he was standing in the entrance hall, she sent word that he should come in and join them. So for the next hour this unlikely trio sat around drinking tea together and making polite conversation: the Russian nobleman who sought to bring down all organized government, the ex-slave turned writer and educator, and the wife of the man who led America into its bloodiest war in defense of the institution of slavery. Only Sachs could have known something like that. Only Sachs could have informed you that when the film actress Louise Brooks was growing up in a small town in Kansas at the beginning of the century, her next-door playmate was Vivian Vance, the same woman who later starred in the *I Love Lucy* show. It thrilled him to have discovered this: that the two sides of American womanhood, the vamp and the frump, the libidinous sex-devil and the dowdy housewife, should have started in the same place, on the same dusty street in the middle of America. Sachs loved these ironies, the vast follies and contradictions of history, the way in which facts were constantly turning themselves on their head. By gorging himself on those facts, he was able to read the world as though it were a work of the imagination, turning documented events into literary symbols, tropes that pointed to some dark, complex pattern embedded in the real. I could never be quite sure how seriously he took this game, but he played it often, and at times it was almost as if he were unable to stop himself. The business about his birth was part of this same compulsion. On the one hand, it was a form of gallows humor, but it was also an attempt to define who he was, a way of implicating himself in the horrors of his own time. Sachs often talked about 'the bomb.' It was a central fact of the world for him, an ultimate demarcation of the spirit, and in his view it separated us from all other generations in history. Once we acquired the power to destroy ouselves, the very notion of human life had been altered; even the air we breathed was contaminated with the stench of death. Sachs was hardly the first person to come up with this idea, but considering what happened to him nine days ago, there's a certain eeriness to the obsession, as if it were a kind of deadly pun, a mixed-up word that took root inside him and proliferated beyond his control.

His father was an Eastern European Jew, his mother was an Irish Catholic. As with most American families, disaster had brought them here (the potato famine of the 1840s, the pogroms of the 1880s), but beyond these rudimentary details, I have no information about Sachs's ancestors. He was fond of saying that a poet was responsible for bringing his mother's family to Boston, but that was only a reference to Sir Walter Ralegh, the man who introduced the potato to Ireland and hence had caused the blight that occurred three hundred years later. As for his father's family, he once told me that they had come to New York because of the death of God. This was another one of Sachs's enigmatic allusions, and until you penetrated the nursery-rhyme logic behind it, it seemed devoid of sense. What he meant was that the pogroms began after the assassination of Czar Alexander II; that Alexander had been killed by Russian Nihilists; that the Nihilists were nihilists because they believed there was no God. It was a simple equation, finally, but incomprehensible until the middle terms were restored to the sequence. Sachs's remark was like someone telling you that the kingdom had been lost for want of a nail. If you knew the poem, you got it. If you didn't know it, you didn't.

When and where his parents met, who they had been in early life, how their respective families reacted to the prospect of a mixed marriage, at what point they moved to Connecticut – all this falls outside the realm of what I am able to discuss. As far as I know, Sachs had a secular upbringing. He was both a Jew and a Catholic, which meant that he was neither one nor the other. I don't recall that he ever talked about going to religious school, and to the best of my knowledge he was neither confirmed nor bar-mitzvahed. The fact that he was circumcised was no more than a medical detail. On several occasions, however, he alluded to a religious crisis that took place in his middle teens, but evidently it burned itself out rather quickly. I was always impressed by his familiarity with the Bible (both Old and New Testaments), and perhaps he started reading it back then, during that period of inner struggle. Sachs was more interested in politics and history than in spiritual questions, but his politics were nevertheless tinged with something I would call a religious quality, as if political engagement were more than a way of confronting problems in the here and now, but a means to personal salvation as well. I believe this is an important point. Sachs's political ideas never fell into any of the conventional categories. He was wary of systems and ideologies, and though he could talk about them with considerable understanding and sophistication, political action for him boiled down to a matter of conscience. That was what made him decide to go to prison in

1968. It wasn't because he thought he could accomplish anything there, but because he knew he wouldn't be able to live with himself if he didn't go. If I had to sum up his attitude toward his own beliefs, I would begin by mentioning the Transcendentalists of the nineteenth century. Thoreau was his model, and without the example of *Civil Disobedience*, I doubt that Sachs would have turned out as he did. I'm not just talking about prison now, but a whole approach to life, an attitude of remorseless inner vigilance. Once, when *Walden* came up in conversation, Sachs confessed to me that he wore a beard 'because Henry David had worn one' – which gave me a sudden insight into how deep his admiration was. As I write these words now, it occurs to me that they both lived the same number of years. Thoreau died at forty-four, and Sachs wouldn't have passed him until next month. I don't suppose there's anything to be made of this coincidence, but it's the kind of thing that Sachs always liked, a small detail to be noted for the record.

His father worked as a hospital administrator in Norwalk, and from all I can gather the family was neither well-to-do nor particularly strapped. Two daughters were born first, then Sachs came along, and then there was a third daughter, all four of them arriving within a span of six or seven years. Sachs seems to have been closer to his mother than his father (she is still alive, he is not), but I never sensed that there were any great conflicts between father and son. As an example of his stupidity as a little boy, Sachs once mentioned to me how upset he had been when he learned that his father hadn't fought in World War II. In light of Sachs's later position, that response becomes almost comical, but who knows how severely his disappointment affected him back then? All his friends used to brag about their fathers' exploits as soldiers, and he envied them for the battle trophies they would trot out for the war games they played in their suburban backyards: the helmets and cartridge belts, the holsters and canteens, the dog tags, hats, and medals. But why his father hadn't served in the army was never explained to me. On the other hand, Sachs always spoke proudly of his father's socialist politics in the thirties, which apparently involved union organizing or some other job connected with the labor movement. If Sachs gravitated more toward his mother than his father, I think it was because their personalities were so alike: both of them garrulous and blunt, both of them endowed with an uncanny talent for getting others to talk about themselves. According to Fanny (who told me as much about these things as Ben ever did), Sachs's father was quieter and more evasive then his mother, more closed in on himself, less inclined to let you know what he was thinking. Still, there must have been a strong bond between them. The most certain proof I can think of comes from a story that Fanny once told me. Not long after Ben's arrest, a local reporter came to the house to interview her father-in-law about the trial. The journalist was clearly looking to write a story about generational conflict (a big subject back in those days), but once Mr Sachs caught wind of his intentions, this normally subdued and taciturn man pounded his fist on the arm of the chair, looked the journalist straight in eye, and said: 'Ben is a terrific kid. We always taught him to stand up for what he believes in, and I'd be crazy not to be proud of what he's doing now. If there were more young men like my son in this country, it would be a hell of a lot better place.'

I never met his father, but I remember a Thanksgiving that I spent at his mother's house extremely well. The visit came a few weeks after Ronald Reagan was elected president, which means it was November 1980 – going on ten years now. It was a bad time in my life. My first marriage had broken up two years before, and I wasn't destined to meet Iris until the end of February, a good three months down the road. My son David was just over three then, and his mother and I had arranged for him to spend the holiday with me, but the plans I made for us had fallen through at the last minute. The alternatives seemed rather grim: either go out to a restaurant somewhere or eat frozen turkey dinners at my small apartment in Brooklyn. Just when I was beginning to feel sorry for myself (it could have been as late as Monday or Tuesday), Fanny rescued the situation by asking us up to Ben's mother's house in Connecticut. All the nieces and nephews would be there, she said, and it was bound to be fun for David.

Mrs Sachs has since moved to a retirement home, but at the time she was still living in the house in New Canaan where Ben and his sisters had grown up. It was a big place just outside town that looked to have been built in the second half of the nineteenth century, one of those gabled Victorian labyrinths with pantry closets, back staircases, and odd little passageways on the second floor. The interiors were dark, and the living room was cluttered with piles of books, newspapers, and magazines. Mrs Sachs must have been in her mid to late sixties then, but there was nothing old or grandmotherly about her. She had been a social worker for many years in the poor neighborhoods of Bridgeport, and it wasn't hard to see that she had been good at her job: an outspoken woman, full of opinions, with a brash, cockeyed sense of humor. She seemed to be amused by many things, a person given neither to sentimentality nor to bad temper, but whenever the subject turned to politics (as it did quite often that day), she proved to have a wickedly sharp tongue. Some of her remarks were downright raunchy, and at one point, when she called Nixon's convicted associates 'the sort of men who fold up their underpants before they go to bed at night,' one of her daughters glanced at me with an embarrassed look on her face, as if to apologize for her mother's unladylike behavior. She needn't have worried. I took an immense liking to Mrs Sachs that day. She was a subversive matriarch who still enjoyed throwing punches at the world, and she seemed as ready to laugh at herself as at everyone else – her children and grandchildren included. Not long after I got there, she confessed to me that she was a terrible cook, which was why she had delegated the responsibility of preparing the dinner to her daughters. But, she added (and here she drew close to me and whispered in my ear), those three girls were none too swift in the kitchen either. After all, she said, she had taught them everything they knew, and if the teacher was an absent-minded clod, what could you expect of the disciples?

It's true that the meal was dreadful, but we scarcely had time to notice. What with so many people in the house that day, and the constant racket of five children under the age of ten, our mouths were kept busier with talk than with food. Sachs's family was a noisy bunch. His sisters and their husbands had flown in from various parts of the country, and since most of them hadn't seen each other in a long while, the dinner conversation quickly became a free-for-all, with everyone talking at once. At any given moment, four or five separate dialogues were going on across the table, but because people weren't necessarily talking to the person next to them, these dialogues kept intersecting with one another, causing abrupt shifts in the pairings of the speakers, so that everyone seemed to be taking part in all the conversations at the same time, simultaneously chattering away about his or her own life and eavesdropping on everyone else as well. Add to this the frequent interruptions from the children, the comings and going of the different courses, the pouring of wine, the dropped plates, overturned glasses, and spilled condiments, the dinner began to resemble an elaborate, hastily improvised vaudeville routine.

It was a sturdy family, I thought, a teasing, fractious group of individuals who cared for one another but didn't cling to the life they had shared in the past. It was refreshing for me to see how little animosity there was among them, how few old rivalries and resentments came to the surface, but at the same time there wasn't much intimacy, they didn't seem as connected to one another as the members of most successful families are. I know that Sachs was fond of his sisters, but only in an automatic and somewhat distant sort of way, and I don't think he was particularly involved with any of them during his adult life. It might have had something to do with his being the only boy, but whenever I happened to catch a glimpse of him during the course of that long afternoon and evening, he seemed to be talking either to his mother or to Fanny, and he probably showed more interest in my son David than in any of his own nephews or nieces. I doubt that I'm trying to make a specific point about this. These kinds of partial observations are subject to any number of errors and misreadings, but the fact is that Sachs behaved like something of a loner in his own family, a figure who stood slightly apart from the rest. That isn't to say that he shunned anyone, but there were moments when I sensed that he was ill at ease, almost bored by having to be there.

Based on the little I know about it, his childhood seems to have been unremarkable. He didn't do especially well in school, and if he won honors for himself in any way, it was only to the extent that he excelled at pranks. He was apparently fearless in confronting authority, and to listen to him tell it, he spent the years from about six to twelve in a continuous ferment of creative sabotage. He was the one who designed the booby traps, who fastened the Kick Me signs on the teacher's back, who set off the fire crackers in the cafeteria garbage cans. He spent hundreds of hours sitting in the principal's office during those years, but punishment was a small price to pay for the satisfaction these triumphs gave him. The other boys respected him for his boldness and invention, which was probably what inspired him to take such risks in the first place. I've seen some of Sachs's early photographs, and there's no question that he was an ugly duckling, a genuine sore thumb: one of those beanstalk assemblages with big ears, buck teeth, and a goofy, lopsided grin. The potential for ridicule must have been enormous; he must have been a walking target for all sorts of jokes and savage stings. If he managed to avoid that fate, it was because he forced himself to be a little wilder than everyone else. It couldn't have been the most pleasant role to play, but he worked hard at mastering it, and after a while he held undisputed dominion over the territory.

Braces aligned his crooked teeth; his body filled out; his limbs gradually learned to obey him. By the time he reached adolescence, Sachs began to resemble the person he would later become. His height worked to his advantage in sports, and when he started to play basketball at thirteen or fourteen, he quickly developed into a promising player. The practical jokes and renegade antics died out then, and while his academic performance in high school was hardly outstanding (he always described himself as a lazy student, with only minimal interest in getting good grades), he read books constantly and was already beginning to think of himself as a future writer. By his own admission, his first works were awful – 'romantico-absurdist soul-searchings,' he once called them, wretched little stories and poems that he kept an absolute secret from everyone. But he stuck with it, and as a sign of his growing seriousness, he went out and bought himself a pipe at the age of seventeen. This was the badge of every true writer, he thought, and during his last year of high school he spent every evening sitting at his desk, pen in one hand, pipe in the other, filling his room with smoke.

These stories came straight from Sachs himself. They helped to define my sense of what he had been like before I met him, but as I repeat his comments now, I realize that they could have been entirely false. Self-deprecation was an important element of his personality, and he often used himself as the butt of his own jokes. Especially when talking about the past, he liked to portray himself in the most unflattering terms. He was always the ignorant kid, the pompous fool, the mischief-maker, the bungling oaf. Perhaps that was how he wanted me to see him, or perhaps he found some perverse pleasure in pulling my leg. For the fact is that it takes a great deal of self-confidence for a person to poke fun at himself, and a person with that kind of self-confidence is rarely a fool or a bungler.

There is only one story from that early period that I feel at all confident about. I heard it toward the end of my visit to Connecticut in 1980, and since it came as much from his mother as it did from him, it falls into a different category from the rest. In itself, this anecdote is less dramatic than some of the others Sachs told me, but looking at it now from the perspective of his whole life, it stands out in special relief – as though it were the announcement of a theme, the initial statement of a musical phrase that would go on haunting him until his last moments on earth.

Once the table was cleared, the people who hadn't helped with the dinner were assigned to wash-up duty in the kitchen. There were just four of us: Sachs and his mother, Fanny and myself. It was a big job, with mess and crockery jammed onto every counter, and as we took turns scraping and sudsing and rinsing and drying, we chatted about this and that, drifting aimlessly from one topic to another. After a while, we found ourselves talking about Thanksgiving, which led to a discussion of other American holidays, which in turn led to some glancing remarks about national symbols. The Statue of Liberty was mentioned, and then, almost as if the memory had returned to both of them at the same time, Sachs and his mother started reminiscing about a trip they had made to Bedloes Island back in the early fifties. Fanny had never heard the story before, so she and I became the audience, standing there with dish towels in our hands as the two of them performed their little act.

'Do you remember that day, Benjy?' Mrs Sachs began.

'Of course I remember,' Sachs said. 'It was one of the turning points of my childhood.'

'You were just a wee little man back then. No more than six or seven.'

'It was the summer I turned six. Nineteen fifty-one.'

'I was a few years older than that, but I'd never been to the Statue of Liberty. I figured it was about time, so one day I hustled you into the car, and off we went to New York. I don't remember where the girls were that morning, but I'm pretty sure it was just the two of us.'

'Just the two of us. And Mrs Something-stein and her two sons. We met them when we got down there.'

'Doris Saperstein, my old friend from the Bronx. She had two boys about your age. Regular little ragamuffins they were, a couple of wild Indians.'

'Just normal kids. They were the ones who caused the whole dispute.'

'What dispute?'

'You don't remember that part, do you?'

'No, I only remember what happened later. That wiped out everything else.'

'You made me wear those terrible short pants with the white

knee socks. You always dressed me up when we went out, and I hated it. I felt like a sissy in those clothes, a Fauntleroy in full regalia. It was bad enough on family outings, but the thought of turning up like that in front of Mrs Saperstein's sons was intolerable to me. I knew they'd be wearing T-shirts, dungarees, and sneakers, and I didn't know how I was going to face them.'

'But you looked like an angel in that outfit,' his mother said.

'Maybe so, but I didn't want to look like an angel. I wanted to look like a regular American boy. I begged to wear something else, but you refused to budge. Visiting the Statue of Liberty isn't like playing in the backyard, you said. It's the symbol of our country, and we have to show it the proper respect. Even then, the irony of the situation didn't escape me. There we were, about to pay homage to the concept of freedom, and I myself was in chains. I lived in an absolute dictatorship, and for as long as I could remember my rights had been trampled underfoot. I tried to explain about the other boys, but you wouldn't listen to me. Nonsense, you said, they'll be wearing their dress-up clothes, too. You were so damned sure of yourself, I finally plucked up my courage and offered to make a bargain with you. All right, I said, I'll wear the clothes today. But if the other boys are wearing dungarees and sneakers, then it's the last time I ever have to do it. From then on, you'll give me permission to wear whatever I want.'

'And I agreed to that? I allowed myself to bargain with a six-year-old?'

'You were just humoring me. The possibility of losing the bet didn't even occur to you. But lo and behold, when Mrs Saperstein arrived at the Statue of Liberty with her two sons, the boys were dressed exactly as I had predicted. And just like that, I became the master of my own wardrobe. It was the first major victory of my life. I felt as if I'd struck a blow for democracy, as if I'd risen up in the name of oppressed peoples all over the world.'

'Now I know why you're so partial to blue jeans,' Fanny said. 'You discovered the principle of self-determination, and at that point you determined to be a bad dresser for the rest of your life.'

'Precisely,' Sachs said. 'I won the right to be a slob, and I've been carrying the banner proudly ever since.'

'And then,' Mrs Sachs continued, impatient to get on with the story, 'we started to climb.'

'The spiral staircase,' her son added. 'We found the steps and started to go up.'

'It wasn't so bad at first,' Mrs Sachs said. 'Doris and I let the boys go on ahead, and we took the stairs nice and easy, holding onto the rail. We got as far as the crown, looked out at the harbor for a couple of minutes, and everything was more or less okay. I thought that was it, that we'd start back down then and go for an ice cream somewhere. But they still let you into the torch in those days, which meant climbing up another staircase – right through Miss Battle-Axe's arm. The boys were crazy to go up there. They kept hollering and whining about how they wanted to see everything, and so Doris and I gave in to them. As it turned out, this staircase didn't have a railing like the other one. It was the narrowest, twistingest little set of iron rungs you ever saw, a fire pole with bumps on it, and when you looked down through the arm, you felt like you were three hundred miles up in the air. It was pure nothingness all around, the great void of heaven. The boys scampered up into the torch by themselves, but by the time I was two-thirds of the way up, I realized I wasn't going to make it. I'd always thought of myself as a pretty tough cookie. I wasn't one of those hysterical women who screamed when she saw a mouse. I was a hefty, down-to-earth broad who'd been around the block a few times, but standing on those stairs that day, I got all weak inside, I had the cold sweats, I thought I was going to throw up. By then, Doris wasn't in such good shape herself, and so we each sat down on one of the steps, hoping that might steady our nerves. It helped a little, but not much, and even with my backside planted on something solid, I still felt I was about to fall, that any second I'd find myself hurtling head-first to the bottom. It was the worst panic I ever felt in my life. I was completely rearranged. My heart was in my throat, my head was in my hands, my stomach was in my feet. I got so scared thinking about Benjamin that I started screaming for him to come down. It was hideous. My voice echoing through the Statue of Liberty like the howls of some tormented spirit. The boys finally left the torch, and then we all went down the stairs sitting, one step at a time. Doris and I tried to make a game out of it for the boys, pretending that this was the fun way to travel. But nothing was going to make me stand up on those stairs again. I'd have sooner jumped off than allow myself to do that. It must have taken us half an hour to get to the bottom again, and by then I was a wreck, a blob of flesh and bone. Benjy and I stayed with the Sapersteins on the Grand Concourse that night, and since then I've had a mortal fear of high places. I'd rather be dead than set foot in an airplane, and once I get above the third or fourth story of a building, I turn to jello inside. How do you like that? And it all started that day when Benjamin was a little boy, climbing into the torch of the Statue of Liberty.'

'It was my first lesson in political theory,' Sachs said, turning his eyes away from his mother to look at Fanny and me. 'I learned that freedom can be dangerous. If you don't watch out, it can kill you.'

I don't want to make too much of this story, but at the same time I don't think it should be entirely neglected. In itself, it was no more than a trivial episode, a bit of family folklore, and Mrs Sachs told it with enough humor and self-mockery to sweep aside its rather terrifying implications. We all laughed when she was finished, and then the conversation moved on to something else. If not for Sachs's novel (the same book he carried through the snow to our aborted reading in 1975), I might have forgotten all about it. But since that book is filled with references to the Statue of Liberty, it's hard to ignore the possibility of a connection – as if the childhood experience of witnessing his mother's panic somehow lay at the heart of what he wrote as a grown man twenty years later. I asked him about it as we were driving back to the city that night, but Sachs only laughed at my question. He hadn't even remembered that part of the story, he said. Then, dismissing the subject once and for all, he launched into a comic diatribe against the pitfalls of psychoanalysis. In the end, none of that matters. Just because Sachs denied the connection doesn't mean that it didn't exist. No one can say where a book comes from, least of all the person who writes it. Books are born out of ignorance, and if they go on living after they are written, it's only to the degree that they cannot be understood.

The New Colossus was the one novel Sachs ever published. It was also the first piece of writing I read by him, and there's no doubt that it played a significant role in getting our friendship off the ground. It was one thing to have liked Sachs in person, but when I learned that I could admire his work as well, I became that much more eager to know him, that much more willing to see him and talk to him again. That instantly set him apart from all the other people I had met since moving back to America. He was more than just a potential drinking companion, I discovered, more than just another acquaintance. An hour after cracking open Sachs's book fifteen years ago, I understood that it would be possible for us to become friends.

I have just spent the morning scanning through it again (there are several copies here in the cabin) and am astonished by how little my feelings for it have changed. I don't think I have to say much more than that. The book continues to exist, it's available in bookstores and libraries, and anyone who cares to read it can do so without difficulty. It was issued in paperback a couple of months after Sachs and I first met, and since then it has stayed mostly in print, living a quiet but healthy life in the margins of recent literature, a crazy hodgepodge of a book that has kept its own small spot on the shelf. The first time I read it, however, I walked into it cold. After listening to Sachs in the bar, I assumed that he had written a conventional first novel, one of those thinly veiled attempts to fictionalize the story of his own life. I wasn't planning to hold that against him, but he had talked so disparagingly about the book that I felt I had to brace myself for some kind of letdown. He autographed a copy for me that day in the bar, but the only thing I noticed at the time was that it was big, a book that ran to more than four hundred pages. I started reading it the next afternoon, sprawled out in bed after drinking six cups of coffee to kill the hangover from Saturday's binge. As Sachs had warned me, it was a young man's book – but not in any of the ways I was expecting it to be. *The New Colossus* had nothing to do with the sixties, nothing to do with Vietnam or the antiwar movement, nothing to do with the seventeen months he had served in prison. That I had been looking for all that stemmed from a failure of imagination on my part. The idea of prison was so terrible to me, I couldn't imagine how anyone who had been there could not write about it.

As every reader knows, *The New Colossus* is a historical novel, a meticulously researched book set in America between 1876 and 1890 and based on documented, verifiable facts. Most of the characters are people who actually lived at the time, and even when the characters are imaginary, they are not inventions so much as borrowings, figures stolen from the pages of other novels. Otherwise, all the events are true – true in the sense that they follow the historical record – and in those places where the record is unclear, there is no tampering with the laws of probability. Everything is made to seem plausible, matter-of-fact, even banal in the accuracy of its depiction. And yet Sachs continually throws the reader off guard, mixing so many genres and styles to tell his story that the book begins to resemble a pinball machine, a fabulous contraption with blinking lights and ninety-eight different sound effects. From chapter to chapter, he jumps from traditional third-person narratives to first-person diary entries and letters, from chronological charts to small anecdotes, from newspaper articles to essays to dramatic dialogues. It's a whirlwind performance, a marathon sprint from the first line to the last, and whatever you might think of the book as a whole, it's impossible not to respect the author's energy, the sheer gutsiness of his ambitions.

Among the characters who appear in the novel are Emma Lazarus, Sitting Bull, Ralph Waldo Emerson, Joseph Pulitzer,

Buffalo Bill Cody, Auguste Bartholdi, Catherine Weldon, Rose Hawthorne (Nathaniel's daughter), Ellery Channing, Walt Whitman, and William Tecumseh Sherman. But Raskalnikov is also there (straight from the epilogue of *Crime and Punishment* – released from prison and newly arrived as an immigrant in the United States, where his name is anglicized to Ruskin), as is Huckleberry Finn (a middle-aged drifter who befriends Ruskin), and Ishmael from *Moby Dick* (who has a brief walk-on role as a bartender in New York). *The New Colossus* begins in the year of America's centennial and works its way through the major events of the next decade and a half: Custer's defeat at the Little Big Horn, the building of the Statue of Liberty, the general strike of 1877, the exodus of Russian Jews to America in 1881, the invention of the telephone, the Haymarket riots in Chicago, the spread of the Ghost Dance religion among the Sioux, the massacre at Wounded Knee. But small events are also recorded, and these are finally what give the book its texture, what turn it into something more than a jigsaw puzzle of historical facts. The opening chapter is a good case in point. Emma Lazarus goes to Concord, Massachusetts to stay as a guest in Emerson's house. While there, she is introduced to Ellery Channing, who accompanies her on a visit to Walden Pond and talks about his friendship with Thoreau (dead now for fourteen years). The two are drawn to each other and become friends, another of those odd juxtapositions that Sachs was so fond of: the white-haired New Englander and the young Jewish poet from Millionaire's Row in New York. At their last meeting, Channing hands her a gift, which he tells her not to open until she is on the train heading back home. When she unwraps the parcel, she finds a copy of Channing's book on Thoreau, along with one of the relics the old man has been hoarding since his friend's death: Thoreau's pocket compass. It's a beautiful moment, very sensitively handled by Sachs, and it plants an important image in the reader's head that will recur in any number of guises throughout the book. Although it isn't said in so many words, the message couldn't be clearer. America has lost its way. Thoreau was the one man who could read the compass for us, and now that he is gone, we have no hope of finding ourselves again.

There is the strange story of Catherine Weldon, the middle-class woman from Brooklyn who goes out west to become one of Sitting Bull's wives. There is a farcical account of the Russian Grand Duke Alexei's tour of the United States – hunting buffalo with Bill Cody, traveling down the Mississippi with General and Mrs George Armstrong Custer. There is General Sherman, whose middle name gives homage to an Indian warrior, receiving an appointment in 1876 (just one month after Custer's last stand) 'to assume military control of all reservations in the Sioux country and to treat the Indians there as prisoners of war,' and then, one year later, receiving another appointment from the American Committee on the Statue of Liberty 'to decide whether the statue should be located on Governor's or Bedloe's Island.' There is Emma Lazarus dying from cancer at age thirty-seven, attended by her friend Rose Hawthorne – who is so transformed by the experience that she converts to Catholicism, enters the order of St Dominic as Sister Alphonsa, and devotes the last thirty years of her life to caring for the terminally ill. There are dozens of such episodes in the book. All of them are true, each is grounded in the real, and yet Sachs fits them together in such a way that they become steadily more fantastic, almost as if he were delineating a nightmare or a hallucination. As the book progresses, it takes on a more and more unstable character – filled with unpredictable associations and departures, marked by increasingly rapid shifts in tone – until you reach a point when you feel the whole thing begin to levitate, to rise ponderously off the ground like some gigantic weather balloon. By the last chapter, you've traveled so high up into the air, you realize that you can't come down again without falling, without being crushed.

There are definite flaws, however. Although Sachs works hard to mask them, there are times when the novel feels too con-structed, too mechanical in its orchestration of events, and only rarely do any of the characters come fully to life. Midway through my first reading of it, I remember telling myself that Sachs was more of a thinker than an artist, and his heavy-handedness often disturbed me – the way he kept hammering home his points, manipulating his characters to underscore his ideas rather than letting them create the action themselves. Still, in spite of the fact that he wasn't writing about himself, I understood how deeply personal the book must have been for him. The dominant emotion was anger, a full-blown, lacerating anger that surged up on nearly every page: anger against America, anger against political hypocrisy, anger as a weapon to destroy national myths. But given that the war in Vietnam was still being fought then, and given that Sachs had gone to jail because of that war, it wasn't hard to understand where his anger had come from. It gave the book a strident, polemical tone, but I also believe it was the secret of its power, the engine that pushed the book forward and made you want to go on reading it. Sachs was only twenty-three when he started *The New Colossus*, and he stuck with the project for five years, writing seven or eight drafts in the process. The published version came to four hundred and thirty-six pages, and I had read them all by the time I went to sleep on Tuesday night. Whatever reservations I might have had were dwarfed by my admiration for what he had accomplished. When I came home from work on Wednesday afternoon, I immediately sat down and wrote him a letter. I told him that he had written a great novel. Any time he wanted to share another bottle of bourbon with me, I would be honored to match him glass for glass.

We started seeing each other regularly after that. Sachs had no job, and that made him more available than most of the people I knew, more flexible in his routines. Social life in New York tends to be quite rigid. A simple dinner can take weeks of advance planning, and the best of friends can sometimes go months without any contact at all. With Sachs, however, impromptu meetings were the norm. He worked when the spirit moved him (most often late at night), and the rest of the time he roamed free, prowling the streets of the city like some nineteenth-century *flâneur*, following his nose wherever it happened to take him. He walked, he went to museums and art galleries, he saw movies in the middle of the day, he read books on park benches. He wasn't beholden to the clock in the way other people are, and as a consequence he never felt as if he were wasting his time. That doesn't mean he wasn't productive, but the wall between work and idleness had crumbled to such a degree for him that he scarcely noticed it was there. This helped him as a writer, I think, since his best ideas always seemed to come to him when he was away from his desk. In that sense, then, everything fell into the category of work for him. Eating was work, watching basketball games was work, sitting with a friend in a bar at midnight was work. In spite of appearances, there was hardly a moment when he wasn't on the job.

My days weren't nearly as open as his were. I had returned from Paris the previous summer with nine dollars in my pocket, and rather than ask my father for a loan (which he probably wouldn't have given me anyway), I had snatched at the first job I was offered. By the time I met Sachs, I was working for a rare-book dealer on the Upper East Side, mostly sitting in the back room of the shop writing catalogues and answering letters. I went in every morning at nine and left at one. In the afternoons, I translated at home, working on a history of modern China by a French journalist who had once been stationed in Peking – a slapdash, poorly written book that demanded more effort than it deserved. My hope was to quit the job with the book dealer and start earning my living as a translator, but it still wasn't clear that my plan would work. In the meantime, I was also writing stories and doing occasional book reviews, and what with one thing and another, I wasn't getting a lot of sleep. Still, I saw Sachs more often than seems possible now, considering the circumstances. One advantage was that we had turned out to live in the same neighborhood, and our apartments were within easy walking distance of each other. This led to quite a few late-night meetings in bars along Broadway, and then, after we discovered a mutual passion for sports, weekend afternoons as well, since the ball-games were always on in those places and neither one of us owned a television set. Almost at once, I began seeing Sachs on the average of twice a week, far more than I saw anyone else.

Not long after these get-togethers began, he introduced me to his wife. Fanny was a graduate student in the art history department at Columbia then, teaching courses at General Studies and finishing up her dissertation on nineteenth-century American landscape painting. She and Sachs had met at the University of Wisconsin ten years before, literally bumping into each other at a peace rally that had been organized on campus. By the time Sachs was arrested in the spring of 1967, they had already been married for close to a year. They lived at Ben's parents' house in New Canaan during the period of the trial, and once the sentence was handed down and Ben went off to prison (early in 1968), Fanny moved back to her own parents' apartment in Brooklyn. At some point during all this, she applied to the graduate program at Columbia and was accepted with a faculty fellowship – which included free tuition, a living stipend of several thousand dollars, and responsibility for teaching a couple of courses. She spent the rest of that summer working as an office temp in Manhattan, found a small apartment on West 112th Street in late August, and then started classes in September, all the while commuting up to Danbury every Sunday on the train to visit Ben. I mention these things now because I happened to see her a number of times during that year – without having the slightest idea who she was. I was still an undergraduate at Columbia then, and my apartment was only five blocks away from hers, on West 107th Street. As chance would have it, two of my closest friends lived in her building, and on several of my visits I actually ran into her in the elevator or the downstairs lobby. Beyond that, there were the times when I saw her walking along Broadway, the times when I found her standing ahead of me at the counter of the discount cigarette store, the times when I caught a glimpse of her entering a building on campus. In the spring, we were even in a class together, a large lecture course on the history of aesthetics given by a professor in the philosophy department. I noticed her in all these places because I found her attractive, but I could never quite

muster the courage to talk to her. There was something intimidat-
ing about her elegance, a walled-off quality that seemed to
discourage strangers from approaching her. The wedding ring on
her left hand was partly responsible, I suppose, but even if she
hadn't been married, I'm not sure it would have made any
difference. Still, I made a conscious effort to sit behind her in that
philosophy class, just so I could spend an hour every week
watching her out of the corner of my eye. We smiled at each other
once or twice as we were leaving the lecture hall, but I was too
timid to push it any farther than that. When Sachs finally
introduced me to her in 1975, we recognized each other immediately. It was an unsettling experience, and it took me several
minutes to regain my composure. A mystery from the past had
suddenly been solved. Sachs was the missing husband of the
woman I had watched so attentively six or seven years before. If I
had stayed in the neighborhood, it's almost certain that I would
have seen him after he was released from prison. But I graduated
from college in June, and Sachs didn't come to New York until
August. By then, I had already moved out of my apartment and
was on my way to Europe.

There's no question that it was a strange match. In almost every
way that I can think of, Ben and Fanny seemed to exist in
mutually exclusive realms. Ben was all arms and legs, an erector
set of sharp angles and bony protrusions, whereas Fanny was
short and round, with a smooth face and olive skin. Ben was
ruddy by comparison, with frizzy, unkempt hair, and skin that
burned easily in the sun. He took up a lot of room, seemed to be
constantly in motion, changed facial expressions every five or six
seconds, whereas Fanny was poised, sedentary, catlike in the
way she inhabited her body. She wasn't beautiful to me so much
as exotic, although that might be too strong a word for what I'm
trying to express. An ability to fascinate is probably closer to what
I'm looking for, a certain air of self-sufficiency that made you
want to watch her, even when she just sat there and did nothing.
She wasn't funny in the way Ben could be, she wasn't quick, she
never ran off at the mouth. And yet I always felt that she was the

43

more articulate of the two, the more intelligent, the one with greater analytical powers. Ben's mind was all intuition. It was bold but not especially subtle, a mind that loved to take risks, to leap into the dark, to make improbable connections. Fanny, on the other hand, was thorough and dispassionate, unremitting in her patience, not prone to quick judgments or ungrounded remarks. She was a scholar, and he was a wise guy; she was a sphinx, and he was an open wound; she was an aristocrat, and he was the people. To be with them was like watching a marriage between a panther and a kangaroo. Fanny, always superbly dressed, stylish, walking alongside a man nearly a foot taller than she was, an oversize kid in black Converse All-Stars, blue jeans, and a gray hooded sweatshirt. On the surface, it seemed to make no sense. You saw them together, and your first response was to think they were strangers.

But that was only on the surface. Underneath his apparent clumsiness, Sachs had a remarkable understanding of women. Not just of Fanny, but of nearly all the women he met, and again and again I was surprised by how naturally they were drawn to him. Growing up with three sisters might have had something to do with it, as if the intimacies learned in childhood had impregnated him with some occult knowledge, a way into feminine secrets that other men spend their whole lives trying to discover. Fanny had her difficult moments, and I don't imagine she was ever an easy person to live with. Her outward calm was often a mask for inner turbulence, and on several occasions I saw for myself how quickly she could fall into dark, depressive moods, overcome by some indefinable anguish that would suddenly push her to the point of tears. Sachs protected her at those times, handling her with a tenderness and discretion that could be very moving, and I think Fanny learned to depend on him for that, to realize that no one was capable of understanding her as deeply as he did. More often than not, this compassion was expressed indirectly, in a language that outsiders couldn't penetrate. The first time I went to their apartment, for example, the dinner conversation came around to the subject of children – whether or

44

not to have them, when was the best time if you did, how many changes they caused, and so on. I remember talking strongly in favor of having them. Sachs, on the other hand, went into a long song and dance about why he disagreed. The arguments he used were fairly conventional (the world is too terrible a place, the population is too big, too much freedom would be lost), but he delivered them with such vehemence and conviction that I assumed he was speaking for Fanny as well and that both of them were dead-set against becoming parents. Years later, I discovered that just the opposite was true. They had desperately wanted to have children, but Fanny was unable to conceive. After numerous attempts to get her pregnant, they had consulted doctors, had tried fertility drugs, had gone through any number of herbal remedies, but nothing had helped. Just days before that dinner in 1975, they had been given definitive word that nothing they did would ever help. It was a crushing blow to Fanny. As she later confessed to me, it was her worst sorrow, a loss she would go on mourning for the rest of her life. Rather than make her talk about it in front of me that evening, Sachs had boiled up a concoction of spontaneous lies, a kettle of steam and hot air to obscure the issue on the table. I heard only a fragment of what he actually said, but that was because I thought he was addressing his remarks to me. As I later understood, he had been talking to Fanny all along. He was telling his wife that he loved her. He was telling her that she didn't have to give him a child to make him go on loving her.

I saw Ben more often than I saw Fanny, and the times when I did see her Ben was always there, but little by little we managed to form a friendship on our own. In some ways, my old infatuation made this closeness seem inevitable, but it also stood as a barrier between us, and several months went by before I was able to look at her without feeling embarrassed. Fanny was an ancient daydream, a phantom of secret desire buried in my past, and now that she had unexpectedly materialized in a new role – as flesh-and-blood woman, as wife of my friend – I admit that I was thrown off balance. It led me to say some stupid things when I first met her, and these blunders only compounded my sense of guilt and confusion. During one of the early evenings I spent at their apartment, I even told her that I hadn't listened to a single word in the class we had taken together. 'Every week, I would spend the whole hour staring at you,' I said. 'Practice is more important than theory, after all, and I figured why waste my time listening to lectures on aesthetics when the beautiful was sitting there right in front of me.'

It was an attempt to apologize for my past behavior, I think, but it came out sounding awful. Such things should never be said under any circumstances, least of all in a flippant tone of voice. They put a terrible burden on the person they're addressed to, and no good can possibly come of them. The moment I spoke those words, I could see that Fanny was startled by my bluntness. 'Yes,' she said, forcing a little smile, 'I remember that class. It was pretty dry stuff.'

'Men are monsters,' I said, unable to stop myself. 'They have ants in their pants, and their heads are crammed with filth. Especially when they're young.'

'Not filth,' Fanny said. 'Just hormones.'

'Those too. But sometimes it's hard to tell the difference.'

'You always wore an earnest look on your face,' she said. 'I remember thinking that you must have been a very serious person. One of those young men who was either going to kill himself or change the world.'

'So far, I haven't done either. I guess that means I've given up my old ambitions.'

'And a good thing, too. You don't want to get stuck in the past. Life is too interesting for that.'

In her own cryptic way, Fanny was letting me off the hook – and also giving me a warning. As long as I behaved myself, she wouldn't hold my past sins against me. It made me feel as though I were on trial, but the fact was that she had every reason to be wary of her husband's new friend, and I don't blame her for keeping me at a distance. As we got to know each other better, the awkwardness began to fade. Among other things, we discovered that we had the same birthday, and though neither one

46

of us had any use for astrology, the coincidence helped to form a link between us. That Fanny was a year older than I was allowed me to treat her with mock deference whenever the subject came up, a standing gag that never failed to get a laugh out of her. Since she was not someone who laughed readily, I took it as a sign of progress on my part. More importantly, there was her work, and my discussions with her about early American painting led to an abiding passion for such artists as Ryder, Church, Blakelock, and Cole – who were scarcely even known to me before I met Fanny. She defended her dissertation at Columbia in the fall of 1975 (one of the first monographs to be published on Albert Pinkham Ryder) and was then hired as an assistant curator of American art at the Brooklyn Museum, where she has continued to work ever since. As I write these words now (July 11), she still has no idea what happened to Ben. She went off on a trip to Europe last month and isn't scheduled to return until after Labour Day. I suppose it would be possible for me to contact her, but I don't see what purpose that would serve. There isn't a damned thing she can do for him at this point, and unless the FBI comes up with an answer before she returns, it's probably best that I keep it to myself. At first, I thought it might be my duty to call her, but now that I've had time to mull it over, I've decided not to ruin her vacation. She's been through enough as it is, and the telephone is hardly an appropriate way to break this kind of news. I'll hold off until she comes back, and then I'll sit her down and tell her what I know in person.

Remembering the early days of the friendship now, I am struck most of all by how much I admired the two of them, both separately and as a couple. Sachs's book had made a deep impression on me, and beyond simply liking him for who he was, I was flattered by the interest he took in my work. He was only two years older than I was, and yet compared to what he had accomplished so far, I felt like a rank beginner. I had missed the reviews of *The New Colossus*, but by all accounts the book had generated a good deal of excitement. Some critics slammed it – largely on political grounds, condemning Sachs for what they

47

saw as his blatant 'anti-Americanism' – but there were others who raved, calling him one of the most promising young novelists to have come along in years. Not much happened on the commercial front (sales were modest, it took two years before a paperback was published), but Sachs's name had been put on the literary map. One would think he would have been gratified by all this, but as I quickly learned about him, Sachs could be maddeningly oblivious when it came to such things. He rarely talked about himself in the way other writers do, and my sense was that he had little or no interest in pursuing what people refer to as a 'literary career.' He wasn't competitive, he wasn't worried about his reputation, he wasn't puffed-up about his talent. That was one of the things that most appealed to me about him: the purity of his ambitions, the absolute simplicity of the way he approached his work. It sometimes made him stubborn and cantankerous, but it also gave him the courage to do exactly what he wanted to do. After the success of his first novel, he immediately started to write another, but once he was a hundred pages into it, he tore up the manuscript and burned it. Inventing stories was a sham, he said, and just like that he decided to give up fiction writing. This was some time in late 1973 or early 1974, about a year before I met him. He began writing essays after that, all kinds of essays and articles on a countless variety of subjects: politics, literature, sports, history, popular culture, food, whatever he felt like thinking about that week or that day. His work was in demand, so he never had trouble finding magazines to publish his pieces, but there was something indiscriminate in the way he went about it. He wrote with equal fervor for national magazines and obscure literary journals, hardly noticing that some publications paid large sums of money for articles and others paid nothing at all. He refused to work with an agent, feeling that would corrupt the process, and therefore he earned considerably less than he should have. I argued with him on this point for many years, but it wasn't until the early eighties that he finally broke down and hired someone to do his negotiating for him.

I was always astonished by how quickly he worked, by his ability to crank out articles under the pressure of deadlines, to produce so much without seeming to exhaust himself. It was nothing for Sachs to write ten or twelve pages at a single sitting, to start and finish an entire piece without once standing up from his typewriter. Work was like an athletic contest for him, an endurance race between his body and his mind, but since he was able to bear down on his thoughts with such concentration, to think with such unanimity of purpose, the words always seemed to be there for him, as if he had found a secret passageway that ran straight from his head to the tips of his fingers. 'Typing for Dollars,' he sometimes called it, but that was only because he couldn't resist making fun of himself. His work was never less than good, I thought, and more often than not it was brilliant. The better I got to know him, the more his productivity awed me. I have always been a plodder, a person who anguishes and struggles over each sentence, and even on my best days I do no more than inch along, crawling on my belly like a man lost in the desert. The smallest word is surrounded by acres of silence for me, and even after I manage to get that word down on the page, it seems to sit there like a mirage, a speck of doubt glimmering in the sand. Language has never been accessible to me in the way that it was for Sachs. I'm shut off from my own thoughts, trapped in a no-man's-land between feeling and articulation, and no matter how hard I try to express myself, I can rarely come up with more than a confused stammer. Sachs never had any of these difficulties. Words and things matched up for him, whereas for me they are constantly breaking apart, flying off in a hundred different directions. I spend most of my time picking up the pieces and gluing them back together, but Sachs never had to stumble around like that, hunting through garbage dumps and trash bins, wondering if he hadn't fit the wrong pieces next to each other. His uncertainties were of a different order, but no matter how hard life became for him in other ways, words were never his problem. The act of writing was remarkably free of pain for him, and when he was working well, he could put words

49

down on the page as fast as he could speak them. It was a curious talent, and because Sachs himself was hardly even aware of it, he seemed to live in a state of perfect innocence. Almost like a child, I sometimes thought, like a prodigious child playing with his toys.

The initial phase of our friendship lasted for approximately a year and a half. Then, within several months of each other, we both left the Upper West Side, and another chapter began. Fanny and Ben went first, moving to an apartment in the Park Slope section of Brooklyn. It was a roomier, more comfortable place than Fanny's old student digs near Columbia, and it put her within walking distance of her job at the museum. That was the fall of 1976. In the time that elapsed between their finding the apartment and moving into it, my wife Delia discovered that she was pregnant. Almost at once, we began making plans to move as well. Our place on Riverside Drive was too cramped to accommodate a child, and with things already growing rocky between us, we figured we might have a better chance if we left the city altogether. I was translating books full-time by then, and as far as work was concerned, it made no difference where we lived.

I can't say that I have any desire to talk about my first marriage now. To the extent that it touches on Sachs's story, however, I don't see how I can entirely avoid the subject. One thing leads to another, and whether I like it or not, I'm as much a part of what happened as anyone else. If not for the breakup of my marriage to Delia Bond, I never would have met Maria Turner, and if I hadn't met Maria Turner, I never would have known about Lillian Stern, and if I hadn't known about Lillian Stern, I wouldn't be sitting here writing this book. Each one of us is connected to Sachs's death in some way, and it won't be possible for me to tell his story without telling each of our stories at the same time. Everything is connected to everything else, every story overlaps with every other story. Horrible as it is for me to say it, I understand now that I'm the one who brought all of us together. As much as Sachs himself, I'm the place where everything begins.

The sequence breaks down like this: I pursued Delia off and on for seven years (1967–74), I convinced her to marry me (1975), we moved to the country (March 1977), our son David was born (June 1977), we separated (November 1978). During the eighteen months I was out of New York, I stayed in close touch with Sachs, but we saw each other less often than before. Postcards and letters took the place of late-night talks in bars, and our contacts were necessarily more circumscribed and formal. Fanny and Ben occasionally drove up to spend weekends with us in the country, and Delia and I visited their house in Vermont for a short stretch one summer, but these get-togethers lacked the anarchic and improvisational quality of our meetings in the past. Still, it wasn't as if the friendship suffered. Every now and then I would have to go down to New York on business: delivering manuscripts, signing contracts, picking up new work, discussing projects with editors. This happened two or three times a month, and whenever I was there I would spend the night at Fanny's and Ben's place in Brooklyn. The stability of their marriage had a calming effect on me, and if I was able to keep some semblance of sanity during that period, I think they were at least partly responsible for it. Going back to Delia the next morning could be difficult, however. The spectacle of domestic happiness I had just witnessed made me understand how seriously I had botched things for myself. I began to dread plunging back into my own turmoil, the deep thickets of disorder that had grown up all around me.

I'm not about to speculate on what did us in. Money was in short supply during our last couple of years together, but I wouldn't want to cite that as a direct cause. A good marriage can withstand any amount of external pressure, a bad marriage cracks apart. In our case, the nightmare began no more than hours after we left the city, and whatever fragile thing that had been holding us together came permanently undone.

Given our lack of money, our original plan had been quite cautious: to rent a house somewhere and see if living in the country suited us or not. If it did, we would stay; if it didn't, we would go back to New York after the lease ran out. But then

Delia's father stepped in and offered to advance us ten thousand dollars for a down payment on a place of our own. With country houses selling for as little as thirty or forty thousand at the time, this sum represented much more than it would now. It was a generous thing for Mr Bond to do, but in the end it worked against us, locking us into a situation neither one of us was prepared to handle. After searching for a couple of months, we found an inexpensive place in Dutchess County, an old and somewhat sagging house with plenty of room inside and a splendid set of lilac bushes in the yard. The day after we moved in, a ferocious thunderstorm swept through the town. Lightning struck the branch of a tree next to the house, the branch caught fire, the fire spread to an electric line that ran through the tree, and we lost our electricity. The moment that happened, the sump pump shut off, and in less than an hour the cellar was flooded. I spent the better part of the night knee-deep in cold rain, working by flashlight as I bailed out the water with buckets. When the electrician arrived the next afternoon to assess the damage, we learned that the entire electrical system had to be replaced. That cost several hundred dollars, and when the septic tank gave out the following month, it cost us more than a thousand dollars to remove the smell of shit from our backyard. We couldn't afford any of these repairs, and the assault on our budget left us dizzy with apprehension. I stepped up the pace of my translation work, taking any assignments that came along, and by mid-spring I had all but abandoned the novel I had been writing for the past three years. Delia was hugely pregnant by then, but she continued to plug away at her own job (free-lance copyediting), and in the last week before she went into labor, she sat at her desk from morning to night correcting a manuscript of over nine hundred pages.

After David was born, the situation only grew worse. Money became my single, overriding obsession, and for the next year I lived in a state of continual panic. With Delia no longer able to contribute much in the way of work, our income fell at the precise moment our expenses began to go up. I took the responsibilities of fatherhood seriously, and the thought of not being able to provide for my wife and son filled me with shame. Once, when a publisher was slow in paying me for work I had handed in, I drove down to New York and stormed into his office, threatening him with physical violence unless he wrote out a check to me on the spot. At one point, I actually grabbed him by the collar and pushed him against the wall. This was utterly implausible behavior for me, a betrayal of everything I believed in. I hadn't fought with anyone since I was a child, and if I let my feelings run away from me in that man's office, it only proves how unhinged I had become. I wrote as many articles as I could, I took on every translation job I was offered, but still it wasn't enough. Assuming that my novel was dead, that my dreams of becoming a writer were finished, I went out and started hunting for a permanent job. But times were bad just then, and opportunities in the country were sparse. Even the local community college, which had advertised for someone to teach a full load of freshman composition courses at the paltry wage of eight thousand dollars a year, received more than three hundred applications for the post. Without any prior teaching experience, I was rejected without an interview. After that, I tried to join the staffs of several of the magazines I had written for, figuring I could commute down to the city if I had to, but the editors only laughed at me and treated my letters as a joke. This is no job for a writer, they answered back, you'd just be wasting your time. But I wasn't a writer anymore, I was a drowning man. I was a man at the end of his rope.

Delia and I were both exhausted, and as time went on our quarreling became automatic, a reflex that neither one of us could control. She nagged and I sulked; she harangued and I brooded; we went days without having the courage to talk to each other. David was the only thing that seemed to bring us pleasure anymore, and we talked about him as if no other subject existed, wary of overstepping the boundaries of that neutral zone. As soon as we did, the snipers would jump back into their trenches, shots would be exchanged, and the war of attrition would begin

54

all over again. It seemed to drag on interminably, a subtle conflict with no definable objective, fought with silences, misunderstandings, and hurt, bewildered looks. For all that, I don't think that either one of us was willing to surrender. We had both dug in for the long haul, and the idea of giving up had never even occurred to us.

All that changed very suddenly in the fall of 1978. One evening, while we were sitting in the living room with David, Delia asked me to fetch her glasses from a shelf in her upstairs study, and when I entered the room I saw her journal lying open on the desk. Delia had been keeping a journal since the age of thirteen or fourteen, and by now it ran to dozens of volumes, notebook after notebook filled with the ongoing saga of her inner life. She had often read passages from it to me, but until that evening I had never so much as dared to look at it without her permission. Standing there at that moment, however, I found myself gripped by a tremendous urge to read those pages. In retrospect, I understand that this meant our life together was already finished, that my willingness to break this trust proved that I had given up any hope for our marriage, but I wasn't aware of it then. At the time, the only thing I felt was curiosity. The pages were open on the desk, and Delia had just asked me to go into the room for her. She must have understood that I would notice them. Assuming that was true, it was almost as if she were inviting me to read what she had written. In all events, that was the excuse I gave myself that night, and even now I'm not so sure I was wrong. It would have been just like her to act indirectly, to provoke a crisis she would never have to claim responsibility for. That was her special talent: taking matters into her own hands, even as she convinced herself that her hands were clean.

So I looked down at the open journal, and once I crossed that threshold, I wasn't able to turn back. I saw that I was the subject of that day's entry, and what I found there was an exhaustive catalogue of complaints and grievances, a grim little document set forth in the language of a laboratory report. Delia had covered everything, from the way I dressed to the foods I ate to my incorrigible lack of human understanding. I was morbid and self-centered, frivolous and domineering, vengeful and lazy and distracted. Even if every one of those things had been true, her portrait of me was so ungenerous, so mean-spirited in its tone, that I couldn't even bring myself to feel angry. I felt sad, hollowed out, dazed. By the time I reached the last paragraph, her conclusion was already self-evident, a thing that no longer needed to be expressed. 'I have never loved Peter,' she wrote. 'It was a mistake to think I ever could. Our life together is a fraud, and the longer we go on like this, the closer we come to destroying each other. We never should have gotten married. I let Peter talk me into it, and I've been paying for it ever since. I didn't love him then, and I don't love him now. No matter how long I stay with Peter, I will never love him.'

It was all so abrupt, so final, that I almost felt relieved. To understand that you are despised in this way eliminates any excuse for self-pity. I couldn't doubt where things stood anymore, and however shaken I might have been in those first moments, I knew that I had brought this disaster down on myself. I had thrown away eleven years of my life in search of a figment. My whole youth had been sacrificed to a delusion, and yet rather than crumple up and mourn what I had just lost, I felt strangely invigorated, set free by the bluntness and brutality of Delia's words. All this strikes me as inexplicable now. But the fact was that I didn't hesitate. I went downstairs with Delia's glasses, told her that I had read her journal, and the next morning I moved out. She was stunned by my decisiveness, I think, but given how thoroughly we had always misread each other, that was probably to be expected. As far as I was concerned, there was nothing to talk about anymore. The deed had already been done, and there wasn't any room for second thoughts.

Fanny helped me find a sublet in lower Manhattan, and by Christmas I was living in New York again. A painter friend of hers was about to go off to Italy for a year, and she had talked him into renting me his spare room for only fifty dollars a month –

which was the absolute limit of what I could afford. It was located directly across the hall from his loft (which was occupied by other tenants), and until I moved in, it had served as a kind of enormous storage closet. All manner of junk and debris was stashed away in there: broken bicycles, abandoned paintings, an old washing machine, empty cans of turpentine, newspapers, magazines, and innumerable fragments of copper wire. I shoved these things to one side of the room, which left me half the space to live in, but after a short period of adjustment, that proved to be large enough. My only household possessions that year were a mattress, a small table, two chairs, a hotplate, a smattering of kitchen utensils, and a single carton of books. It was basic, no-nonsense survival, but the truth is that I was happy in that room. As Sachs put it the first time he came to visit me, it was a sanctuary of inwardness, a room in which the only possible activity was thought. There was a sink and a toilet, but no bath, and the wooden floor was in such poor condition that it gave me splinters whenever I walked on it with bare feet. But I started working on my novel again in that room, and little by little my luck changed. A month after I moved in, I won a grant of ten thousand dollars. The application had been sent in so long before, I had completely forgotten that I was a candidate. Then, just two weeks after that, I won a second grant of seven thousand dollars, which had been applied for in the same flurry of desperation as the first. All of a sudden, miracles had become a common occurrence in my life. I handed over half the money to Delia, and still there was enough to keep me going in a state of relative splendor. Every week, I would shuttle up to the country to spend a day or two with David, sleeping at a neighbor's house down the road. This arrangement lasted for roughly nine months, and when Delia and I finally sold our house the following September, she moved to an apartment in South Brooklyn, and I was able to see David for longer stretches at a time. We both had lawyers by then, and our divorce was already in the works.

Fanny and Ben took an active interest in my new career as a single man. To the degree that I talked to anyone about what I was up to, they were my confidants, the ones I kept abreast of my comings and goings. They had both been upset by the breakup with Delia, but less so Fanny than Ben, I think, although she was the one who worried more about David, zeroing in on that aspect of the problem once she understood that Delia and I had no chance of getting back together. Sachs, on the other hand, did everything he could to talk me into giving it another try. That went on for several weeks, but once I moved back to the city and settled into my new life, he stopped belaboring the point. Delia and I had never let our differences show in public, and our separation came as a shock to most of the people we knew, particularly to close friends like Sachs. Fanny, however, seemed to have had her suspicions all along. When I announced the news in their apartment on the first night I spent away from Delia, she paused for a moment at the end of my story and then said, 'It's a hard thing to swallow, Peter, but in some ways it's probably for the best. As time goes on, I think you're going to be much happier.'

They gave a lot of dinner parties that year, and I was invited to nearly all of them. Fanny and Ben knew an astounding number of people, and at one time or another it seemed that half of New York wound up sitting at the large oval table in their dining room. Artists, writers, professors, critics, editors, gallery owners – they all tramped out to Brooklyn and gorged themselves on Fanny's food, drinking and talking well into the night. Sachs was always the master of ceremonies, an effusive maniac who kept conversations humming along with well-timed jokes and provocative remarks, and I grew to depend on these dinners as my chief source of entertainment. My friends were watching out for me, doing everything in their power to show the world that I was back in circulation. They never talked about matchmaking in so many words, but enough unmarried women turned up at their house on those evenings for me to understand that they had my best interests at heart.

Early in 1979, about three or four months after I returned to New York, I met someone there who played a central role in

Sachs's death. Maria Turner was twenty-seven or twenty-eight at the time, a tall, self-possessed young woman with closely cropped blonde hair and a bony, angular face. She was far from beautiful, but there was an intensity in her gray eyes that attracted me, and I liked the way she carried herself in her clothes, with a kind of prim, sensual grace, a reserve that would unmask itself in little flashes of erotic forgetfulness – letting her skirt drift up along her thighs as she crossed and uncrossed her legs, for example, or the way she touched my hand whenever I lit a cigarette for her. It wasn't that she was a tease or explicitly tried to arouse. She struck me as a good bourgeois girl who had mastered the rules of social behavior, but at the same time it was as if she no longer believed in them, as if she were walking around with a secret she might or might not be willing to share with you, depending on how she felt at that moment.

She lived in a loft on Duane Street, not far from my place on Varick, and after the party broke up that night, we shared a ride with a Brooklyn car service back to Manhattan. That was the beginning of what turned out to be a sexual alliance that lasted for close to two years. I use that phrase as a precise, clinical description, but that doesn't mean our relations were only physical, that we had no interest in each other beyond the pleasures we found in bed. Still, what went on between us was devoid of romantic trappings or sentimental illusions, and the nature of our understanding did not change significantly after that first night. Maria wasn't hungry for the sorts of attachments that most people seem to want, and love in the traditional sense was something alien to her, a passion that lay outside the sphere of what she was capable of. Given my own inner state at the time, I was perfectly willing to accept the conditions she imposed on me. We made no claims on each other, saw each other only intermittently, pursued strictly independent lives. And yet there was a solid affection between us, an intimacy that I had never quite managed to achieve with anyone else. It took me a while to catch on, however. In the beginning, I found her a little scary, perhaps even perverse (which lent a certain excitement to our initial contacts), but as time went on I understood that she was merely eccentric, an unorthodox person who lived her life according to an elaborate set of bizarre, private rituals. Every experience was systematized for her, a self-contained adventure that generated its own risks and limitations, and each one of her projects fell into a different category, separate from all the others. In my case, I belonged to the category of sex. She appointed me as her bed partner on that first night, and that was the function I continued to serve until the end. In the universe of Maria's compulsions, I was just one ritual among many, but I was fond of the role she had picked for me, and I never found any reason to complain.

Maria was an artist, but the work she did had nothing to do with creating objects commonly defined as art. Some people called her a photographer, others referred to her as a conceptualist, still others considered her a writer, but none of these descriptions was accurate, and in the end I don't think she can be pigeonholed in any way. Her work was too nutty for that, too idiosyncratic, too personal to be thought of as belonging to any particular medium or discipline. Ideas would take hold of her, she would work on projects, there would be concrete results that could be shown in galleries, but this activity didn't stem from a desire to make art so much as from a need to indulge her obsessions, to live her life precisely as she wanted to live it. Living always came first, and a number of her most time-consuming projects were done strictly for herself and never shown to anyone.

Since the age of fourteen, she had saved all the birthday presents that had ever been given to her – still wrapped, neatly arranged on shelves according to the year. As an adult, she held an annual birthday dinner in her own honor, always inviting the same number of guests as her age. Some weeks, she would indulge in what she called 'the chromatic diet,' restricting herself to foods of a single color on any given day. Monday orange: carrots, cantaloupe, boiled shrimp. Tuesday red: tomatoes, persimmons, steak tartare. Wednesday white: flounder, potatoes, cottage cheese. Thursday green: cucumbers, broccoli, spinach –

and so on, all the way through the last meal on Sunday. At other times, she would make similar divisions based on the letters of the alphabet. Whole days would be spent under the spell of *b*, *c*, or *w*, and then, just as suddenly as she had started it, she would abandon the game and go on to something else. These were no more than whims, I suppose, tiny experiments with the idea of classification and habit, but similar games were just as likely to go on for many years. There was the long-term project of dressing Mr L., for example, a stranger she had once met at a party. Maria found him to be one of the handsomest men she had ever seen, but his clothes were a disgrace, she thought, and so without announcing her intentions to anyone, she took it upon herself to improve his wardrobe. Every year at Christmas she would send him an anonymous gift – a tie, a sweater, an elegant shirt – and because Mr L. moved in roughly the same social circles that she did, she would run into him every now and again, noting with pleasure the dramatic changes in his sartorial appearance. For the fact was that Mr L. always wore the clothes that Maria sent him. She would even go up to him at these gatherings and compliment him on what he was wearing, but that was as far as it went, and he never caught on that she was the one responsible for those Christmas packages.

She had grown up in Holyoke, Massachusetts, the only child of parents who divorced when she was six. After graduating from high school in 1970, she had gone down to New York with the idea of attending art school and becoming a painter, but she lost interest after one term and dropped out. She bought herself a secondhand Dodge van and took off on a tour of the American continent, staying for exactly two weeks in each state, finding temporary work along the way whenever possible – waitressing jobs, migrant farm jobs, factory jobs, earning just enough to keep her going from one place to the next. It was the first of her mad, compulsive projects, and in some sense it stands as the most extraordinary thing she ever did: a totally meaningless and arbitrary act to which she devoted almost two years of her life. Her only ambition was to spend fourteen days in every state, and beyond that she was free to do whatever she wanted. Doggedly and dispassionately, never questioning the absurdity of her task, Maria stuck it out to the end. She was just nineteen when she started, a young girl entirely on her own, and yet she managed to fend for herself and avoid major catastrophes, living the sort of adventure that boys her age only dream of. At one point in her travels, a co-worker gave her an old thirty-five millimeter camera, and without any prior training or experience, she began taking photographs. When she saw her father in Chicago a few months after that, she told him that she had finally found something she liked doing. She showed him some of her photographs, and on the strength of those early attempts, he offered to make a bargain with her. If she went on taking photographs, he said, he would cover her expenses until she was in a position to support herself. It didn't matter how long it took, but she wasn't allowed to quit. That was the story she told me in any case, and I never had grounds to disbelieve it. All during the years of our affair, a deposit of one thousand dollars showed up in Maria's account on the first of every month, wired directly from a bank in Chicago.

She returned to New York, sold her van, and moved into the loft on Duane Street, a large empty room located on the floor above a wholesale egg and butter business. The first months were lonely and disorienting for her. She had no friends, no life to speak of, and the city seemed menacing and unfamiliar, as if she had never been there before. Without any conscious motives, she began following strangers around the streets, choosing someone at random when she left her house in the morning and allowing that choice to determine where she went for the rest of the day. It became a method of acquiring new thoughts, of filling up the emptiness that seemed to have engulfed her. Eventually, she began going out with her camera and taking pictures of the people she followed. When she returned home in the evening, she would sit down and write about where she had been and what she had done, using the strangers' itineraries to speculate about their lives and, in some cases, to compose brief, imaginary biographies. That was more or less how Maria stumbled into her career as an artist. Other works followed, all of them driven by the same spirit of investigation, the same passion for taking risks. Her subject was the eye, the drama of watching and being watched, and her pieces exhibited the same qualities one found in Maria herself: meticulous attention to detail, a reliance on arbitrary structures, patience bordering on the unendurable. In one work, she hired a private detective to follow her around the city. For several days, this man took pictures of her as she went about her rounds, recording her movements in a small notebook, omitting nothing from the account, not even the most banal and transitory events: crossing the street, buying a newspaper, stopping for a cup of coffee. It was a completely artificial exercise, and yet Maria found it thrilling that anyone should take such an active interest in her. Microscopic actions became fraught with new meaning, the driest routines were charged with uncommon emotion. After several hours, she grew so attached to the detective that she almost forgot she was paying him. When he handed in his report at the end of the week and she studied the photographs of herself and read the exhaustive chronologies of her movements, she felt as if she had become a stranger, as if she had been turned into an imaginary being.

For her next project, Maria took a temporary job as a chambermaid in a large midtown hotel. The point was to gather information about the guests, but not in any intrusive or compromising way. She intentionally avoided them in fact, restricting herself to what could be learned from the objects scattered about their rooms. Again she took photographs; again she invented life stories for them based on the evidence that was available to her. It was an archeology of the present, so to speak, an attempt to reconstitute the essence of something from only the barest fragments: a ticket stub, a torn stocking, a blood stain on the collar of a shirt. Some time after that, a man tried to pick up Maria on the street. She found him distinctly unattractive and rebuffed him. That same evening, by pure coincidence, she ran into him at a gallery opening in SoHo. They talked once again, and this time she learned from the man that he was leaving the next morning on a trip to New Orleans with his girlfriend. Maria would go there as well, she decided, and follow him around with her camera for the entire length of his visit. She had absolutely no interest in him, and the last thing she was looking for was an amorous adventure. Her intention was to keep herself hidden, to resist all contact with him, to explore his outward behavior and make no effort to interpret what she saw. The next morning, she caught a flight from LaGuardia to New Orleans, checked into a hotel, and bought herself a black wig. For three days she made inquiries at dozens of hotels, trying to track down the man's whereabouts. She discovered him at last, and for the rest of the week she walked behind him like a shadow, taking hundreds of photographs, documenting every place he went to. She kept a written diary as well, and when the time came for him to go back to New York, she returned on an earlier flight – in order to be waiting at the airport for a last sequence of pictures as he stepped off the plane. It was a complex and disturbing experience for her, and it left her feeling that she had abandoned her life for a kind of nothingness, as though she had been taking pictures of things that weren't there. The camera was no longer an instrument that recorded presences, it was a way of making the world disappear, a technique for encountering the invisible. Desperate to undo the process she had set in motion, Maria launched into a new project just days after returning to New York. Walking through Times Square with her camera one afternoon, she got into a conversation with the doorman of a topless go-go bar. The weather was warm, and Maria was dressed in shorts and a T-shirt, an unusually skimpy outfit for her. But she had gone out that day in order to be noticed. She wanted to affirm the reality of her body, to make heads turn, to prove to herself that she still existed in the eyes of others. Maria was well put together, with long legs and attractive breasts, and the whistles and lewd remarks she received that day helped to revive her spirits. The doorman told her that she was a pretty girl, just as pretty as the girls inside, and as their conversation continued, she suddenly found herself being offered a job. One of the dancers had called in sick, he said, and if she wanted to fill in for her, he'd introduce her to the boss and see if something couldn't be worked out. Scarcely pausing to think about it, Maria accepted. That was how her next work came into being, a piece that eventually came to be known as *The Naked Lady*. Maria asked a friend to come along that night and take pictures of her as she performed – not to show anyone, but for herself, in order to satisfy her own curiosity about what she looked like. She was consciously turning herself into an object, a nameless figure of desire, and it was crucial to her that she understand precisely what that object was. She only did it that once, working in twenty-minute shifts from eight o'clock in the evening until two in the morning, but she didn't hold back, and the whole time she was on stage, perched behind the bar with colored strobe lights bouncing off her bare skin, she danced her heart out. Dressed in a rhinestone G-string and a pair of two-inch heels, she shook her body to loud rock and roll and watched the men stare at her. She wiggled her ass at them, she ran her tongue over her lips, she winked seductively as they slipped her dollar bills and urged her on. As with everything else she tried, Maria was good at it. Once she got herself going, there was hardly any stopping her.

As far as I know, she went too far only once. That was in the spring of 1976, and the ultimate effects of her miscalculation proved to be catastrophic. At least two lives were lost, and even though it took years for that to happen, the connection between the past and the present is inescapable. Maria was the link between Sachs and Lillian Stern, and if not for Maria's habit of courting trouble in whatever form she could find it, Lillian Stern never would have entered the picture. After Maria turned up at Sachs's apartment in 1979, a meeting between Sachs and Lillian Stern became possible. It took several more unlikely twists before that possibility was realized, but each of them can be traced directly back to Maria. Long before any of us knew her, she went out one morning to buy film for her camera, saw a little black address book lying on the ground, and picked it up. That was the event that started the whole miserable story. Maria opened the book, and out flew the devil, out flew a scourge of violence, mayhem, and death.

It was one of those standard little address books manufactured by the Schaeffer Eaton Company, about six inches tall and four inches across, with a flexible imitation leather cover, spiral binding, and thumb tabs for each letter of the alphabet. It was a well-worn object, filled with over two hundred names, addresses, and telephone numbers. The fact that many of the entries had been crossed out and rewritten, that a variety of writing instruments had been used on almost every page (blue ballpoints, black felt tips, green pencils) suggested that it had belonged to the owner for a long time. Maria's first thought was to return it, but as is often the case with personal property, the owner had neglected to write his name in the book. She searched in all the logical places – the inside front cover, the first page, the back – but no name was to be found. Not knowing what to do with it after that, she dropped the book into her bag and carried it home.

Most people would have forgotten about it, I think, but Maria wasn't one to shy away from unexpected opportunities, to ignore the promptings of chance. By the time she went to bed that night, she had already come up with a plan for her next project. It would be an elaborate piece, much more difficult and complicated than anything she had attempted before, but the sheer scope of it threw her into a state of intense excitement. She was almost certain that the owner of the address book was a man. The handwriting had a masculine look to it; there were more listings for men than for women; the book was in ragged condition, as if it had been treated roughly. In one of those sudden, ridiculous flashes that everyone is prey to, she imagined that she was destined to fall in love with the owner of the book. It lasted only a second or two, but in that time she saw him as the man of her dreams: beautiful, intelligent, warm; a better man than she had ever loved before. The vision dispersed, but by then it was already too late. The book had been transformed into a magical object for her, a storehouse of obscure passions and unarticulated desires. Chance had led her to it, but now that it was hers, she saw it as an instrument of fate.

She studied the entries that first evening and found no names that were familiar to her. That was the perfect starting point, she felt. She would set out in the dark, knowing absolutely nothing, and one by one she would talk to all the people listed in the book. By finding out who they were, she would begin to learn something about the man who had lost it. It would be a portrait *in absentia*, an outline drawn around an empty space, and little by little a figure would emerge from the background, pieced together from everything he was not. She hoped that she would eventually track him down that way, but even if she didn't, the effort would be its own reward. She wanted to encourage people to open up to her when she saw them, to tell her stories about enchantment and lust and falling in love, to confide their deepest secrets in her. She fully expected to work on these interviews for months, perhaps even for years. There would be thousands of photographs to take, hundreds of statements to transcribe, an entire universe to explore. Or so she thought. As it happened, the project was derailed after just one day.

With only one exception, every person in the book was listed under his or her last name. In among the Ls, however, there was an entry for someone named Lilli. Maria assumed it was a woman's first name. If that were so, then this unique departure from the directory style could have been significant, a sign of some special intimacy. What if Lilli was the girlfriend of the man who had lost the address book? Or his sister, or even his mother? Rather than go through the names in alphabetical order as she had originally planned, Maria decided to jump ahead to L and pay a call on the mysterious Lilli first. If her hunch was correct, she might suddenly find herself in a position to learn who the man was.

She couldn't approach Lilli directly. Too much hinged on the meeting, and she was afraid of destroying her chances by blundering into it unprepared. She had to get a sense of who this woman was before she talked to her, to see what she looked like, to follow her around for a while and discover what her habits were. On the first morning, she traveled uptown to the East eighties to stake out Lilli's apartment. She entered the vestibule of the small building to check the buzzers and mailboxes, and just then, as she began to study the list of names on the wall, a woman stepped out of the elevator and opened the inner door. Maria turned to look at her, but before the face had registered, she heard the woman speak her name. 'Maria?' she said. The word was uttered as a question, and an instant later Maria understood that she was looking at Lillian Stern, her old friend from Massachusetts. 'I can't believe it,' Lillian said. 'It's really you, isn't it?'

They hadn't seen each other in more than five years. After Maria set off on her strange journey around America, they had lost contact, but until then they had been close, and their friendship went all the way back to childhood. In high school, they had been nearly inseparable, two offbeat girls struggling through adolescence together, plotting their escape from small-town life. Maria had been the serious one, the quiet intellectual, the one who had trouble making friends, whereas Lillian had been the girl with a reputation, the wild one who slept around and took drugs and played hooky from school. For all that, they were unshakeable allies, and in spite of their differences there was much more that drew them together than pulled them apart. Maria once confessed to me that Lillian had been a great example to her, and it was only by knowing her that she had ever learned how to be herself. But the influence seemed to work both ways. Maria was the one who talked Lillian into moving down to New York after high school, and for the next several months they had shared a cramped, roach-filled apartment on the Lower East Side. While Maria went to art classes, Lillian studied acting and worked as a waitress. She also took up with a rock-and-roll drummer named Tom, and by the time Maria left New York in her van, he had become a permanent fixture in the apartment. She wrote Lillian a number of postcards during her two years on the road, but without an address there was no way that Lillian could write back. When Maria returned to the city, she did everything she could to find her friend, but someone else was living in the old apartment, and there was no listing for her in the phone book. She tried calling Lillian's parents in Holyoke, but they had apparently moved to another town, and suddenly she was out of options. When she ran into Lillian in the vestibule that day, she had given up hope of ever seeing her again.

It was an extraordinary encounter for both of them. Maria told me that they both screamed, then fell into each other's arms, then broke down and wept. Once they were able to talk again, they took the elevator upstairs and spent the rest of the day in Lillian's apartment. There was so much catching up to do, Maria said, the stories just poured out of them. They ate lunch together, and then dinner, and by the time she went home and crawled into bed, it was close to three o'clock in the morning.

Curious things had happened to Lillian in those years, things that Maria never would have thought possible. My knowledge of them is only secondhand, but after talking to Sachs last summer, I believe that the story Maria told me was essentially accurate. She could have been wrong about some of the minor details (as Sachs could have been), but in the long run that's unimportant. Even if Lillian is not always to be trusted, even if her penchant for exaggeration is as pronounced as I'm told it is, the basic facts are not in question. At the time of her accidental meeting with Maria in 1976, Lillian had spent the past three years supporting herself as a prostitute. She entertained her clients in her apartment on East Eighty-seventh Street, and she worked entirely on her own – a part-time hustler with a thriving, independent business. All that is certain. What remains in doubt is exactly how it began. Her boyfriend Tom seems to have been involved in some way, but the full extent of his responsibility is unclear. In both versions of the story, Lillian described him as having a serious drug habit, an addiction to heroin that eventually got him thrown out of his band. According to the story Maria heard, Lillian remained desperately in love with him. She was the one who cooked up the idea herself, volunteering to sleep with other men in order to provide Tom with money. It was fast and painless, she discovered, and as long as she kept his connection happy, she knew that Tom would never leave her. At that point in her life, she said, she was willing to do anything to hold onto him, even if it meant going down the tubes herself. Eleven years later, she told Sachs something altogether different. Tom was the one who talked her into it, she said, and because she was scared of him, because he had threatened to kill her if she didn't go along with it, she'd had no choice but to give in. In this second version, Tom was the one who arranged the appointments for her, literally pimping for his own girlfriend as a way to cover the costs of his addiction. In the end, I don't suppose it matters which version was true. They were equally sordid, and they both led to the same result. After six or seven months, Tom vanished. In Maria's story, he ran off with someone else; in Sachs's story, he died of an overdose. One way or another, Lillian was alone again. One way or another, she continued sleeping with men to pay her bills. What astonished Maria was how matter-of-factly Lillian talked to her about it – with no shame or embarrassment. It was just a job like any other, she said, and when push came to shove, it was a damn sight better than serving drinks or waiting on tables. Men were going to drool wherever you went, and there was nothing you could do to stop them. It made a lot more sense to get paid for it than to fight them off – and besides, a little extra fucking never harmed anyone. If anything, Lillian was proud of how well she had done for herself. She met with clients only three days a week, she had money in the bank, she lived in a comfortable apartment in a good neighborhood. Two years earlier, she had enrolled in acting school again. She felt that she was making progress now, and in the past few weeks she had begun to audition for some parts, mostly in small downtown theaters. It wouldn't be long before something came her way, she said. Once she managed to build up another ten or fifteen thousand dollars, she was planning to close down her business and pursue acting full-time. She was just twenty-four years old, after all, and everything was still in front of her.

Maria had brought along her camera that day, and she took a

number of photographs of Lillian during the time they spent together. When she told me the story three years later, she spread out these pictures in front of me as we talked. There must have been thirty or forty of them, full-size black-and-white photographs that caught Lillian from a variety of angles and distances – some of them posed, some of them not. These portraits were my one and only encounter with Lillian Stern. More than ten years have gone by since that day, but I have never forgotten the experience of looking at those pictures. The impression they made on me was that strong, that lasting.

'She's beautiful, isn't she?' Maria said.

'Yes, extremely beautiful,' I said.

'She was on her way out to buy groceries when we bumped into each other. You see what she's wearing. A sweatshirt, blue jeans, old sneakers. She was dressed for one of those five-minute dashes to the corner store and then back again. No makeup, no jewelry, no props. And still she's beautiful. Enough to take your breath away.'

'It's her darkness,' I said, searching for an explanation. 'Women with dark features don't need a lot of makeup. You see how round her eyes are. The long lashes set them off. And her bones are good, too, we mustn't forget that. Bones make all the difference.'

'It's more than that, Peter. There's a certain inner quality that's always coming to the surface with Lillian. I don't know what to call it. Happiness, grace, animal spirits. It makes her seem more alive than other people. Once she catches your attention, it's hard to stop looking at her.'

'You get the feeling that she's comfortable in front of the camera.'

'Lillian's always comfortable. She's completely relaxed in her own skin.'

I flipped through some more of the photographs and came to a sequence that showed Lillian standing in front of an open closet, in various stages of undress. In one picture, she was taking off her blue jeans; in another, she was removing her sweatshirt; in

71

the next one, she was down to a pair of minuscule white panties and a white sleeveless undershirt; in the next, the panties were gone; in the next one after that, the undershirt was gone as well. Several nude shots followed. In the first, she was facing the camera, head thrown back, laughing, her small breasts almost flattened against her chest, taut nipples protruding over the horizon; her pelvis was thrust forward, and she was clutching the meat of her inner thighs with her two hands, her thatch of dark pubic hair framed by the whiteness of her curled fingers. In the next one she was turned the other way, ass front, jutting her hip to one side and looking over her other shoulder at the camera, still laughing, striking the classic pinup pose. She was clearly enjoying herself, clearly delighted by the opportunity to show herself off.

'This is pretty racy stuff,' I said. 'I didn't know you took girlie pictures.'

'We were getting ready to go out for dinner, and Lillian wanted to change her clothes. I followed her into the bedroom so we could continue talking. I still had my camera with me, and when she started to undress, I took some more pictures. It just happened. I wasn't planning to do it until I saw her peeling off her clothes.'

'And she didn't mind?'

'It doesn't look like she minded, does it?'

'Did it turn you on?'

'Of course it did. I'm not made of wood, you know.'

'What happened next? You didn't sleep together, did you?'

'Oh no, I'm too much of a prude for that.'

'I'm not trying to force a confession out of you. Your friend looks pretty irresistible to me. As much to women as to men, I would think.'

'I admit that I was aroused. If Lillian had made some kind of move then, maybe something would have happened. I've never slept with another woman, but that day with her, I might have done it. It crossed my mind, in any case, and that's the only time I ever felt like that. But Lillian was just fooling around for the

72

camera, and it never got any farther than the strip-tease. It was all in fun, and both of us were laughing the whole time.'

'Did you ever get around to showing her the address book?'

'Eventually. I think it was after we came back from the restaurant. Lillian spent a long time looking through it, but she couldn't really say who it belonged to. It had to be a client, of course. Lilli was the name she used for her work, but beyond that she wasn't sure.'

'It narrowed down the list of possibilities, though.'

'True, but it might not have been someone she'd met. A potential client, for example. Maybe one of Lillian's satisfied customers had passed on her name to someone else. A friend, a business associate, who knows. That's how Lillian got her new clients, by word of mouth. The man wrote down her name in his book, but that doesn't mean he'd gotten around to calling her yet. Maybe the man who'd given him the name hadn't called either. Hookers circulate like that – their names ripple out in concentric circles, weird networks of information. For some men, it's enough to carry around a name or two in their little black book. For future reference, as it were. In case their wife leaves them, or for sudden fits of horniness or frustration.'

'Or when they happen to be passing through town.'

'Exactly.'

'Still, you had your first clues. Until Lillian turned up, the owner of the book could have been anyone. At least you had a fighting chance now.'

'I suppose. But things didn't work out that way. Once I started talking to Lillian, the whole project changed.'

'You mean she wouldn't give you the list of her clients?'

'No, nothing like that. She would have done it if I'd asked her.'

'What was it, then?'

'I'm not quite sure how it happened, but the more we talked, the more definite our plan became. It didn't come from either one of us. It was just floating in the air, a thing that already seemed to exist. Running into each other had a lot to do with it, I think. It was all so wonderful and unexpected, we were sort of beside ourselves. You have to understand how close we'd been. Bosom buddies, sisters, pals for life. We really cared about each other, and I thought I knew Lillian as well as I knew myself. And then what happens? After five years, I discover that my best friend has turned into a whore. It knocked me off balance. I felt awful about it, almost as if I'd been betrayed. But at the same time – and this is where it starts to get murky – I realized that I envied her, too. Lillian hadn't changed. She was the same terrific kid I'd always known. Crazy, full of mischief, exciting to be with. She didn't think of herself as a slut or fallen woman, her conscience was clear. That was what impressed me so much: her absolute inner freedom, the way she lived by her own rules and didn't give a damn what anybody thought. I had already done some fairly excessive things myself by then. The New Orleans project, the 'Naked Lady' project, I was pushing myself a little farther along each time, testing the limits of what I was capable of. But next to Lillian I felt like some spinster librarian, a pathetic virgin who hadn't done much of anything. I thought to myself: If she can do it, why can't I?'

'You're kidding.'

'Wait, let me finish. It was more complicated than that. When I told Lillian about the address book and the people I was going to talk to, she thought it was fantastic, the greatest thing she'd ever heard. She wanted to help me. She wanted to go around and talk to the people in the book, just like I was going to do. She was an actress, remember, and the idea of pretending to be me got her all worked up. She was positively inspired.'

'So you switched. Is that what you're trying to tell me? Lillian talked you into trading places with her.'

'No one talked anyone into anything. We decided on it together.'

'Still . . .'

'Still nothing. We were equal partners from beginning to end. And the fact was, Lillian's life changed because of it. She fell in love with one of the people in the book and wound up marrying him.'

'It gets stranger and stranger.'

'It was strange, all right. Lillian went out with one of my cameras and the address book, and the fifth or sixth person she saw was the man who became her husband. I knew there was a story hidden in that book – but it was Lillian's story, not mine.'

'And you actually met this man? She wasn't making it up?'

'I was their witness at the wedding in City Hall. As far as I know, Lillian never told him how she'd been earning her living, but why should he have to know? They live in Berkeley, California, now. He's a college teacher, a terrifically nice guy.'

'And how did things turn out for you?'

'Not so well. Not so well at all. The same day that Lillian went off with my spare camera, she had an afternoon appointment with one of her regular clients. When he called that morning to confirm, she explained that her mother was sick and she had to leave town. She'd asked a friend to fill in for her, and if he didn't mind seeing someone else this once, she guaranteed he wouldn't regret it. I can't remember her exact words, but that was the general drift. She gave me a big buildup, and after some gentle persuasion the man went along with it. So there I was, sitting alone in Lillian's apartment that afternoon, waiting for the doorbell to ring, getting ready to fuck a man I'd never seen before. His name was Jerome, a squat little man in his forties with hair on his knuckles and yellow teeth. He was a salesman of some sort. Wholesale liquor, I think it was, but it might have been pencils or computers. It doesn't make any difference. He rang the doorbell on the dot of three, and the moment he walked into the apartment, I realized I couldn't go through with it. If he'd been halfway attractive, I might have been able to pluck up my courage, but with a charmer like Jerome it just wasn't possible. He was in a hurry and kept looking at his watch, eager to get started, to get it over with and get out. I played along, not knowing what else to do, trying to think of something as we went into the bedroom and took off our clothes. Dancing naked in a topless bar had been one thing, but standing there with that fat, furry salesman was so intimate, I couldn't even look him in the eyes. I'd hidden my camera in the bathroom, and I figured if I was going to get any pictures out of this fiasco, I'd have to act now. So I excused myself and trotted off to the potty, leaving the door open just a crack. I turned on both faucets in the sink, took out my loaded camera, and started snapping shots of the bedroom. I had a perfect angle. I could see Jerome sprawled out on the bed. He was looking up at the ceiling and wiggling his dick in his hand, trying to get a hard on. It was disgusting, but also comical in some way, and I was glad to be getting it on film. I guessed there'd be time for ten or twelve pictures, but after I'd taken six or seven of them, Jerome suddenly bounced up from the bed, walked over to the bathroom, and yanked open the door before I had a chance to shut it. When he saw me standing there with the camera in my hands, he went crazy. I mean really crazy, out of his mind. He started yelling, accusing me of taking pictures so I could black-mail him and ruin his marriage, and before I knew it he'd snatched the camera from me and was smashing it against the bathtub. I tried to run away, but he grabbed hold of my arm before I could get out, and then he started pounding me with his fists. It was a nightmare. Two naked strangers, slugging it out in a pink tiled bathroom. He kept grunting and shouting as he hit me, yelling at the top of his lungs, and then he landed one that knocked me out. It broke my jaw, if you can believe it. But that was only part of the damage. I also had a broken wrist, a couple of cracked ribs, and bruises all over my body. I spent ten days in the hospital, and afterward my jaw was wired shut for six weeks. Little Jerome beat me to a pulp. He kicked the living shit out of me.'

When I met Maria at Sachs's apartment in 1979, she hadn't slept with a man in close to three years. It took her that long to recover from the shock of the beating, and abstinence was not a choice so much as a necessity, the only possible cure. As much as the physical humiliation she had suffered, the incident with Jerome had been a spiritual defeat. For the first time in her life, Maria had been chastened. She had stepped over the boundaries of herself, and the brutality of that experience had altered her sense of who she was. Until then, she had imagined herself capable of anything: any adventure, any transgression, any dare. She had felt stronger than other people, immunized against the ravages and failures that afflict the rest of humanity. After the switch with Lillian, she learned how badly she had deceived herself. She was weak, she discovered, a person hemmed in by her own fears and inner constraints, as mortal and confused as anyone else.

It took three years to repair the damage (to the extent that it was ever repaired), and when we crossed paths at Sachs's apartment that night, she was more or less ready to emerge from her shell. If I was the one she offered her body to, it was only because I happened to come along at the right moment. Maria always scoffed at that interpretation, insisting that I was the only man she could have gone for, but I would be crazy to think it was because I possessed any supernatural charms. I was just one man among many possible men, damaged goods in my own right, and if I corresponded to what she was looking for just then, so much the better for me. She was the one who set the rules of our friendship, and I stuck to them as best I could, a willing accomplice to her whims and urgent demands. At Maria's request, I agreed that we would never sleep together two nights in a row. I agreed that I would never talk to her about any other woman. I agreed that I would never ask her to introduce me to any of her friends. I agreed to act as though our affair were a secret, a clandestine drama to be hidden from the rest of the world. None of these restraints bothered me. I dressed in the clothes that Maria wanted me to wear, I indulged her appetite for odd meeting places (subway token booths, Off-Track Betting parlors, restaurant bathrooms), I ate the same color-coordinated meals that she did. Everything was play for Maria, a call to constant invention, and no idea was too outlandish not to be tried at least once. We made love with our clothes off and our clothes on, with lights and without lights, indoors and outdoors, on her bed and under it. We put on togas, caveman suits, and rented tuxedos. We pretended to be strangers, we pretended to be married. We acted out doctor-and-nurse routines, waitress-and-customer routines, teacher-and-student routines. It was all fairly childish, I suppose, but Maria took these escapades seriously – not as diversions but as experiments, studies in the shifting nature of the self. If she hadn't been so earnest, I doubt that I could have carried on with her in the way I did. I saw other women during that time, but Maria was the only one who meant anything to me, the only one who is still part of my life today.

In September of that year (1979), someone finally bought the house in Dutchess County, and Delia and David moved back to New York, settling into a brownstone apartment in the Cobble Hill section of Brooklyn. This made things both better and worse for me. I was able to see my son more often, but it also meant more frequent contacts with my soon-to-be ex-wife. Our divorce was well underway by then, but Delia was starting to have misgivings, and in those last months before the papers went through, she made an obscure, halfhearted attempt to win me back. If there had been no David in the picture, I would have been able to resist this campaign without any trouble. But the little boy was clearly suffering from my absence, and I held myself responsible for his bad dreams, his bouts with asthma, his tears. Guilt is a powerful persuader, and Delia instinctively pushed all the right buttons whenever I was around. Once, for example, after a man she was acquainted with had come to her house for dinner, she reported to me that David had crawled into his lap and asked him if he was going to be his new father. Delia wasn't throwing this incident in my face, she was simply sharing her concern with me, but each time I heard another one of these stories, I sank a little deeper into the quicksand of my remorse. It wasn't that I wanted to live with Delia again, but I wondered if I shouldn't resign myself to it, if I wasn't destined to be married to her after all. I considered David's welfare more important than my own, and yet for close to a year I had been cavorting like an idiot with Maria Turner and the others, ignoring every thought that touched on the future. It was difficult to justify this life to myself. Happiness wasn't the only thing that counted, I argued. Once you became a parent, there were duties that couldn't be shirked, obligations that had to be fulfilled, no matter what the cost.

Fanny was the one who saved me from what would have been a terrible decision. I can say that now in the light of what happened later, but back then nothing was clear to me. When the lease on my Varick Street sublet ran out, I rented an apartment just six or seven blocks from Delia's place in Brooklyn. I hadn't been intending to move so close to her, but the prices in Manhattan were too steep for me, and once I started looking on the other side of the river, every apartment I was shown seemed to be in her neighborhood. I wound up with a shabby floor-through in Carroll Gardens, but the rent was affordable, and the bedroom was large enough for two beds – one for me and one for David. He started spending two or three nights a week with me, which was a good change in itself, but one that pushed me into a precarious position with Delia. I had allowed myself to slip back into her orbit, and I could feel my resolve beginning to waver. By an unfortunate coincidence, Maria had left town for a couple of months at the time of my move, and Sachs was gone as well – off to California to work on a screenplay of *The New Colossus*. An independent producer had bought the film rights to his novel, and Sachs had been hired to write the script in collaboration with a professional screenwriter who lived in Hollywood. I will return to that story later, but for now the point is that I was alone, stranded in New York without my usual companions. My whole future was being thrown into question again, and I needed someone to talk to, to hear myself think out loud.

One night, Fanny called me at my new apartment and invited me to dinner. I assumed it would be one of her standard parties, with five or six other guests, but when I showed up at her house the following evening, I discovered that I was the only person she had asked. This came as a surprise to me. In all the years we had known each other, Fanny and I had never spent any time by ourselves. Ben had always been around, and except for the odd moments when he left the room or was called away to the telephone, we had scarcely even spoken to each other without someone else listening to what we said. I had become so accustomed to this arrangement, I didn't bother to question it anymore. Fanny had always been a remote and idealized figure for me, and it seemed fitting that our relations should be indirect, perpetually mediated by others. In spite of the affection that had grown up between us, it still made me a little nervous to be with her. My self-consciousness tended to make me rather whimsical, and I often went out of my way to make her laugh, cracking bad jokes and delivering atrocious puns, translating my awkwardness into a blithe and puerile banter. All this disturbed me, since I never acted that way with anyone else. I am not a jocular person, and I knew that I was giving her a false impression of who I was, but it wasn't until that night that I understood why I had always hidden myself from her. Some thoughts are too dangerous, and you mustn't allow yourself to get near them.

I remember the white silk blouse she wore that evening and the white pearls around her brown neck. I think she noticed how puzzled I was by her invitation, but she didn't let on about it, acting as though it were perfectly normal for friends to have dinner in this way. It probably was, but not from my point of view, not with the history of evasions that existed between us. I asked her if there was anything special she wanted to talk about. No, she said, she just felt like seeing me. She had been working hard ever since Ben left town, and when she woke up yesterday morning, it suddenly occurred to her that she missed me. That was all. She missed me and wanted to know how I was.

We started with drinks in the living room, mostly talking about Ben for the first few minutes. I mentioned a letter he had written to me the week before, and then Fanny described a phone conversation she'd had with him earlier that day. She didn't believe the movie would ever get made, she said, but Ben was earning good money for the script, and that was bound to help. The house in Vermont needed a new roof, and maybe they'd be able to go ahead with it before the old one caved in. We might have talked about Vermont after that, or else her work at the museum, I forget. By the time we sat down for dinner, we had somehow moved on to my book. I told Fanny that I was still making progress, but less than before, since several days a week were now given over entirely to David. We lived like a couple of old bachelors, I said, shuffling around the apartment in our slippers, smoking pipes in the evening, talking philosophy over a glass of brandy as we studied the embers in the fireplace.

'A little like Holmes and Watson,' Fanny said.

'We're getting there. Defecation remains a lively topic these days, but once my colleague is out of diapers, I'm sure we'll be tackling other subjects.'

'It could be worse.'

'Of course it could. You don't hear me complaining, do you?'

'Have you introduced him to any of your lady friends?'

'Maria, for example?'

'For example.'

'I've thought about it, but there never seems to be a good time. It's probably because I don't want to. I'm afraid he'll get confused.'

'And what about Delia? Has she been seeing other men?'

'I think so, but she isn't very forthcoming about her private business.'

'Just as well, I suppose.'

'I can't really say. From the looks of things now, she seems fairly happy that I've moved into her neighborhood.'

'Good God. You're not encouraging this, are you?'

'I'm not sure. It's not as though I'm thinking about marrying anyone else.'

'David's not a good enough reason, Peter. If you went back to Delia now, you'd begin to hate yourself for it. You'd turn into a bitter old man.'

'Maybe that's what I am already.'

'Nonsense.'

'I try not to be, but it gets harder and harder to look at the mess I've made without feeling pretty stupid.'

'You feel responsible, that's all. It's tugging you in opposite directions.'

81

'Whenever I leave, I tell myself I should have stayed. Whenever I stay, I tell myself I should have left.'

'It's called ambivalence.'

'Among other things. If that's the term you want to use, I'll let it stand.'

'Or, as my grandmother once put it to my mother: "Your father would be a wonderful man, if only he were different." '

'Ha.'

'Yes, ha. A whole epic of pain and suffering reduced to a single sentence.'

'Matrimony as a swamp, as a lifelong exercise in self-delusion.'

'You just haven't met the right person yet, Peter. You've got to give yourself more time.'

'You're saying I don't know what real love is. And once I do, my feelings will change. It's nice of you to think that, but what if it never happens? What if it's not in the cards for me?'

'It is, I guarantee it.'

'And what makes you so sure?'

Fanny paused for a moment, put down her knife and fork, and then reached across the table and took hold of my hand. 'You love me, don't you?'

'Of course I love you,' I said.

'You've always loved me, haven't you? From the first moment you laid eyes on me. It's true, isn't it? You've loved me for all these years, and you still love me now.'

I pulled my hand away and looked down at the table, overcome by embarrassment. 'What is this?' I said. 'A forced confession?'

'No, I'm just trying to prove that you married the wrong woman.'

'You're married to someone else, remember? I always thought that kept you off the list of candidates.'

'I'm not saying you should have married me. But you shouldn't have married the person you did.'

'You're talking in circles, Fanny.'

'It's perfectly clear. You just don't want to understand what I'm saying.'

'No, there's a flaw in your argument. I grant you that marrying Delia was a mistake. But loving you doesn't prove that I can love someone else. What if you're the only woman I could ever love? I pose this question hypothetically, of course, but it's a crucial point. If it's true, then your argument makes no sense.'

'Things don't work that way, Peter.'

'That's the way they work for you and Ben. Why make an exception for yourself?'

'I'm not.'

'And what's that supposed to mean?'

'I don't have to spell everything out for you, do I?'

'You'll have to forgive me, but I'm beginning to feel a little confused. If I didn't know I was talking to you, I'd swear you were coming on to me.'

'Are you saying you'd object?'

'Jesus, Fanny, you're married to my best friend.'

'Ben has nothing to do with it. This is strictly between us.'

'No it's not. It has everything to do with him.'

'And what do you think Ben is doing out in California?'

'He's writing a movie script.'

'Yes, he's writing a movie script. And he's also fucking a girl named Cynthia.'

'I don't believe you.'

'Why don't you call him and find out for yourself? Just ask him. He'll tell you the truth. Just say: Fanny tells me you're fucking a girl named Cynthia; what about it, old man? He'll give you a straight answer, I know he will.'

'I don't think we should be having this conversation.'

'And then ask him about the other ones before Cynthia. Grace, for example. And Nora, and Martine, and Val. Those are the first names that spring to mind, but if you give me a minute, I'll think of some more. Your friend is a cunt-hound, Peter. You never knew that about him, did you?'

'Don't talk that way. It's disgusting.'

'I'm only giving you the facts. It's not as though Ben hides it

83

from me. He has my permission, you see. He can do anything he wants. And I can do anything I want.'

'Why bother to stay married, then? If all this is true, there's no reason for you to be together.'

'We love each other, that's why.'

'It certainly doesn't sound like it.'

'But we do. This is the way we've arranged things. If I didn't give Ben his freedom, I'd never be able to hold onto him.'

'So he runs around while you stay put, waiting for your prodigal husband to come home again. It doesn't sound like a fair arrangement to me.'

'It's fair. It's fair because I accept it, because I'm happy with it. Even if I've used my own freedom only sparingly, it's still mine, it still belongs to me. It's a right I can exercise whenever I choose.'

'Such as now.'

'This is it, Peter. You're finally going to get what you've always wanted. And you don't have to feel that you're betraying Ben. What happens tonight is strictly between you and me.'

'You said that before.'

'Maybe you understand it a little better now. You don't have to tie yourself up in knots. If you want me, you can have me.'

'Just like that.'

'Yes, just like that.'

I found her assertiveness daunting, incomprehensible. If I hadn't been so thrown by it, I probably would have stood up from the table and left; but as it was, I just sat in my chair and said nothing. Of course I wanted to sleep with her. She had understood that all along, and now that I had been exposed, now that she had turned my secret into a blunt and vulgar proposition, I scarcely knew who she was anymore. Fanny had become someone else. Ben had become someone else. In the space of one brief conversation, all my certainties about the world had collapsed.

Fanny took hold of my hand again, and instead of trying to talk her out of it, I responded with a weak, embarrassed smile. She must have interpreted that as capitulation, for a moment later she stood up from her chair and walked around the table to where I was sitting. I opened my arms to her, and without saying a word she crawled into my lap, planted her haunches firmly against my thighs, and took hold of my face with her hands. We started kissing. Mouths open, tongues thrashing, slobbering onto each other's chins, we started kissing like a couple of teenagers in the back seat of a car.

We carried on like that for the next three weeks. Almost at once, Fanny became recognizable to me again, a familiar and enigmatic point of stillness. She was no longer the same, of course, but not in any of the ways that had stunned me that first night, and the aggressiveness she had shown then was never repeated. I began to forget all about it, accustoming myself to our altered relations, to the ongoing rush of desire. Ben was still out of town, and except for the nights David was with me, I spent every night at his house, sleeping in his bed and making love to his wife. I took it for granted that I was going to marry Fanny. Even if it meant destroying my friendship with Sachs, I was fully prepared to go ahead with it. For the time being, however, I kept this knowledge to myself. I was still too awed by the strength of my feelings, and I didn't want to overwhelm her by speaking too soon. That was how I justified my silence, in any case, but the truth was that Fanny showed little inclination to talk about anything but the day-to-day, the logistics of the next meeting. Our lovemaking was wordless and intense, a swoon to the depths of immobility. Fanny was all languor and compliance, and I fell in love with the smoothness of her skin, with the way she would close her eyes whenever I stole up behind her and kissed the back of her neck. For the first couple of weeks, I didn't want anything more than that. Touching her was enough, and I lived for the barely audible purrings that came from her throat, for the feel of her back slowly arching against my palms.

I imagined Fanny as David's stepmother. I imagined the two of us setting up house in a different neighborhood and living there for the rest of our lives. I imagined storms, dramatic scenes, immense shouting matches with Sachs before any of this could happen. Perhaps it would finally come to blows, I thought. I found myself ready for anything, and even the idea of squaring off against my friend failed to shock me. I pressed Fanny to talk about him, hungry to listen to her grievances in order to vindicate myself in my own eyes. If I could establish that he had been a bad husband, then my plan to steal her away from him would be given the weight and sanctity of a moral purpose. I wouldn't be stealing her, I would be rescuing her, and my conscience would remain clear. What I was too naïve to grasp was that enmity can also be a dimension of love. Fanny suffered from Ben's sexual conduct; his strayings and pecadillos were a source of constant pain for her, but once she began to confide in me about these things, the bitterness I was expecting to hear from her never advanced beyond a sort of mild rebuke. Opening up to me seemed to relieve some pressure inside her, and now that she had committed a sin of her own, perhaps she was able to pardon him for the sins he had committed against her. This was the economy of justice, so to speak, the quid pro quo that turns the victim into the one who victimizes, the act that puts the scales in balance. In the end, I learned a great deal about Sachs from Fanny, but it never provided me with the ammunition I was looking for. If anything, her disclosures had just the opposite effect. One night, for example, when we started talking about the time he had spent in prison, I found out that those seventeen months had been far more terrible for him than he had ever allowed me to know. I don't think that Fanny was specifically trying to defend him, but when I heard about the things he had lived through (random beatings, continual harassment and threats, a possible incident of homosexual rape), I found it difficult to muster any resentment against him. Sachs as seen through Fanny's eyes was a more complicated and troubled person than the one I thought I knew. He wasn't just the ebullient and gifted extrovert who had become my friend, he was also a man who hid himself from others, a man burdened with secrets he had never shared with anyone. I wanted an excuse to turn against him, but all through those weeks I spent with Fanny, I felt as close to him as ever before. Strangely enough, none of that interfered with my feelings for her. Loving her was simple, even if everything that surrounded that love was fraught with ambiguity. She was the one who had thrown herself at me, after all, and yet the more tightly I held her, the less sure I became of what I was holding.

The affair coincided exactly with Ben's absence. A couple of days before he was scheduled to return, I finally brought up the subject of what we were going to do once he was back in New York. Fanny proposed that we go on in the same way, seeing each other whenever we wished. I told her that wasn't possible, that she would have to make a break with Ben and move in with me if we were going to continue. There wasn't any room for duplicity, I said. We should tell him what had happened, resolve things as quickly as we could, and then plan on getting married. It never occurred to me that this wasn't what Fanny wanted, but that only proves how ignorant I was, how badly I had misread her intentions from the start. She wouldn't leave Ben, she said. She had never even considered it. No matter how much she loved me, it wasn't something she was prepared to do.

It turned into an agonizing conversation that lasted for several hours, a vortex of circular arguments that never took us anywhere. We both did a lot of crying, each one imploring the other to be reasonable, to give in, to look at the situation from a new perspective, but it didn't work. Perhaps it never could have worked, but as it was happening, I felt it was the worst conversation of my life, a moment of absolute ruin. Fanny wouldn't leave Ben, and I wouldn't stay with her unless she did. It's got to be all or nothing, I kept telling her. I loved her too much to settle for just a part of her. As far as I was concerned, anything less than all would be nothing, a misery I could never bring myself to live with. So I got my misery and my nothing, and the affair ended with our conversation that night. Over the months that followed, there was scarcely a moment when I didn't regret it, when I didn't grieve over my stubbornness, but there was never any chance to undo the finality of my words.

Even now, I'm at a loss to understand Fanny's behavior. One could dismiss the whole thing, I suppose, and say that she was simply amusing herself with a brief romp while her husband was out of town. But if sex was all she'd been after, it made no sense to have chosen me as the person to have it with. Given my friendship with Ben, I was the last person she would have turned to. She might have been acting out of revenge, of course, seizing on me as a way to square her accounts with Ben, but in the long run I don't think that explanation goes deep enough. It presupposes a kind of cynicism that Fanny never really possessed, and too many questions are left unanswered. It's also possible that she thought she knew what she was doing and then began to lose her nerve. A classic case of cold feet, as it were, but then what to make of the fact that she never hesitated, that she never showed the slightest glimmer of regret or indecision? Right up to the last moment, it never even crossed my mind that she had any doubts about me. If the affair ended as abruptly as it did, it had to be because she was expecting it to, because she had known it would happen that way all along. This seems perfectly plausible. The only problem is that it contradicts everything she said and did during the three weeks we spent together. What looks like a clarifying thought is finally no more than another snag. The moment you accept it, the conundrum starts all over again.

It wasn't all bad for me, however. In spite of how it ended, the episode had a number of positive results, and I look back on it now as a critical juncture in my own private story. For one thing, I gave up the idea of returning to my marriage. Loving Fanny had shown me how futile that would have been, and I laid those thoughts to rest once and for all. There's no question that Fanny was directly responsible for this change of heart. If not for her, I never would have been in a position to meet Iris, and from then on my life would have developed in an altogether different way. A worse way, I'm convinced; a way that would have turned me toward the bitterness that Fanny had warned me against the first night we spent together. By falling in love with Iris, I fulfilled the prophecy she made about me that same night – but before I could

88

believe that prophecy, I first had to fall in love with Fanny. Was that what she was trying to prove to me? Was that the hidden motive behind our whole crazy affair? It seems preposterous even to suggest it, and yet it tallies with the facts more closely than any other explanation. What I'm saying is that Fanny threw herself at me in order to save me from myself, that she did what she did to prevent me from going back to Delia. Is such a thing possible? Can a person actually go that far for the sake of someone else? If so, then Fanny's actions become nothing less than extraordinary, a pure and luminous gesture of self-sacrifice. Of all the interpretations I've considered over the years, this is the one I like best. That doesn't mean it's true, but as long as it could be true, it pleases me to think it is. After eleven years, it's the only answer that still makes any sense.

Once Sachs returned to New York, I planned to avoid seeing him. I had no idea if Fanny was going to tell him what we'd done, but even if she kept it a secret, the prospect of having to hide it from him myself struck me as intolerable. Our relations had always been too honest and straightforward for that, and I was in no mood to start telling him stories now. I figured he would see through me anyway, and if Fanny happened to tell him what we'd been up to, I would be laying myself open to all kinds of disasters. One way or the other, I wasn't prepared to see him. If he knew, then acting as if he didn't know would be an insult. And if he didn't know, then every minute I spent with him would be a torture.

I worked on my novel, I took care of David, I waited for Maria to return to the city. Under normal circumstances, Sachs would have called me within two or three days. We rarely went longer than that without being in touch, and now that he was back from his Hollywood adventure, I fully expected to hear from him. But three days went by, and then another three days, and little by little I understood that Fanny had let him in on the secret. No other explanation was possible. I assumed that meant our friendship was over and that I would never see him again. Just when I was beginning to come to grips with this idea (on the seventh or eighth day), the telephone rang, and there was Sachs on the other end of the line, sounding in top form, cracking jokes with the same enthusiasm as ever. I tried to match his cheerfulness, but I was too taken aback to do a very good job of it. My voice shook, and I said all the wrong things. When he asked me to come to dinner that night, I made up an excuse and said I would call back tomorrow to work out something else. I didn't call. Another day or two went by, and then Sachs rang up again, still sounding chipper, as though nothing had changed between us. I did my best to fend him off, but this time he wouldn't take no for an answer. He offered to buy me lunch that same afternoon, and before I could think of a way to wriggle out of it, I heard myself accept his invitation. In less than two hours, we were supposed to meet at Costello's Restaurant, a little diner on Court Street just a few blocks from my house. If I didn't show up, he would simply walk over to my place and knock on the door. I hadn't been quick enough, and now I was going to have to face the music.

He was already there when I arrived, sitting in a booth at the back of the restaurant. *The New York Times* was spread out on the Formica table in front of him, and he seemed engrossed in what he was reading, smoking a cigarette and absentmindedly flicking ashes onto the floor after each puff. This was early 1980, the days of the hostage crisis in Iran, the Khmer Rouge atrocities in Cambodia, the war in Afghanistan. Sachs's hair had grown lighter in the California sun, and his bronzed face was smattered with freckles. He looked good, I thought, more rested than the last time I'd seen him. As I walked toward the table, I wondered how close I would have to get before he noticed I was there. The sooner it happened, the worse our conversation was going to be, I said to myself. If he looked up, that would mean he was anxious – which would prove that Fanny had already talked to him. On the other hand, if he kept his nose buried in his paper, that would show he was calm, which might mean that Fanny hadn't talked to him. Each step I took through the crowded restaurant would be a sign in my favor, I felt, a small piece of evidence that he was still in the dark, that he still didn't know I had betrayed him. As it happened, I got all the way to the booth without receiving a single glance.

'That's a nice suntan you've got there, Mr Hollywood,' I said.

As I slid onto the bench across from him, Sachs jerked up his head, stared blankly at me for a moment or two, and then smiled. It was as though he hadn't been expecting to see me, as though I had suddenly appeared in the booth by accident. That was taking it too far, I thought, and in the small silence that preceded his answer, it occurred to me that he had only been pretending to be distracted. In that case, the newspaper was no more than a prop. The whole time he'd been sitting there waiting for me to come, he'd merely been turning pages, blindly scanning the words without bothering to read them.

'You don't look too bad yourself,' he said. 'The cold weather must agree with you.'

'I don't mind it. After spending last winter in the country, this feels like the tropics.'

'And what have you been up to since I went out there to massacre my book?'

'Massacring my own book,' I said. 'Every day, I add another few paragraphs to the catastrophe.'

'You must have quite a bit by now.'

'Eleven chapters out of thirteen. I suppose that means the end is in sight.'

'Any idea when you'll be finished?'

'Not really. Three or four months, maybe. But it could be twelve. And then again, it could be two. It gets harder and harder to make any predictions.'

'I hope you'll let me read it when you're done.'

'Of course you can read it. You'll be the first person I give it to.'

At that point, the waitress arrived to take our orders. That's how I remember it in any case: an early interruption, a brief pause in the flow of our talk. Since moving into the neighborhood, I had been going to Costello's for lunch about twice a week, and the waitress knew who I was. She was an immensely fat and friendly woman who waddled among the tables in a pale green uniform and kept a yellow pencil stuck in her frizzy gray hair at all times. She never wrote with that pencil, using one she stored in her apron pocket instead, but she liked to have it on hand in case there was an emergency. I've forgotten this woman's name now, but she used to call me 'hon' and to stand around and chat with me whenever I came in – never about anything in particular, but always in a way that made me feel welcome. Even with Sachs there that afternoon, we went through one of our typically long-winded exchanges. It doesn't matter what we talked about, but I mention it in order to show what kind of mood Sachs was in that day. Not only did he not talk to the waitress (which was highly unusual for him), but the moment she walked off with our orders, he picked up the conversation exactly where we had stopped, as if we had never been interrupted. It was only then that I began to understand how agitated he must have been. Later on, when the food was served, I don't think he ate more than two or three bites of it. He smoked and drank coffee, dousing his cigarettes in the flooded saucers.

'The work is what counts,' he said, closing up the newspaper and tossing it onto the bench beside him. 'I just want you to know that.'

'I don't think I follow you,' I said, realizing that I followed him all too well.

'I'm telling you not to worry, that's all.'

'Worry? Why should I worry?'

'You shouldn't,' Sachs said, breaking into a warm, astonishingly radiant smile. For a moment or two, he looked almost beatific. 'But I've known you long enough to feel pretty certain that you will.'

'Am I missing something, or have we decided to talk in circles today?'

'It's all right, Peter. That's the only point I'm trying to make. Fanny told me, and you don't have to walk around feeling bad about it.'

'Told you what?' It was a ridiculous question, but I was too stunned by his composure to say anything else.

'What happened while I was gone. The bolt of lightning. The fucking and sucking. The whole bloody thing.'

'I see. Not much left to the imagination.'

'No, not a hell of a lot.'

'So what happens now? Is this the moment when you hand me your card and tell me to contact my seconds? We'll have to meet at dawn, of course. Somewhere good, somewhere with the appropriate scenic value. The walkway of the Brooklyn Bridge, for example, or maybe the Civil War monument at Grand Army Plaza. Something majestic. A place where the sky can dwarf us, where the sunlight can glint off our raised pistols. What do you say, Ben? Is that how you want to do it? Or would you rather get it over with now? American-style. You reach across the table, you punch me in the nose, and then you walk out. Either way is fine with me. I leave it up to you.'

'There's also a third possibility.'

'Ah, the third path,' I said, all anger and facetiousness. 'I hadn't realized there were so many options available to us.'

'Of course there are. More than we can count. The one I'm thinking of is quite simple. We wait for our food to arrive, we eat it, then I pay the check and we leave.'

'That's not good enough. There's no drama in it, no confrontation. We have to force things out into the open. If we back down now, I won't feel satisfied.'

'There's nothing to quarrel about, Peter.'

'Yes there is. There's everything to quarrel about. I asked your wife to marry me. If that isn't sufficient grounds for a quarrel, then neither one of us deserves to live with her.'

'If you want to get it off your chest, go ahead. I'm perfectly willing to listen. But you don't have to talk about it if you don't want to.'

'No one can care so little about his own life. It's almost criminal to be so indifferent.'

'I'm not indifferent. It's just that it was bound to happen sooner or later. I'm not dumb, after all. I know how you feel about

Fanny. You've always felt that way. It's written all over you every time you come near her.'

'Fanny was the one who made the first move. If she hadn't wanted it, nothing would have happened.'

'I'm not blaming you. If I were in your position, I would have done the same thing.'

'That doesn't make it right, though.'

'It's not a question of right and wrong. That's the way the world works. Every man is the prisoner of his pecker, and there's not a damned thing we can do about it. We try to fight it sometimes, but it's always a losing battle.'

'Is this a confession of guilt, or are you trying to tell me you're innocent?'

'Innocent of what?'

'Of what Fanny told me. Your carryings-on. Your extra-curricular activities.'

'She told you that?'

'At great length. She wound up giving me quite an earful. Names, dates, descriptions of the victims, the whole works. It's had an impact. Since then, my idea of who you are has been completely altered.'

'I'm not sure you want to believe everything you hear.'

'Are you calling Fanny a liar?'

'Of course not. It's just that she doesn't always have a firm grasp of the truth.'

'That sounds like the same thing to me. You're saying it differently, that's all.'

'No, I'm telling you that Fanny can't help what she thinks. She's convinced herself that I'm unfaithful, and no amount of talk is ever going to dissuade her.'

'And you're saying that you're not?'

'I've had my lapses, but never to the extent she imagines. Considering how long we've been together, it's not a bad record. Fanny and I have had our ups and downs, but there's never been a moment when I haven't wanted to be married to her.'

'So where does she get the names of all these other women?'

'I tell her stories. It's part of a game we play. I make up stories about my imaginary conquests, and Fanny listens. It excites her. Words have power, after all. For some women, there's no stronger aphrodisiac. You must have learned that about Fanny by now. She loves dirty talk. And the more graphic you make it, the more turned on she gets.'

'That wasn't what it sounded like to me. Every time Fanny talked about you, she was dead serious. Not a word about "imaginary conquests." They were all very real to her.'

'Because she's jealous, and a part of her insists on believing the worst. It's happened many times now. At any given moment, Fanny has me conducting a passionate affair with someone or other. It's been going on for years, and the list of women I've slept with keeps getting longer. After a while, I learned it didn't do any good to deny it. That only made her more suspicious of me, and so rather than tell her the truth, I tell her what she wants to hear. I lie in order to keep her happy.'

'Happiness is hardly the word I'd use for it.'

'To keep us together, then. To keep us in some kind of balance. The stories help. Don't ask me why, but once I start telling them to her, things clear up between us again. You thought I'd stopped writing fiction, but I'm still at it. My audience is down to just one person now, but she's the only one who really counts.'

'And you expect me to believe this?'

'Don't think I'm enjoying myself. It's not easy to talk about it. But I figure you have a right to know, and I'm doing the best I can.'

'And Valerie Maas? You're telling me that nothing ever went on with her?'

'That's a name that used to come up often. She's an editor at one of the magazines I've written for. A year or two ago, we had a number of lunches together. Strictly business. We'd discuss my pieces, talk about future projects, that kind of thing. Eventually, Fanny got it into her head that Val and I were having an affair. I can't say that I wasn't attracted to her. If the circumstances had been different, I might have done something stupid. Fanny sensed all that, I think. I probably mentioned Val's name once too often around the house or made too many flattering remarks about what a good editor she was. But the truth is that Val isn't interested in men. She's been living with another woman for the past five or six years, and I couldn't have gotten anywhere with her even if I'd tried.'

'Didn't you tell that to Fanny?'

'There wouldn't have been any point. Once she's made up her mind, there's never any talking her out of it.'

'You make her sound so unstable. But Fanny isn't like that. She's a solid person, one of the least deluded people I've ever met.'

'She is. In many ways, she's as strong as they come. But she's also suffered a lot, and the last few years have been hard on her. She wasn't always like this, you understand. Until four or five years ago, there wasn't a jealous bone in her body.'

'Five years ago is when I met her. Officially, that is.'

'It's also when the doctor told her she'd never have any children. Things changed for her after that. She's been seeing a therapist for the past couple of years, but I don't think it's done much good. She feels undesirable. She feels that no man can possibly love her. That's why she imagines I'm carrying on with other women. Because she thinks she's failed me. Because she thinks I must be punishing her for having let me down. Once you turn against yourself, it's hard not to believe that everyone else is against you, too.'

'None of this ever shows.'

'That's part of the problem. Fanny doesn't talk enough. She bottles up things inside her, and when they do come out, it's always in oblique ways. That only makes the situation worse. Half the time, she suffers without being aware of it.'

'Until last month, I always thought you had a perfect marriage.'

'We never know anything about anyone. I used to think the same thing about your marriage, and look what happened to you and Delia. It's hard enough keeping track of ourselves. Once it comes to other people, we don't have a clue.'

'But Fanny knows I love her. I must have said it a thousand times, and I'm sure she believes me. I can't imagine that she doesn't.'

'She does. And that's why I think what happened is a good thing. You've helped her, Peter. You've done more for her than anyone else.'

'So now you're thanking me for going to bed with your wife?'

'Why not? Because of you, there's a chance that Fanny will start believing in herself again.'

'Just call Doctor Fixit, huh? He repairs broken marriages, mends wounded souls, saves couples in distress. No appointment necessary, house calls twenty-four hours a day. Dial our toll-free number now. That's Doctor Fixit. He gives you his heart and asks for nothing in return.'

'I don't blame you for feeling resentful. It can't be a very good time for you now, but for whatever it's worth, Fanny thinks you're the greatest man who ever lived. She loves you. She's never going to stop loving you.'

'Which doesn't change the fact that she wants to go on being married to you.'

'It goes too far back, Peter. We've been through too much together. Our whole lives are bound up in it.'

'And where does that leave me?'

'Where you've always been. As my friend. As Fanny's friend. As the person we care most about in the world.'

'So it starts up all over again.'

'If you want it to, yes. As long as you can stand it, it's as if nothing has changed.'

I was suddenly on the verge of tears. 'Just don't blow it,' I said. 'That's all I've got to say to you. Just don't blow it. Make sure you take good care of her. You've got to promise me that. If you don't keep your word, I think I'll kill you. I'll hunt you down and strangle you with my own two hands.'

I stared down at my plate, struggling to keep myself under

control. When I finally looked up again, I saw that Sachs was staring at me. His eyes were somber, his expression fixed in an attitude of pain. Before I could get up from the table to leave, he stretched out his right hand and held it in midair, unwilling to drop it until I took it in my own. 'I promise,' he said, squeezing hard, steadily tightening his grip. 'I give you my word.'

After that lunch, I no longer knew what to believe. Fanny had told me one thing, Sachs had told me another, and as soon as I accepted one story, I would have to reject the other. There wasn't any alternative. They had presented me with two versions of the truth, two separate and distinct realities, and no amount of pushing and shoving could ever bring them together. I understood that, and yet at the same time I realized that both stories had convinced me. In the morass of sorrow and confusion that bogged me down over the next several months, I hesitated to choose between them. I don't think it was a question of divided loyalties (although that might have been part of it), but rather a certainty that both Fanny and Ben had been telling me the truth. The truth as they saw it, perhaps, but nevertheless the truth. Neither one of them had been out to deceive me; neither one had intentionally lied. In other words, there was no universal truth. Not for them, not for anyone else. There was no one to blame or to defend, and the only justifiable response was compassion. I had looked up to them both for too many years not to feel disappointed by what I had learned, but I wasn't disappointed only in them. I was disappointed in myself. I was disappointed in the world. Even the strongest were weak, I told myself; even the bravest lacked courage; even the wisest were ignorant.

I found it impossible to rebuff Sachs anymore. He had been so forthright during our conversation over lunch, so clear about wanting our friendship to continue, that I couldn't bring myself to turn my back on him. But he had been wrong to assume that nothing would change between us. Everything had changed, and like it or not, our friendship had lost its innocence. Because of Fanny, we had each crossed over into the other s life, had each made a mark on the other's internal history, and what had once been pure and simple between us was now infinitely muddy and complex. Little by little, we began to adjust to these new conditions, but with Fanny it was another story. I kept my distance from her, always seeing Sachs alone, always begging off when he invited me to their house. I accepted the fact that she belonged with Ben, but that didn't mean I was ready to see her. She understood my reluctance, I think, and though she continued to send me her love through Sachs, she never pressed me to do anything I didn't want to do. It wasn't until November that she finally called, a good six or seven months later. That was when she invited me to Thanksgiving dinner at Ben's mother's house in Connecticut. In the intervening half year, I had talked myself into thinking there had never been any hope for us, that even if she had left Ben to live with me, it wouldn't have worked. That was a fiction, of course, and I have no way of knowing what would have happened, no way of knowing anything. But it helped to get me through those months without losing my mind, and when I suddenly heard Fanny's voice again on the telephone, I figured the moment had come to test myself in a real situation. So David and I drove up to Connecticut and back, and I spent an entire day in her company. It wasn't the happiest day I've ever spent, but I managed to survive it. Old wounds opened, I bled a little bit, but when I returned home that night with the sleeping David in my arms, I discovered that I was still more or less in one piece.

I don't want to suggest that I accomplished this cure on my own. Once Maria returned to New York, she played a large part in holding me together, and I immersed myself in our private escapades with the same passion as before. Nor was she the only one. When Maria wasn't available, I found still others to distract me from my broken heart. A dancer named Dawn, a writer named Laura, a medical student named Dorothy. At one time or another, each of them held a singular place in my affections. Whenever I stopped and examined my own behavior, I concluded that I wasn't cut out for marriage, that my dreams of settling down with Fanny had been misguided from the start. I wasn't a monogamous person, I told myself. I was too drawn by the mystery of first encounters, too infatuated with the theater of seduction, too hungry for the excitement of new bodies, and I couldn't be counted on over the long haul. That was the logic I used on myself in any case, and it functioned as an effective smokescreen between my head and my heart, between my groin and my intelligence. For the truth was that I had no idea what I was doing. I was out of control, and I fucked for the same reason that other men drink: to drown my sorrows, to dull my senses, to forget myself. I became *homo erectus*, a heathen phallus gone amok. Before long I was entangled in several affairs at once, juggling girlfriends like a demented acrobat, hopping in and out of different beds as often as the moon changes shape. In that this frenzy kept me occupied, I suppose it was successful medicine. But it was the life of a crazy person, and it probably would have killed me if it had lasted much longer than it did.

But there was more to it than just sex. I was working well, and my book was finally coming to the end. No matter how many disasters I created for myself, I managed to work through them, to push on without slackening my pace. My desk had become a sanctuary, and as long as I continued to sit there, struggling to find the next word, nothing could touch me anymore: not Fanny, not Sachs, not even myself. For the first time in all the years I had been writing, I felt as though I had caught fire. I couldn't tell if the book was good or bad, but that no longer seemed important. I had stopped questioning myself. I was doing what I had to do, and I was doing it in the only way that was possible for me. Everything else followed from that. It wasn't that I began to believe in myself so much as that I was inhabited by a sublime indifference. I had become interchangeable with my work, and I accepted that work on its own terms now, understanding that nothing could relieve me of the desire to do it. This was the bedrock epiphany, the illumination in which doubt gradually dissolved. Even if my life fell apart, there would still be something to live for.

I finished *Luna* in mid-April, two months after my talk with

Sachs in the restaurant. I kept my word and gave him the manuscript, and four days later he called to tell me that he'd finished it. To be more exact, he started shouting into the telephone, heaping me with such outlandish praise that I felt myself blush on the other end. I hadn't dared to dream of a response like that. It so buoyed up my spirits that I was able to shrug off the disappointments that followed, and even as the book made the rounds of the New York publishing houses, collecting one rejection after another, I didn't let it interfere with my work. Sachs's encouragement made all the difference. He kept assuring me that I had nothing to worry about, that everything would work out in the end, and in spite of the evidence, I continued to believe him. I began writing a second novel. When Luna was finally taken (seven months and sixteen rejections later), I was already well into my new project. That happened in late November, just two days before Fanny invited me to Thanksgiving dinner in Connecticut. No doubt that contributed to my decision to go. I said yes to her because I'd just heard the news about my book. Success made me feel invulnerable, and I knew there would never be a better moment to face her.

Then came my meeting with Iris, and the madness of those two years abruptly ended. That was on February 23, 1981: three months after Thanksgiving, one year after Fanny and I cut off our affair, six years after my friendship with Sachs had begun. It strikes me as both strange and fitting that Maria Turner should have been the person who made that meeting possible. Again, it had nothing to do with intentionality, nothing to do with a conscious desire to make things happen. But things did happen, and if not for the fact that February twenty-third was the night that Maria's second exhibition opened in a small gallery on Wooster Street, I'm certain that Iris and I never would have met. Decades would have passed before we found ourselves standing in the same room again, and by then the opportunity would have been lost. It's not that Maria actually brought us together, but our meeting took place under her influence, so to speak, and I feel indebted to her because of that. Not to Maria as flesh-and-blood woman, perhaps, but to Maria as the reigning spirit of chance, as goddess of the unpredictable.

Because our affair continued to be a secret, there was no question of my serving as her escort that night. I showed up at the gallery just like any other guest, gave Maria a quick kiss of congratulations, and then stood among the crowd with a plastic cup in my hand, sipping cheap white wine as I scanned the room for familiar faces. I didn't see anyone I knew. At one point, Maria looked over in my direction and winked, but other than the brief smile I threw her in return, I kept my end of the bargain and avoided contact with her. Less than five minutes after that wink, someone came up from behind and tapped me on the shoulder. It was a man named John Johnston, a passing acquaintance whom I hadn't seen in a number of years. Iris was standing next to him, and after he and I exchanged greetings, he introduced us to each other. Based on her appearance, I gathered that she was a fashion model – an error that most people still make when seeing her for the first time. Iris was just twenty-four back then, a dazzling blonde presence, six feet tall with an exquisite Scandinavian face and the deepest, merriest blue eyes to be found between heaven and hell. How could I have guessed that she was a graduate student in English literature at Columbia University? How could I have known that she had read more books that I had and was about to begin a six-hundred-page dissertation on the works of Charles Dickens?

Since I assumed that she and Johnston were intimate friends, I shook her hand politely and did my best not to stare at her. Johnston had been married to someone else the last time I'd seen him, but I figured he was divorced now, and I didn't question him about it. As it happened, he and Iris scarcely knew each other. The three of us talked for several minutes, and then Johnston suddenly turned around and started talking to someone else, leaving me alone with Iris. It was only then that I began to suspect how casual their relations were. Unaccountably, I pulled out my wallet and showed her some snapshots of David, bragging about my little son as though he were a well-known public figure. To listen to Iris recall that evening now, it was at that moment that she decided she was in love with me, that she understood I was the person she was going to marry. It took me a little longer to understand how I felt about her, but only by a few hours. We continued talking over dinner in a nearby restaurant and then on through drinks at yet another place. It must have been past eleven o'clock by the time we finished. I waved down a cab for her on the street, but before I opened the door to let her in, I reached out and grabbed her, drawing her close to me and kissing her deep inside the mouth. It was one of the most impetuous things I have ever done, a moment of insane, unbridled passion. The cab drove off, and Iris and I continued standing in the middle of the street, wrapped in each other's arms. It was as though we were the first people who had ever kissed, as though we invented the art of kissing together that night. By the next morning, Iris had become my happy ending, the miracle that had fallen down on me when I was least expecting it. We took each other by storm, and nothing has ever been the same for me since.

Sachs was my best man at the wedding in June. There was a dinner after the ceremony, and about halfway through the meal he stood up from the table to make a toast. It turned out to be very short, and because he said so little, I can bring back every word of it. 'I'm taking this out of the mouth of William Tecumseh Sherman,' he said. 'I hope the general doesn't mind, but he got there before I did and I can't think of a better way to express it.' Then, turning in my direction, Sachs lifted his glass and said: 'Grant stood by me when I was crazy. I stood by him when he was drunk, and now we stand by each other always.'

3

The era of Ronald Reagan began. Sachs went on doing what he had always done, but in the new American order of the 1980s, his position became increasingly marginalized. It wasn't that he had no audience, but it grew steadily smaller, and the magazines that published his work became steadily more obscure. Almost imperceptibly, Sachs came to be seen as a throwback, as someone out of step with the spirit of the time. The world had changed around him, and in the present climate of selfishness and intolerance, of moronic, chest-pounding Americanism, his opinions sounded curiously harsh and moralistic. It was bad enough that the Right was everywhere in the ascendant, but even more disturbing to him was the collapse of any effective opposition to it. The Democratic Party had caved in; the Left had all but disappeared; the press was mute. All the arguments had suddenly been appropriated by the other side, and to raise one's voice against it was considered bad manners. Sachs continued to make a nuisance of himself, to speak out for what he had always believed in, but fewer and fewer people bothered to listen. He pretended not to care, but I could see that the battle was wearing him down, that even as he tried to take comfort from the fact that he was right, he was gradually losing faith in himself.

If the movie had been made, it might have turned things around for him. But Fanny's prediction proved to be correct, and after six or eight months of revisions, renegotiations, and ditherings back and forth, the producer finally let the project drop. It's difficult to gauge the full extent of Sachs's disappointment. On the surface, he affected a jocular attitude about the whole business, cracking jokes, telling Hollywood stories, laughing about the large sums of money he had earned. This might or might not have been a bluff, but I'm convinced that a part of him had set great store in the possibility of seeing his book turned into a film. Unlike some writers, Sachs bore no grudge against popular culture, and he had never felt any conflict about the project. It wasn't a question of compromising himself, it was an opportunity to reach large numbers of people, and he didn't hesitate when the offer came. Although he never said it in so many words, I sensed that the call from Hollywood had flattered his vanity, stunning him with a brief, intoxicating whiff of power. It was a perfectly normal response, but Sachs was never easy on himself, and chances are that he later regretted these overblown dreams of glory and success. That would have made it more difficult for him to talk about his true feelings once the project failed. He had looked to Hollywood as a way to escape the impending crisis growing inside him, and once it became clear that there was no escape, I believe he suffered a lot more than he ever let on.

All this is speculation. As far as I could tell, there were no abrupt or radical shifts in Sachs's behavior. His work schedule was the same mad scramble of overcommitments and deadlines, and once the Hollywood episode was behind him, he went on producing as much as ever, if not more. Articles, essays, and reviews continued to pour out of him at a staggering rate, and I suppose it could be argued that far from having lost his direction, he was in fact barreling ahead at full tilt. If I question this optimistic portrait of Sachs during those years, it's only because I know what happened later. Immense changes occurred inside him, and while it's simple enough to pinpoint the moment when these changes began, to zero in on the night of his accident and blame everything on that freakish occurrence, I no longer believe that explanation is adequate. Is it possible for someone to change overnight? Can a man fall asleep as one person and then wake up as another? Perhaps, but I wouldn't be willing to bet on it. It's not that the accident wasn't serious, but there are a thousand different ways in which a person can respond to a brush with death. That Sachs responded in the way he did doesn't mean I think he had any choice in the matter. On the contrary, I look on it as a reflection of his state of mind before the accident ever took place. In other words, even if Sachs seemed to be doing more or less well just then, even if he was only dimly aware of his own distress during the months and years that preceded that night, I am convinced that he was in a very bad way. I have no proof to offer in support of this statement – except the proof of hindsight. Most men would have considered themselves lucky to have lived through what happened to Sachs that evening and then shrugged it off. But Sachs didn't, and the fact that he didn't – or, more precisely, the fact that he couldn't – suggests that the accident did not change him so much as make visible what had previously been hidden. If I'm wrong about this, then everything I've written so far is rubbish, a heap of irrelevant musings. Perhaps Ben's life did break in two that night, dividing into a distinct before and after – in which case everything from before can be struck from the record. But if that's true, it would mean that human behavior makes no sense. It would mean that nothing can ever be understood about anything.

I didn't witness the accident, but I was there the night it happened. There must have been forty or fifty of us at the party, a mass of people crowded into the confines of a cramped Brooklyn Heights apartment, sweating, drinking, raising a ruckus in the hot summer air. The accident took place at around eleven o'clock, but by then most of us had gone up to the roof to watch the fireworks. Only two people actually saw Sachs fall: Maria Turner, who was standing next to him on the fire escape, and a woman named Agnes Darwin, who inadvertently caused him to lose his balance by tripping into Maria from behind. There is no question that Sachs could have been killed. Given that he was four stories off the ground, it seems almost a miracle that he wasn't. If not for the clothesline that broke his fall about five feet from the bottom, there's no way he could have escaped without some permanent injury: a broken back, a fractured skull, any one of countless misfortunes. As it was, the rope snapped under the weight of his falling body, and instead of tumbling head-first onto the bare cement, he landed in a cushioning tangle of bathmats, blankets, and towels. The impact was still tremendous, but nothing close to what it could have been. Not only did Sachs survive, but he emerged from the accident relatively unharmed: a few cracked ribs, a mild concussion, a broken shoulder, some nasty bumps and bruises. One can take comfort from that, I suppose, but in the end the real damage had little to do with Sachs's body. This is the thing I'm still struggling to come to terms with, the mystery I'm still trying to solve. His body mended, but he was never the same after that. In those few seconds before he hit the ground, it was as if Sachs lost everything. His entire life flew apart in midair, and from that moment until his death four years later, he never put it back together again.

It was July 4, 1986, the one hundredth anniversary of the Statue of Liberty. Iris was off on a six-week tour of China with her three sisters (one of whom lived in Taipei), David was spending two weeks at a summer camp in Bucks County, and I was holed up in the apartment, working on a new book and seeing no one. Ordinarily, Sachs would have been in Vermont by then, but he had been commissioned by the *Village Voice* to write an article about the festivities, and he wasn't planning to leave the city until he handed in the article. Three years earlier, he had finally succumbed to my advice and entered into an agreement with a literary agent (Patricia Clegg, who also happened to be my agent), and it was Patricia who threw the party that night. Since Brooklyn was ideally situated for watching the fireworks, Ben and Fanny had accepted Patricia's invitation. I had been invited as well, but I wasn't planning to go. I was too inside my work to want to leave the house, but when Fanny called that afternoon and told me that she and Ben would be there, I changed my mind. I hadn't seen either of them for close to a month, and with everyone about to disperse for the summer, I figured it would be my last chance to talk to them until the fall.

As it happened, I scarcely talked to Ben. The party was in full swing by the time I got there, and within three minutes of saying hello to him we had been pushed to opposite corners of the room.

By pure chance, I was jostled up against Fanny, and before long we were so engrossed in conversation that we lost track of where Ben was. Maria Turner was also there, but I didn't see her in the crowd. It was only after the accident that I learned she had come to the party – had in fact been standing with Sachs on the fire escape before he fell – but by then there was so much confusion (shrieking guests, sirens, ambulances, scurrying paramedics) that the full impact of her presence failed to register with me. In the hours that preceded that moment, I enjoyed myself a good deal more than I had been expecting to. It wasn't the party so much as being with Fanny, the pleasure of talking to her again, of knowing that we were still friends in spite of all the years and all the disasters that stood behind us. To tell the truth, I was feeling rather mawkish that night, in the grip of oddly sentimental thoughts, and I remember looking into Fanny's face and realizing – very suddenly, as if for the first time – that we were no longer young, that our lives were slipping away from us. It could have been the alcohol I had drunk, but this thought struck me with all the force of a revelation. We were all growing old, and the only thing we could count on anymore was each other. Fanny and Ben, Iris and David: this was my family. They were the people I loved, and it was their souls I carried around inside me.

We went up to the roof with the others, and in spite of my initial reluctance, I was glad not to have missed the fireworks. The explosions had turned New York into a spectral city, a metropolis under siege, and I savored the sheer mayhem of it all: the incessant noise, the corollas of bursting light, the colors wafting through immense dirigibles of smoke. The Statue of Liberty stood off to our left in the harbor, incandescent in its floodlit glory, and every so often I felt as if the buildings of Manhattan were about to uproot themselves, just take off from the ground and never come back again. Fanny and I sat a little behind the others, heels dug in to balance ourselves against the pitch of the roof, shoulders touching, talking about nothing in particular. Reminiscences, Iris's letters from China, David, Ben's article, the museum. I don't want to make too much of it, but just moments before Ben fell, we drifted onto the story that he and his mother had told about their visit to the Statue of Liberty in 1951. Under the circumstances, it was natural that the story should have come up, but it was gruesome just the same, for no sooner did we both laugh at the idea of falling through the Statue of Liberty than Ben fell from the fire escape. An instant later, Maria and Agnes started screaming below us. It was as if uttering the word *fall* had precipitated a real fall, and even if there was no connection between the two events, I still gag every time I think of what happened. I still hear those screams coming from the two women, and I still see the look on Fanny's face when Ben's name was called out, the look of fear that invaded her eyes as the colored lights of the explosions continued to ricochet against her skin.

He was taken to Long Island College Hospital, still unconscious. Even though he woke up within an hour, they kept him there for the better part of two weeks, conducting a series of brain tests to measure the precise extent of the damage. They would have discharged him sooner, I think, but Sachs said nothing for the first ten days, uttering not a single syllable to anyone – not to Fanny, not to me, not to Maria Turner (who came to visit every afternoon), not to the doctors or nurses. The garrulous, irrepressible Sachs had fallen silent, and it seemed logical to assume that he had lost the power of speech, that the jolt to his head had caused grave internal damage.

It was a hellish period for Fanny. She took off from work and spent every day sitting in the room with Ben, but he was unresponsive to her, often closing his eyes and pretending to be asleep when she came in, returning her smiles with blank stares, seeming to take no comfort from her presence. It made an already difficult situation nearly intolerable for her, and I don't think I've ever seen her so worried, so distraught, so close to full-scale unhappiness as she was then. Nor did it help that Maria kept turning up as well. Fanny imputed all kinds of motives to these visits, but the fact was that they were unfounded. Maria scarcely knew Ben, and many years had gone by since their last encounter. Seven years, to be exact – the last time having been at the dinner in Brooklyn where Maria and I first met. Maria's invitation to the Statue of Liberty party had nothing to do with her knowing Ben or Fanny or myself. Agnes Darwin, an editor who was preparing a book about Maria's work, happened to be a friend of Patricia Clegg's, and she was the one responsible for bringing her to the gathering that night. Watching Ben fall had been a terrifying experience for Maria, and she came to the hospital out of alarm, out of concern, because it wouldn't have felt right to her not to come. I knew that, but Fanny didn't, and as I watched her distress whenever she and Maria crossed paths (understanding that she suspected the worst, that she had convinced herself that Maria and Ben were carrying on a secret liaison), I invited the two of them to lunch in the hospital cafeteria one afternoon in order to clear the air.

According to Maria, she and Ben had talked for a while in the kitchen. He had been animated and charming, regaling her with arcane anecdotes about the Statue of Liberty. When the fireworks began, he suggested that they climb through the kitchen window and watch from the fire escape instead of going to the roof. She hadn't thought he'd been drinking excessively, but at a certain point, completely out of the blue, he jumped up, swung himself over the railing, and sat down on the edge of the iron banister, legs dangling below him in the darkness. This frightened her, she said, and she rushed over and put her arms around him from behind, grabbing hold of his torso to prevent him from falling. She tried to talk him into coming down, but he only laughed and told her not to worry. Just then, Agnes Darwin walked into the kitchen and saw Maria and Ben through the open window. Their backs were turned, and with all the noise and commotion outside, they didn't have the slightest clue that she was there. A chubby, high-spirited woman who had already drunk more than was good for her, Agnes got it into her head to go out and join them on the fire escape. Carrying a glass of wine in one hand, she maneuvered her ample body through the window, landed on the platform with the heel of her left shoe caught between two iron slats, tried to right her balance, and suddenly lurched forward. There wasn't much room out there, and half a step later she had stumbled into Maria from behind, crashing squarely into her friend's back with the full force of her weight. The shock of the blow caused Maria's arms to fly open, and once she lost her grip on Sachs, he went hurtling over the edge of the railing. Just like that, she said, without any warning at all. Agnes bumped into her, she bumped into Sachs, and an instant later he was falling head-first into the night.

It relieved Fanny to learn that her suspicions were groundless, but at the same time nothing had really been explained. Why had Sachs climbed onto the banister in the first place? He had always been scared of heights, and it seemed like the last thing he would have done under the circumstances. And if all had been well between him and Fanny before the accident, why had he turned against her now, why did he recoil from her every time she entered the room? Something had happened, something more than the physical injuries caused by the accident, and until Sachs was able to speak, or until he decided he wanted to speak, Fanny would never know what it was.

It took nearly a month before Sachs told me his side of the story. He was home then, still recuperating but no longer forced to lie in bed, and I went over to his apartment one afternoon while Fanny was at work. It was a sweltering day in early August. We drank beer in the living room, I remember, watching a baseball game on television with the sound off, and whenever I think of that conversation now, I see the silent ballplayers on the small, flickering screen, prancing about in a procession of dimly observed movements, an absurd counterpoint to the painful confidences that my friend poured out to me.

At first, he said, he was only vaguely aware of who Maria Turner was. He recognized her when he saw her at the party, but he couldn't recall the context of their previous meeting. I never forget a face, he told her, but I'm having trouble attaching a name to yours. Elusive as ever, Maria just smiled, saying that it would probably come to him after a while. I was at your house once, she added, by way of a hint, but she wouldn't divulge more than that. Sachs understood that she was playing with him, but he rather enjoyed the way she went about it. He was intrigued by her amused and ironic smile, and he had no objection to being led into a little game of cat and mouse. She clearly had the wit for it, and that was already interesting, already something worth taking the trouble to pursue.

If she had told him her name, Sachs said, he probably wouldn't have acted in the way he did. He knew that Maria Turner and I had been involved with each other before I met Iris, and he knew that Fanny still had some contact with her, since every now and then she would talk to him about Maria's work. But there had been a mixup the night of the dinner party seven years earlier, and Sachs had never properly understood who Maria Turner was. Three or four young women artists had been sitting at the table that evening, and since Sachs was meeting all of them for the first time, he had made the common enough error of jumbling up their names and faces, assigning the wrong name to each face. In his mind, Maria Turner was a short woman with long brown hair, and whenever I had mentioned her to him, that was the image he saw.

They carried their drinks into the kitchen, which was somewhat less crowded than the living room, and sat down on a radiator by the open window, thankful for the slight breeze blowing against their backs. Contrary to Maria's statement about his sober condition, Sachs told me that he was already quite drunk. His head was spinning, and even though he kept warning himself to stop, he belted back at least three bourbons in the next hour. Their conversation developed into one of those mad, elliptical exchanges that come to life when people are flirting with each other at parties, a series of riddles, *non sequiturs*, and clever jabs of one-upmanship. The trick is to say nothing about oneself in as elegant and circuitous manner as possible, to make the other person laugh, to be deft. Both Sachs and Maria were good at that kind of thing, and they managed to keep it up through the three bourbons and a couple of glasses of wine.

Because the weather was hot, and because Maria had been hesitant about going to the party (thinking it would be dull), she had put on the skimpiest outfit in her wardrobe: a sleeveless, skin-tight, crimson leotard with a plunging neckline on top, a tiny black miniskirt below, bare legs, spike heels, a ring on each finger and a bracelet on each wrist. It was an outrageous, provocative costume, but Maria was in one of those moods, and if nothing else it guaranteed that she wouldn't be lost in the crowd. As Sachs told it to me that afternoon in front of the silent television, he had been on his best behavior for the past five years. He hadn't looked at another woman in all that time, and Fanny had learned how to trust him again. Saving his marriage had been hard work; it had called for an immense effort from both of them over a long and difficult period, and he had vowed never to put his life with Fanny in jeopardy again. Now here he was, sitting on the radiator next to Maria at the party, pressed up against a half-naked woman with splendid, inviting legs – already half out of control, with too much drink circulating in his bloodstream. Little by little, Sachs was engulfed by an almost uncontrollable urge to touch those legs, to run his hand up and down the smoothness of that skin. To make matters worse, Maria was wearing an expensive and dangerous perfume (Sachs had always had a weakness for perfume), and as their teasing, bantering conversation continued, it was all he could do to fight against committing a serious, humiliating blunder. Fortunately, his inhibitions won out over his desires, but that did not prevent him from imagining what would have happened if they had lost. He saw his fingertips falling gently on a spot just above her left knee; he saw his hand as it traveled up into the silky regions of her inner thigh (those small areas of flesh still hidden by the skirt), and then, after allowing his fingers to roam there for several seconds, felt them slip past the rim of her undies into an Eden of buttocks and dense, tingling pubes. It was a lurid mental performance, but once the projector started rolling in his head, Sachs was powerless to turn it off. Nor did it help that Maria seemed to know precisely what he was thinking. If she had looked offended, the spell might have been broken, but Maria evidently liked being the object of such lascivious thoughts, and from the way she looked at him whenever he looked at her, Sachs began to suspect that she was silently egging him on, daring him to go ahead and do what he wanted to do. Knowing Maria, I said, I could think of any number of obscure motives to account for her behavior. It could have been connected to a project she was working on, for example, or else she was enjoying herself because she knew something that Sachs didn't know, or else, somewhat more perversely, she had decided to punish him for not remembering her name. (Later on, when I had a chance to talk to her about it in private, she confessed that this last reason was in fact true.) But Sachs wasn't aware of any of this at the time. He could only be certain of what he felt, and that was very simple: he was lusting after a strange, attractive woman, and he despised himself for it.

'I don't see that you have anything to be ashamed of,' I said. 'You're human, after all, and Maria can be pretty fetching when she puts her mind to it. As long as nothing happened, it's hardly worth reproaching yourself for.'

'It's not that I was tempted,' Sachs said slowly, carefully choosing his words. 'It's that I was tempting her. I wasn't going to do that kind of thing anymore, you see. I'd promised myself that it was over, and here I was doing it again.'

'You're confusing thoughts with deeds,' I said. 'There's a world of difference between doing something and just thinking about it. If we didn't make that distinction, life would be impossible.'

'I'm not talking about that. The point was that I wanted to do something that just a moment before I hadn't been aware of wanting to do. It wasn't a question of being unfaithful to Fanny, it was a question of self-knowledge. I found it appalling to discover that I was capable of tricking myself like that. If I'd put a stop to it right then and there, it wouldn't have been so bad, but even after I understood what I was up to, I went on flirting with her anyway.'

114

'But you didn't touch her. In the end, that's the only thing that counts.'

'No, I didn't touch her. But I worked things out so she would have to touch me. As far as I'm concerned, that's even worse. I was dishonest with myself. I stuck to the letter of the law like a good little Boy Scout, but I utterly betrayed its spirit. That's why I fell off the fire escape. It wasn't really an accident, Peter. I caused it myself. I acted like a coward, and then I had to pay for it.'

'Are you telling me you jumped?'

'No, nothing as simple as that. I ran a stupid risk, that's all. I did something unforgivable because I was too ashamed to admit to myself that I wanted to touch Maria Turner's leg. In my opinion, a man who goes to such lengths of self-deception deserves whatever he gets.'

That was why he took her out onto the fire escape. It was an exit from the awkward scene that had developed in the kitchen, but it was also the first step of an elaborate plan, a ruse that would allow him to rub up against Maria Turner's body and still keep his honor intact. This was what so galled him in retrospect: not the fact of his desire, but the denial of that desire as a duplicitous means of fulfilling it. Everything was chaos out there, he said. Cheering crowds, exploding fireworks, a frenetic, pulsing din in his ears. They stood on the platform for several moments watching a volley of rockets illuminate the sky, and then he put the first part of his plan into effect. Given a lifetime of fear in such situations, it was remarkable that he did not hesitate. Moving forward to the edge of the platform, he swung his right leg over the railing, briefly steadied himself by taking hold of the bar with his two hands, and then swung his left leg over as well. Rocking slightly back and forth as he corrected his balance, he heard Maria gasp behind him. She thought he was about to jump, Sachs realized, and so he quickly reassured her, insisting that he was only trying to get a better view. Fortunately, Maria wasn't satisfied with his answer. She pleaded with him to climb down, and when he wouldn't do that, she did the very thing he was hoping she would do, the very thing his reckless stratagems had been calculated to make happen. She rushed up from behind him and wrapped her arms around his chest. That was all: a tiny act of concern that disguised itself as a passionate, full-fledged embrace. If it didn't quite produce the ecstatic response he had been looking forward to (he was too scared to give it his full attention), neither did it wholly disappoint him. He could feel the warmth of her breath fluttering against the back of his neck, he could feel her breasts pushing into his spine, he could smell her perfume. It was the briefest of moments, the smallest of small, ephemeral pleasures, but as her bare, slender arms tightened around him, he experienced something that resembled happiness – a microscopic shudder, a surge of transitory bliss. His gamble seemed to have paid off. He had only to get himself down from there, and the whole masquerade would have been worth it. His plan was to lean back against Maria and use her body for support as he lowered himself to the platform (which would prolong the contact between them until the last possible second), but just as Sachs started shifting his weight to carry out this operation, Agnes Darwin was catching the heel of her shoe and stumbling into Maria from behind. Sachs had loosened his grip from the bar of the railing, and when Maria suddenly crashed into him with a violent forward thrust, his fingers opened and his hands lost contact with the bar. His center of gravity heaved upward, he felt himself pitching out from the building, and an instant later he was surrounded by nothing but air.

'It couldn't have taken me long to reach the ground,' he said. 'Maybe a second or two, three at most. But I distinctly remember having more than one thought during that time. First came the horror, the moment of recognition, the instant when I understood that I was falling. You'd think that would have been all, that I wouldn't have had time to think of anything else. But the horror didn't last. No, that's wrong, the horror continued, but there was another thought that grew up inside it, something stronger than just horror alone. It's hard to give it a name. A feeling of absolute certainty, perhaps. An immense, overpowering rush of conviction, a taste of some ultimate truth. I've never been so certain of anything in my life. First I realized that I was falling, and then I realized that I was dead. I don't mean that I sensed I was going to die, I mean that I was already dead. I was a dead man falling through the air, and even though I was technically still alive, I was dead, as dead as a man who's been buried in his grave. I don't know how else to put it. Even as I fell, I was already past the moment of hitting the ground, past the moment of impact, past the moment of shattering into pieces. I had turned into a corpse, and by the time I hit the clothesline and landed in those towels and blankets, I wasn't there anymore. I had left my body, and for a split second I actually saw myself disappear.'

There were questions I wanted to ask him then, but I didn't interrupt. Sachs was having trouble getting the story out, talking in a trance of hesitations and awkward silences, and I was afraid that a sudden word from me would throw him off course. To be honest, I didn't quite understand what he was trying to say. There was no question that the fall had been a ghastly experience, but I was confused by how much effort he put into describing the small events that had preceded it. The business with Maria struck me as trivial, of no genuine importance, a trite comedy of manners not worth talking about. In Sachs's mind, however, there was a direct connection. The one thing had caused the other, which meant that he didn't see the fall as an accident or a piece of bad luck so much as some grotesque form of punishment. I wanted to tell him that he was wrong, that he was being overly hard on himself – but I didn't. I just sat there and listened to him as he went on analyzing his own behavior. He was trying to present me with an absolutely precise account, splitting hairs with the patience of a medieval theologian, straining to articulate every nuance of his harmless dalliance with Maria out on the fire escape. It was infinitely subtle, infinitely labored and complex, and after a while I began to understand that this lilliputian drama had taken on the same magnitude for him as the fall itself. There was no difference anymore. A quick, ludicrous embrace had become the moral equivalent of death. If Sachs hadn't been so earnest about it, I would have found it comical. Unfortunately, it didn't occur to me to laugh. I was trying to be sympathetic, to hear him out and accept what he had to say on its own terms. Looking back on it now, I believe I would have served him better if I had told him what I thought. I should have laughed in his face. I should have told him he was crazy and made him stop. If there was ever a moment when I failed Sachs as a friend, it was that afternoon four years ago. I had my chance to help him, and I let the opportunity slip through my fingers.

He never made a conscious decision not to speak, he said. It just happened that way, and even as his silence continued, he felt ashamed of himself for causing so many people to worry. There was never any question of brain damage or shock, never any sign of physical impairment. He understood everything that was said to him, and in his heart he knew that he was capable of expressing himself on any subject. The pivotal moment had come at the beginning, when he opened his eyes and saw an unfamiliar woman staring directly into his face – a nurse, as he later discovered. He heard her announce to someone that Rip Van Winkle had finally woken up – or perhaps those words were addressed to him, he couldn't be sure. He wanted to say something back to her, but his mind was already in a tumult, wheeling in all directions at once, and with the pain in his bones suddenly making itself felt, he decided that he was too weak to answer her just then and let the opportunity pass. Sachs had never done anything like that before, and as the nurse continued to chatter away at him, eventually joined by a doctor and a second nurse, the three of them crowding around his bed, encouraging him to tell them how he felt, Sachs went on thinking his own thoughts as if they weren't there, glad to have released himself from the burden of answering them. He assumed it would happen just that once, but the same thing happened the next time, and then the next time, and the time after that as well. Whenever someone spoke to him, Sachs was seized by the same odd compulsion to hold his tongue. As the days went on, he became ever more steadfast in his silence, acting as though it were a point of honor, a secret challenge to keep faith with himself. He would listen to the words that people directed at him, carefully weighing each sentence as it entered his ears, but then, instead of offering a remark of his own, he would turn away, or close his eyes, or stare back at his interlocutor as though he could see straight through him. Sachs knew how childish and petulant this behavior was, but that didn't make it any less difficult for him to stop. The doctors and nurses meant nothing to him, and he felt no great responsibility toward Maria, or myself, or any of his other friends. Fanny was different, however, and there were several instances when he came close to backing down for her sake. At the very least, a flicker of regret would pass through him whenever she came to visit. He understood how cruel he was being to her, and it filled him with a sense of worthlessness, a loathsome aftertaste of guilt. Sometimes, as he lay there in bed warring with his conscience, he would make a feeble attempt to smile at her, and once or twice he actually went so far as to move his lips, producing some faint gurgling sounds in the back of his throat to convince her that he was doing his best, that sooner or later real words would start coming out of him. He hated himself for these shams, but too many things were happening inside his silence now, and he couldn't summon the will to break it.

Contrary to what the doctors supposed, Sachs remembered every detail of the accident. He had only to think about any one moment of that night for the whole night to return in all its sickening immediacy: the party, Maria Turner, the fire escape, the first moments of his fall, the certainty of death, the clothesline, the cement. None of it was dim, no piece of it was less vivid than any other piece. The entire event stood in a surfeit of clarity, an avalanche of overpowering recall. Something extraordinary had taken place, and before it lost its force within him, he needed to devote his unstinting attention to it. Hence his silence. It was not a refusal so much as a method, a way of holding onto the horror of that night long enough to make sense of it. To be silent was to enclose himself in contemplation, to relive the moments of his fall again and again, as if he could suspend himself in midair for the rest of time – forever just two inches off the ground, forever waiting for the apocalypse of the last moment.

He had no intention of forgiving himself, he told me. His guilt was a foregone conclusion, and the less time he wasted on it the better. 'At any other moment in my life,' he said, 'I probably would have looked for excuses. Accidents happen, after all. Every hour of every day, people are dying when they least expect it. They burn up in fires, they drown in lakes, they drive their cars into other cars, they fall out of windows. You read about it in the paper every morning, and you'd have to be a fool not to know that your life could end just as abruptly and pointlessly as any one of those poor bastards'. But the fact was that my accident wasn't caused by bad luck. I wasn't just a victim, I was an accomplice, an active partner in everything that happened to me, and I can't ignore that, I have to take some responsibility for the role I played. Does this make sense to you, or am I talking gibberish? I'm not saying that flirting with Maria Turner was a crime. It was a shabby business, a despicable little stunt, but not a hell of a lot more than that. I might have felt like a shit for lusting after her, but if that tweak in my gonads was the whole story, I would have forgotten all about it by now. What I'm saying is that I don't think sex had much to do with what happened that night. That's one of the things I figured out in the hospital, lying in bed for all those days without talking. If I'd really been serious about chasing after Maria Turner, why did I go to such ridiculous lengths to trick her into touching me? God knows there were less dangerous ways of going about it, a hundred more effective strategies for achieving the same result. But I turned myself into a daredevil out there on the fire escape, I actually risked my life. For what? For a tiny squeeze in the dark, for nothing at all. Looking back on that scene from my hospital bed, I finally understood that everything was different from how I had imagined it. I had gotten it backwards, I had been looking at it upsidedown. The point of my crazy antics wasn't to get Maria Turner to put her arms around me, it was to risk my life. She was only a pretext, an instrument for getting me onto the railing, a hand to guide me to the edge of disaster. The question was: Why did I do it? Why was I so eager to court that risk? I must have asked myself that question six hundred times a day, and each time I asked it, a tremendous chasm would open up inside me, and immediately after that I would be falling again, plunging headlong into the darkness. I don't want to be overly dramatic about it, but those days in the hospital were the worst days of my life. I had put myself in a position to fall, I realized, and I had done it on purpose. That was my discovery, the unassailable conclusion that rose up out of my silence. I learned that I didn't want to live. For reasons that are still impenetrable to me, I climbed onto the railing that night in order to kill myself.'

'You were drunk,' I said. 'You didn't know what you were doing.'

'I was drunk, and I knew exactly what I was doing. It's just that I didn't know I knew it.'

'That's double-talk. Pure sophistry.'

'I didn't know that I knew, and the drinks gave me the courage to act. They helped me do the thing I didn't know I wanted to do.'

'You told me you fell because you were too afraid to touch Maria's leg. Now you change your story and tell me that you fell on purpose. You can't have it both ways. It's got to be one or the other.'

'It's both. The one thing led to the other, and they can't be separated. I'm not saying I understand it, I'm just telling you how it was, what I know to be true. I was ready to do away with myself that night. I can still feel it in my gut, and it scares the hell out of me to walk around with that feeling.'

'There's a part in everyone that wants to die,' I said, 'a little caldron of self-destructiveness that's always boiling under the surface. For some reason, the fires were stoked too high for you that night, and something crazy happened. But just because it happened once, it doesn't mean it's going to happen again.'

'Maybe so. But that doesn't wash away the fact that it happened, and it happened for a reason. If I could be caught by surprise like that, it must mean there's something fundamentally wrong with me. It must mean that I don't believe in my life anymore.'

'If you didn't believe in it, you wouldn't have started talking again. You must have come to some kind of decision. You must have settled things for yourself by then.'

'Not really. You walked into the room with David, and he came up to my bed and smiled at me. I suddenly found myself saying hello to him. It was as simple as that. He looked so nice. All tanned and healthy from his weeks at camp, a perfect nine-year-old boy. When he walked up to my bed and smiled at me, it never occurred to me not to talk to him.'

'There were tears in your eyes. I thought that meant you had resolved something for yourself, that you were on your way back.'

'It meant that I knew I'd hit bottom. It meant that I understood I had to change my life.'

'Changing your life isn't the same thing as wanting to end it.'

'I want to end the life I've been living up to now. I want everything to change. If I don't manage to do that, I'm going to be in deep trouble. My whole life has been a waste, a stupid little joke, a dismal string of petty failures. I'm going to be forty-one years old next week, and if I don't take hold of things now, I'm going to drown. I'm going to sink like a stone to the bottom of the world.'

'You just need to get back to work. The minute you start writing again, you'll begin to remember who you are.'

'The idea of writing disgusts me. It doesn't mean a goddamned thing to me anymore.'

'This isn't the first time you've talked like this.'

'Maybe not. But this time I mean it. I don't want to spend the rest of my life rolling pieces of blank paper into a typewriter. I want to stand up from my desk and do something. The days of being a shadow are over. I've got to step into the real world now and do something.'

'Like what?'

'Who the hell knows?' Sachs said. His words hung in the air for several seconds, and then, without warning, his face broke into a smile. It was the first smile I had seen on him in weeks, and for that one transitory moment, he almost began to look like his old self again. 'When I figure it out,' he said, 'I'll write you a letter.'

I left Sachs's apartment thinking he would pull through the crisis. Not right away, perhaps, but over the long term I found it difficult to imagine that things wouldn't return to normal for him. He had too much resiliency, I told myself, too much intelligence and stamina to let the accident crush him. It's possible that I was underestimating the degree to which his confidence had been shaken, but I tend to think not. I saw how tormented he was, I saw the anguish of his doubts and self-recriminations, but in spite of the hateful things he said about himself that afternoon, he had also flashed me a smile, and I read that fugitive burst of irony as a signal of hope, as proof that Sachs had it in him to make a full recovery.

Weeks passed, however, and then months, and the situation remained exactly what it had been. It's true that he regained much of his social poise, and as time went on his suffering became less obvious (he no longer brooded in company, he no longer seemed quite so absent), but that was only because he talked less about himself. It wasn't the same silence as the one in the hospital, but its effect was similar. He talked now, he opened his mouth and used words at the appropriate moments, but he never said anything about what really concerned him, never anything about the accident or its aftermath, and little by little I sensed that he had pushed his suffering underground, burying it in a place where no one could see it. If all else had been equal, this might not have troubled me so much. I could have learned to live with this quieter and more subdued Sachs, but the outward signs were too discouraging, and I couldn't shake the feeling that they were symptoms of some larger distress. He turned down assignments from magazines, made no effort to renew his professional contacts, seemed to have lost all interest in ever sitting behind his typewriter again. He had told me as much after he came home from the hospital, but I hadn't believed him. Now that he was keeping his word, I began to grow frightened. For as long as I had known him, Sachs's life had revolved around his work, and to see him suddenly without that work made him seem like a man who had no life. He was adrift, floating in a sea of undifferentiated days, and as far as I could tell, it was all one to him whether he made it back to land or not.

Some time between Christmas and the start of the new year, Sachs shaved off his beard and cut his hair down to normal length. It was a drastic change, and it made him look like an altogether different person. He seemed to have shrunk somehow, to have grown both younger and older at the same time, and a good month went by before I began to get used to it, before I stopped being startled every time he walked into a room. It's not that I preferred him to look one way or the other, but I regretted the simple fact of change, of any change in and of itself. When I asked him why he had done it, his first response was a noncommittal shrug. Then, after a short pause, realizing that I expected a fuller answer than that, he muttered something about not wanting to take the trouble anymore. He was into low maintenance, he said, the no-fuss approach to personal hygiene. Besides, he wanted to do his bit for capitalism. By shaving three or four times a week, he would be helping to keep the razor blade companies in business, which meant that he would be contributing to the good of the American economy, to the health and prosperity of all.

This was pretty lame stuff, but after we talked about it that one time, the subject never came up again. Sachs clearly didn't want to dwell on it, and I didn't press him for further explanations. That doesn't mean it was unimportant to him, however. A man is free to choose how he looks, but in Sachs's case I felt it was a particularly violent and aggressive act, almost a form of self-mutilation. The left side of his face and scalp had been badly cut from his fall, and the doctors had stitched up several areas around his temple and lower jaw. With a beard and long hair, the scars from these wounds had been hidden from sight. Once the hair was gone, the scars had become visible, the dents and gashes

124

stood out nakedly for everyone to see. Unless I've seriously misunderstood him, I think that's why Sachs changed his appearance. He wanted to display his wounds, to announce to the world that these scars were what defined him now, to be able to look at himself in the mirror every morning and remember what had happened to him. The scars were an amulet against forgetting, a sign that none of it would ever be lost.

One day in mid-February, I went out to lunch with my editor in Manhattan. The restaurant was somewhere in the West Twenties, and after the meal was over I started walking up Eighth Avenue toward Thirty-fourth Street, where I planned to catch a subway back to Brooklyn. Five or six blocks from my destination, I happened to see Sachs on the other side of the street. I can't say that I'm proud of what I did after that, but it seemed to make sense at the time. I was curious to know what he did on these rambles of his, desperate for some kind of information about how he occupied his days, and so instead of calling out to him I hung back and kept myself hidden. It was a cold afternoon, with a raw gray sky and a threat of snow in the air. For the next couple of hours, I followed Sachs around the streets, shadowing my friend through the canyons of New York. As I write about this now, it sounds a lot worse than it actually was, at least in terms of what I imagined I was doing. I had no intention of spying on him, no wish to penetrate any secrets. I was looking for something hopeful, some glimmer of optimism to assuage my worry. I said to myself: He's going to surprise me; he's going to do something or go somewhere that will prove he's all right. But two hours went by, and nothing happened. Sachs wandered around the streets like a lost soul, roaming haphazardly between Times Square and Greenwich Village at the same slow and contemplative pace, never rushing, never seeming to care where he was. He gave coins to beggars. He stopped to light a fresh cigarette every ten or twelve blocks. He browsed in a bookstore for several minutes, at one point removing one of my books from the shelf and studying it with some attentiveness. He entered a porno shop and looked at magazines of naked women. He paused in front of an electronics store window. Eventually, he bought a newspaper, walked into a coffee house on the corner of Bleecker and MacDougal Streets, and settled down at a table. That was where I left him, just as the waitress came over to take his order. I found it all so bleak, so depressing, so tragic, that I couldn't even bring myself to talk to Iris about it when I got home.

Knowing what I know now, I can see how little I really understood. I was drawing conclusions from what amounted to partial evidence, basing my response on a cluster of random, observable facts that told only a small piece of the story. If more information had been available to me, I might have had a different picture of what was going on, which might have made me a bit slower to despair. Among other things, I was completely in the dark about the special role Maria Turner had assumed for Ben. Ever since October, they had been seeing each other on a regular basis, spending every Thursday together from ten in the morning until five in the afternoon. I only learned about this two years after the fact. As they each told me (in separate conversations at least two months apart), there was never any sex involved. Given what I know about Maria's habits, and given that Sachs's story tallied with hers, I see no point in doubting what they told me.

As I look back on the situation today, it makes perfect sense that Sachs should have reached out to her. Maria was the embodiment of his catastrophe, the central figure in the drama that had precipitated his fall, and therefore no one could have been as important to him. I have already talked about his determination to hold onto the events of that night. What better method to accomplish this than by staying in touch with Maria? By turning her into a friend, he would be able to keep the symbol of his transformation constantly before his eyes. His wounds would remain open, and every time he saw her he could reenact the same sequence of torments and emotions that had come so close to killing him. He would be able to repeat the experience again and again, and with enough practice and hard work, perhaps he would learn to master it. That was how it must have begun. The challenge wasn't to seduce Maria or to take her to bed, it was to expose himself to temptation and see if he had the strength to resist it. Sachs was searching for a cure, for a way to win back his self-respect, and only the most drastic measures would suffice. In order to find out what he was worth, he had to risk everything all over again.

But there was more to it than that. It wasn't just a symbolic exercise for him, it was a step forward into a real friendship. Sachs had been moved by Maria's visits to the hospital, and even then, as early as the first weeks of his recovery, I think he understood how deeply the accident had affected her. That was the initial bond between them. They had both lived through something terrible, and neither one of them was inclined to dismiss it as a simple piece of bad luck. More importantly, Maria was aware of the part she had played in what happened. She knew that she had encouraged Sachs on the night of the party, and she was honest enough with herself to admit what she had done, to realize that it would have been morally wrong to look for excuses. In her own way, she was just as troubled by the event as Sachs was, and when he finally called in October to thank her for coming to the hospital so often, she saw it as a chance to make amends, to undo some of the damage she had caused. I'm not just guessing when I say this. Maria held nothing back from me when we talked last year, and the whole story comes straight from her mouth.

'The first time Ben came to my place,' she said, 'he asked me a lot of questions about my work. He was probably just being polite. You know how it is: you're feeling awkward, and you don't know what to talk about, so you start asking questions. After a while, though, I could see that he was getting interested. I brought out some old projects for him to look at, and his comments struck me as very intelligent, a lot more perceptive than most of the things I hear. What he especially seemed to like was the combination of documentary and play, the objectification of inner states. He understood that all my pieces were stories, and even if they were true stories, they were also invented. Or even if they were invented, they were also true. So we talked about that for a while, and then we got onto various other things, and by the time he left I was already beginning to cook up one of my weird ideas. The guy was so lost and miserable, I thought maybe it would be a good thing if we started working on a piece together. I didn't have anything specific in mind at that point – just that the piece would be about him. He called again a few days later, and when I told him what I was thinking, he seemed to catch on right away. That surprised me a little. I didn't have to argue my case or talk him into it. He just said yes, that sounds like a promising idea, and we went ahead and did it. From then on, we spent every Thursday together. For the next four or five months, we spent every Thursday working on the piece.'

As far as I am able to judge, it never really amounted to anything. Unlike Maria's other projects, this one had no organizing principle or clearly defined purpose, and rather than start with a fixed idea as she always had in the past (to follow a stranger, for example, or to look up names in an address book), 'Thursdays with Ben' was essentially formless: a series of improvisations, a picture album of the days they spent in each other's company. They had agreed beforehand that they wouldn't follow any rules. The only condition was that Sachs arrive at Maria's house promptly at ten o'clock, and from then on they would play it by ear. For the most part, Maria took pictures of him, maybe two or three rolls' worth, and then they would spend the rest of the day talking. A few times, she asked him to dress up in costumes. At other times, she recorded their conversations and took no pictures at all. When Sachs cut off his beard and shortened his hair, it turned out that he was acting on Maria's advice, and the operation took place in her loft. She recorded the whole thing with her camera: the before, the after, and all the steps in between. It begins with Sachs in front of a mirror, clutching a pair of scissors in his right hand. With each successive shot, a little more of his hair is gone. Then we see him lathering up his stubbled cheeks, and after that he gives himself a shave.

Maria stopped shooting at that point (to put the finishing touches on his haircut), and then there's one last picture of Sachs: short-haired and beardless, grinning into the camera like one of those slick hairdo boys you see on barbershop walls. I found it a nice touch. Not only was it funny in itself, but it proved that Sachs was able to enjoy the fun. After I saw that picture, I realized there were no simple solutions. I had underestimated him, and the story of those months was finally much more complicated than I had allowed myself to believe. Then came the shots of Sachs outside. In January and February, Maria had apparently followed him around the streets with her camera. Sachs had told her that he wanted to know what it felt like to be watched, and Maria had obliged him by resurrecting one of her old pieces: only this time it was done in reverse. Sachs took on the role she had played, and she turned herself into the private detective. That was the scene I had stumbled across in Manhattan when I saw Sachs walking along the other side of the street. Maria had been there as well, and what I had taken as conclusive evidence of my friend's misery was in fact no more than a charade, a little bit of play-acting, a silly reenactment of Spy versus Spy. God knows how I managed to miss seeing Maria that day. I must have been concentrating so hard on Sachs that I was blind to everything else. But she saw me, and when she finally told me about it when we talked last fall, I felt crushed with shame. Luckily, she didn't manage to take any pictures of me and Sachs together. Everything would have been out in the open then, but I had been following him from too far away for her to catch us in the same shot.

She took several thousand pictures of him in all, most of which were still on contact sheets when I saw them last September. Even if the Thursday sessions never developed into a coherent, ongoing work, they had a therapeutic value for Sachs – which was all Maria had hoped to accomplish with them in the first place. When Sachs came to visit her in October, he had with-drawn so far into his pain that he was no longer able to see himself. I mean that in a phenomenological sense, in the same way that one talks about self-awareness or the way one forms an image of oneself. Sachs had lost the power to step out from his thoughts and take stock of where he was, to measure the precise dimensions of the space around him. What Maria achieved over the course of those months was to lure him out of his own skin. Sexual tension was a part of it, but there was also her camera, the constant assault of her cyclops machine. Every time Sachs posed for a picture, he was forced to impersonate himself, to play the game of pretending to be who he was. After a while, it must have had an effect on him. By repeating the process so often, he must have come to a point where he started seeing himself through Maria's eyes, where the whole thing doubled back on him and he was able to encounter himself again. They say that a camera can rob a person of his soul. In this case, I believe it was just the opposite. With this camera, I believe that Sachs's soul was gradually given back to him.

He was getting better, but that didn't mean he was well, that he would ever be the person he had been. Deep down, he knew that he could never return to the life he had led before the accident. He had tried to explain that to me during our conversation in August, but I hadn't understood. I had thought he was talking about work – to write or not to write, to abandon his career or not – but it turned out that he had been talking about everything: not just himself, but his life with Fanny as well. Within a month of coming home from the hospital, I think he was already looking for a way to break free of his marriage. It was a unilateral decision, a product of his need to wipe the slate clean and start over again, and Fanny was no more than an innocent victim of the purge. Months passed, however, and he couldn't bring himself to tell her. This probably accounts for many of the puzzling contradictions in his behavior during that time. He didn't want to hurt Fanny, and yet he knew he was going to hurt her, and this knowledge only increased his despair, only made him hate himself more than he already did. Thus the long period of waffling and inaction, of simultaneous recovery and decline. If nothing else, I believe it points to the essential goodness of Sachs's heart. He had convinced himself that his survival hinged on committing an act of cruelty, and for several months he chose not to commit it, wallowing in the depths of a private torment in order to spare his wife from the brutality of his decision. He came close to destroying himself out of kindness. His bags were already packed, and yet he stayed on because her feelings meant as much to him as his own.

When the truth finally emerged, it was scarcely recognizable anymore. Sachs never managed to come out and tell Fanny that he wanted to leave her. His nerve had failed him too badly for that; his shame was too profound for him to be capable of expressing such a thought. Rather, in a much more oblique and circuitous manner, he began to make it known to Fanny that he was no longer worthy of her, that he no longer deserved to be married to her. He was ruining her life, he said, and before he dragged her down with him into hopeless misery, she should cut her losses and run. I don't think there's any question that Sachs believed this. Whether on purpose or not, he had manufactured a situation in which these words could be spoken in good faith. After months of conflict and indecision, he had hit upon a way to spare Fanny's feelings. He wouldn't have to hurt her by announcing his intention to walk out. Rather, by inverting the terms of the dilemma, he would convince her to walk out on him. She would initiate her own rescue; he would help her to stand up for herself and save her own life.

Even if Sachs's motives were hidden from him, he was at last maneuvering himself into a position to get what he wanted. I don't mean to sound cynical about it, but it strikes me that he subjected Fanny to many of the same elaborate self-deceptions and tricky reversals he had used with Maria Turner out on the fire escape the previous summer. An overly refined conscience, a predisposition toward guilt in the face of his own desires, led a good man to act in curiously underhanded ways, in ways that compromised his own goodness. This is the nub of the catastrophe, I think. He accepted everyone else's frailties, but when it came to himself he demanded perfection, an almost superhuman rigor in even the smallest acts. The result was disappointment, a dumbfounding awareness of his own flawed humanity, which drove him to place ever more stringent demands on his conduct, which in turn led to ever more suffocating disappointments. If he had learned how to love himself a little more, he wouldn't have had the power to cause so much unhappiness around him. But Sachs was driven to do penance, to take on his guilt as the guilt of the world and to bear its marks in his own flesh. I don't blame him for what he did. I don't blame him for telling Fanny to leave him or for wanting to change his life. I just feel sorry for him, inexpressibly sorry for the terrible things he brought down on himself.

It took some time before his strategy had any effect. But what is a woman supposed to think when her husband tells her to fall in love with someone else, to get rid of him, to run away from him and never come back? In Fanny's case, she dismissed this talk as nonsense, as further evidence of Ben's growing instability. She had no intention of doing any of these things, and unless he told her straight out that he was finished, that he no longer wanted to be married to her, she was determined to stay put. The standoff lasted for four or five months. This feels like an unendurable length of time to me, but Fanny refused to back down. He was putting her to a test, she felt, trying to push her out of his life in order to see how tenaciously she would hold on, and if she let go now, his worst fears about himself would come true. Such was the circular logic of her struggle to save their marriage. Every time Ben spoke to her, she interpreted it to mean the opposite of what he said. Leave meant don't leave; love someone else meant love me; give up meant don't give up. In the light of what happened later, I'm not so sure that she was wrong. Sachs thought he knew what he wanted, but once he got it, it no longer had any value to him. But by then it was too late. What he had lost, he had lost forever.

According to what Fanny told me, there was never any decisive break between them. Sachs wore her down instead, exhausting her with his persistence, slowly debilitating her until she no longer had the strength to fight back. There had been a few hysterical scenes in the beginning, she said, a few outbursts of tears and shouting, but all that eventually stopped. Little by little, she had run out of counterarguments, and when Sachs finally spoke the magic words, telling her one day in early March that a trial separation might be a good idea, she just nodded her head and went along with him. At the time, I knew nothing about any of this. Neither one of them had opened up to me about their troubles, and since my own life was particularly frantic just then, I wasn't able to see them as often as I would have wished. Iris was pregnant; we were searching for a new place to live; I was commuting to a teaching job in Princeton twice a week and working hard on my next book. Still, it seems that I played an unwitting part in their marital negotiations. What I did was to provide Sachs with an excuse, a way to walk out on her without appearing to have slammed the door shut. It all goes back to that day in February when I followed him around the streets. I had just spent two and a half hours with my editor, Nan Howard, and during the course of our conversation Sachs's name had been mentioned more than once. Nan knew how close we were. She had been at the Fourth of July party herself, and since she knew about the accident and the tough times he had been going through since then, it was normal that she should ask me how he was. I told her that I was still worried – not so much by his mood anymore, but by the fact that he hadn't done a stitch of work. 'It's been seven months now,' I said, 'and that's too long a holiday, especially for someone like Ben.' So we talked about work for a few minutes, wondering what it would take for him to get going again, and just as we started in on dessert, Nan came up with what struck me as a terrific idea. 'He should put his old pieces together and publish them as a book,' she said. 'It wouldn't be very difficult. All he'd have to do is pick out the best ones, maybe touch up a couple of sentences here and there. But once he sits down with his old work, who knows what might happen? It could make him want to start writing again.'

'Are you saying you'd be interested in publishing this book?' I said.

'I don't know,' she said, 'is that what I'm saying?' Nan paused for a moment and laughed. 'I suppose I just said it, didn't I?' Then she paused again, as if to catch herself before she went too far. 'But still, why the hell not? It's not as though I don't know Ben's stuff. I've been reading it since high school, for Christ's sake. Maybe it's about time someone twisted his arm and got him to do it.'

Half an hour later, when I caught sight of Sachs on Eighth Avenue, I was still thinking about this conversation with Nan. The idea of the book had settled comfortably inside me by then, and for once I was feeling encouraged, more hopeful than I had been in a long time. Perhaps that explains why I became so depressed afterward. I found a man living in what looked like a state of utter abjection, and I couldn't bring myself to accept what I had seen: my once brilliant friend, wandering around for hours in a quasi-trance, scarcely distinguishable from the ruined men and women who begged coins from him in the street. I got home that evening feeling sick at heart. The situation was out of control, I told myself, and unless I acted fast, there wouldn't be a prayer of saving him.

I invited him out to lunch the following week. The moment he sat down in his chair, I plunged in and started talking about the book. This notion had been bandied about a few times in the past, but Sachs had always been reluctant to commit himself. He felt his magazine pieces were things of the moment, written for specific reasons at specific times, and a book would be too permanent a place for them. They should be allowed to die a natural death, he'd once told me. Let people read them once and forget them – there was no need to erect a tomb. I was already familiar with this defense, so I didn't present the idea in literary terms. I talked about it strictly as a money proposition, a cold cash deal. He had been sponging off Fanny for the past seven months, I said, and maybe it was time for him to start pulling his own weight. If he wasn't willing to go out and find a job, the least he could do was publish this book. Forget about yourself for once, I told him. Do it for her.

I don't think I'd ever spoken to him so emphatically. I was so wound up, so filled with passionate good sense, that Sachs started smiling before I was halfway into my harangue. I suppose there was something comical about my behavior that afternoon, but that was only because I hadn't expected to win so easily. As it turned out, Sachs needed little convincing. He made up his mind to do the book as soon as he heard about my conversation with Nan, and everything I said to him after that was unnecessary. He tried to get me to stop, but since I thought that meant he didn't want to talk about it, I kept on arguing with him, which was a bit like telling someone to eat a meal that was already inside his stomach. I'm sure he found me laughable, but none of that makes any difference now. What matters is that Sachs agreed to do the book, and at the time I felt it was a major victory, a gigantic step in the right direction. I knew nothing about Fanny, of course, and therefore I had no idea that the project was simply a ploy, a strategic move to help him bring his marriage to an end. That doesn't mean Sachs wasn't planning to publish the book, but his motives were quite different from the ones I imagined. I saw the book as a way back into the world, whereas he saw it as an escape, as a last gesture of goodwill before he slipped off into the darkness and disappeared.

That was how he found the courage to talk to Fanny about a trial separation. He would go to Vermont to work on the book, she would stay in the city, and meanwhile they would both have a chance to think about what they wanted to do. The book made it possible for him to leave with her blessing, for both of them to ignore the true purpose of his departure. Over the next two weeks, Fanny organized Ben's trip to Vermont as if it were still one of her wifely duties, actively dismantling their marriage as if she believed they would go on being married forever. The habit of caring for him was so automatic by then, so deeply ingrained in who she was, that it probably never occurred to her to stop and consider what she was doing. That was the paradox of the end. I had lived through something similar with Delia: that strange postscript when a couple is neither together nor not together, when the last thing holding you together is the fact that you are apart. Fanny and Ben acted no differently. She helped him move out of her life, and he accepted that help as the most natural thing in the world. She went down to the cellar and lugged up sheafs of old articles for him; she made photocopies of yellowed, crumbling originals; she visited the library and searched through spools of microfilm for errant pieces; she put the whole mass of clippings and tear sheets and jagged pages into chronological order. On the last day, she even went out and bought cardboard file boxes to store the papers in, and the next morning, when it came time for Sachs to leave, she helped him carry these boxes downstairs and load them into the trunk of the car. So much for making a clean break. So much for giving off unambiguous signals. At that point, I don't think either one of them would have been capable of it.

That was some time in late March. Innocently accepting what Sachs had told me, I assumed that he was going to Vermont in order to work. He had gone there alone before, and the fact that Fanny was staying behind in New York didn't strike me as unusual. She had her job, after all, and since no one had mentioned how long Sachs would be gone, I figured it would be a relatively short trip. A month maybe, six weeks at the most. Putting together the book would not be a difficult task, and I didn't see how it could take him longer than that. And even if it did, there was nothing to prevent Fanny from visiting him in the meantime. So I didn't question any of their arrangements. They all made sense to me, and when Sachs called to say good-bye on the last night, I told him how glad I was that he was going. Good luck, I said, I'll see you soon. And that was it. Whatever he might have been planning then, he didn't say a word to make me think he wouldn't be back.

After Sachs left for Vermont, my thoughts turned elsewhere. I was busy with work, with Iris's pregnancy, with David's troubles in school, with deaths of relatives on both sides of the family, and the spring passed very quickly. Perhaps I felt relieved that he was gone, I don't know, but there's no doubt that country life had improved his spirits. We talked on the phone about once a week, and I gathered from these conversations that things were going well for him. He had started work on something new, he told me, and I took this as such a momentous event, such a turnaround from his previous state, that I suddenly allowed myself to stop worrying about him. Even when he kept putting off his return to New York, prolonging his absence through April, then May, and then June, I didn't feel any alarm. Sachs was writing again, I told myself, Sachs was healthy again, and as far as I was concerned, that meant all was right with the world.

Iris and I saw Fanny on several occasions that spring. I remember at least one dinner, a Sunday brunch, and a couple of outings to the movies. To be perfectly honest, I didn't detect any signs of distress or unease in her. It's true that she talked about Sachs very little (which should have alerted me to something), but whenever she did talk about him, she sounded pleased, even excited by what was happening in Vermont. Not only was he writing again, she told us, but he was writing a novel. This was so much better than anything she could have imagined, it made no difference that the essay book had been shunted to the side. He was working up a storm, she said, scarcely even pausing to eat or sleep, and whether these reports were exaggerated or not (either by Sachs or by her), they put an end to all further questions. Iris and I never asked her why she didn't go up to visit Ben. We didn't ask because the answer was already obvious. He was on a roll with his work, and after waiting so long for this to happen, she wasn't about to interfere.

She was holding back on us, of course, but more to the point was that Sachs had been cut out of the picture as well. I only learned about this later, but all during the time he spent in Vermont, it seems that he knew as little about what Fanny was thinking as I did. She hardly could have expected it to work out that way. Theoretically, there was still some hope for them, but once Ben packed the car with his belongings and drove off to the country, she realized that they were finished. It didn't take more than a week or two for this to happen. She still cared about him and wished him well, but she had no desire to see him, no desire to talk to him, no desire to make any more efforts. They had talked about keeping the door open, but now it seemed as if the door had vanished. It wasn't that it had closed, it simply wasn't there anymore. Fanny found herself looking at a blank wall, and after that she turned away. They were no longer married, and what she did with her life from then on was her own business.

In June, she met a man named Charles Spector. I don't feel I have a right to talk about this, but to the degree that it affected Sachs, it's impossible to avoid mentioning it. The crucial thing here is not that Fanny wound up marrying Charles (the wedding took place four months ago) but that once she started falling in love with him that summer, she didn't come forward and let Ben know what was happening. Again, it's not a matter of affixing blame. There were reasons for her silence, and under the circumstances I think she acted properly, with no hint of selfishness or deceit. The affair with Charles caught her by surprise, and in those early stages she was still too confused to know what her feelings were. Rather than rush into telling Ben about something that might not last, she decided to hold off for a while, to spare him from further dramas until she was certain of what she wanted to do. Through no fault of her own, this waiting period lasted too long. Ben found out about Charles purely by accident – returning home to Brooklyn one night and seeing him in bed with Fanny – and the timing of that discovery couldn't have been worse. Considering that Sachs was the one who had pushed for the separation in the first place, this probably shouldn't have mattered. But it did. Other factors were involved as well, but this one counted as much as any of those others. It kept the music playing, so to speak, and what might have ended at that point did not. The waltz of disasters went on, and after that there was no stopping it.

But that was later, and I don't want to run ahead of myself. On the surface, things purred along as they had for the past several months. Sachs worked on his novel in Vermont, Fanny went to her job at the museum, and Iris and I waited for our baby to be born. After Sonia arrived (on June twenty-seventh), I lost touch with everyone for the next six or eight weeks. Iris and I were in Babyland, a country where sleep is forbidden and day is indistinguishable from night, a walled-off kingdom governed by the whims of a tiny, absolute monarch. We asked Fanny and Ben to be Sonia's godparents, and they both accepted with elaborate declarations of pride and gratitude. Gifts poured in after that, Fanny delivering hers in person (clothes, blankets, rattles) and Ben's turning up by mail (books, bears, rubber ducks). I was particularly moved by Fanny's response, by the way she would stop in after work just to hold Sonia for fifteen or twenty minutes, cooing at her with all kinds of affectionate nonsense. She seemed to glow with the baby in her arms, and it always saddened me to think how none of this had been possible for her. 'My little beauty,' she would call Sonia, 'my angel girl,' 'my dark passion flower,' 'my heart.' In his own way, Sachs was no less enthusiastic than she was, and I took the small packages that kept appearing in the mail as a sign of real progress, decisive proof that he was well again. In early August, he began urging us to come up to Vermont to see him. He was ready to show me the first part of his book, he said, and he wanted us to introduce him to his goddaughter. 'You've kept her from me long enough,' he said. 'How can you expect me to take care of her if I don't know what she looks like?'

So Iris and I rented a car and a baby seat and drove up north to spend a few days with him. I remember asking Fanny if she wanted to join us, but it seemed that the timing was bad. She had just started her catalogue essay for the Blakelock exhibition she was curating at the museum that winter (her most important show to date), and she was anxious about meeting the deadline. She planned to visit Ben as soon as it was done, she explained, and because this seemed like a legitimate excuse, I didn't press her to go. Again, I had been confronted with a significant piece of evidence, and again I had ignored it. Fanny and Ben hadn't seen each other in five months, and it still hadn't dawned on me that they were in any trouble. If I had bothered to open my eyes for a few minutes, I might have noticed something. But I was too wrapped up in my own happiness, too absorbed in my own little world to pay any attention.

Still, the trip was a success. After spending four days and three nights in his company, I concluded that Sachs was on firm ground again, and I went away feeling as close to him as I had ever felt in the past. I'm tempted to say that it was just like old times, but that wouldn't be quite accurate. Too much had happened to him since his fall, there had been too many changes in both of us for our friendship to be exactly what it had been. But that doesn't mean these new times were less good than the old. In many ways, they were better. In that they represented something I felt I had lost, something I had despaired of ever finding again, they were much better.

Sachs had never been a well-organized person, and it startled me to see how thoroughly he had prepared for our visit. There were flowers in the room where Iris and I slept, guest towels were neatly folded on the bureau, and he had made the bed with all the precision of a veteran innkeeper. Downstairs, the kitchen had been stocked with food, there was an ample supply of wine and beer, and, as we discovered each night, the dinner menus had been worked out in advance. These small gestures were significant, I felt, and they helped set the tone of our stay. Daily life was easier for him than it had been in New York, and little by little he had managed to regain control of himself. As he put it to me in one of our late-night conversations, it was a bit like being in prison again. There weren't any extraneous preoccupations to bog him down. Life had been reduced to its bare-bones essentials, and he no longer had to question how he spent his time. Every day was more or less a repetition of the day before. Today resembled yesterday, tomorrow would resemble today, and what happened next week would blur into what had happened this week. There was comfort for him in that. The element of surprise had been eliminated, and it made him feel sharper, better able to concentrate on his work. 'It's odd,' he continued, 'but the two times I've sat down and written a novel, I've been cut off from the rest of the world. First in jail when I was a kid, and now up here in Vermont, living like a hermit in the woods. I wonder what the hell it means.'

'It means that you can't live without other people,' I said. 'When they're there for you in the flesh, the real world is sufficient. When you're alone, you have to invent imaginary characters. You need them for the companionship.'

All through the visit, the three of us kept ourselves busy doing nothing. We ate and drank, we swam in the pond, we talked. Sachs had installed an all-weather basketball court behind the house, and for an hour or so each morning we shot hoops and played one-on-one (he whipped me soundly every time). While Iris napped in the afternoons, he and I would take turns carrying Sonia around the yard, rocking her to sleep as we talked. The first night, I stayed up late and read the typescript of his book-in-progress. The other two nights, we stayed up late together, discussing what he had written so far and what was still to come. The sun shone on three of the four days; the temperatures were warm for that time of year. All in all, it was just about perfect.

Sachs's book was only a third written at that point, and the piece I read was still a long way from being finished. Sachs understood that, and when he gave me the manuscript the first night I was there, he wasn't looking for detailed criticisms or suggestions on how to improve this or that passage. He just wanted to know if I thought he should continue. 'I've reached a stage where I don't know what I'm doing anymore,' he said. 'I can't tell if it's good or bad. I can't tell if it's the best thing I've ever done or a pile of garbage.'

It wasn't garbage. That much was clear to me from the first page, but as I worked my way through the rest of the draft, I also realized that Sachs was onto something remarkable. This was the book I had always imagined he could write, and if it had taken a disaster to get him started, then perhaps it hadn't been a disaster at all. Or so I persuaded myself at the time. Whatever problems I found in the manuscript, whatever cuts and changes would ultimately have to be made, the essential thing was that Sachs had begun, and I wasn't going to let him stop. 'Just keep writing and don't look back,' I told him over breakfast the next morning. 'If you can push on to the end, it's going to be a great book. Mark my words: a great and memorable book.'

It's impossible for me to know if he could have pulled it off. At the time, I felt certain that he would, and when Iris and I said good-bye to him on the last day, it never even crossed my mind to doubt it. The pages I had read were one thing, but Sachs and I had also talked, and based on what he said about the book over the next two nights, I was convinced that he had the situation well in hand, that he understood what lay ahead of him. If that's true, then I can't imagine anything more sickening or terrible. Of all the tragedies my poor friend created for himself, leaving this book unfinished becomes the hardest one to bear. I don't mean to say that books are more important than life, but the fact is that everyone dies, everyone disappears in the end, and if Sachs had managed to finish his book, there's a chance it might have outlived him. That's what I've chosen to believe, in any case. As it stands now, the book is no more than the promise of a book, a potential book buried in a box of messy manuscript pages and a smattering of notes. That's all that's left of it, along with our two late-night conversations out in the open air, sitting under a moonless sky crammed full of stars. I thought his life was beginning all over again, that he had come to the brink of an extraordinary future, but it turned out that he was almost at the end. Less than a month after I saw him in Vermont, Sachs stopped working on his book. He went out for a walk one afternoon in the middle of September, and the earth suddenly swallowed him up. That was the long and the short of it, and from that day on he never wrote another word.

To mark what will never exist, I have given my book the same title that Sachs was planning to use for his: *Leviathan*.

4

I didn't see him again for close to two years. Maria was the only person who knew where he was, and Sachs had made her promise not to tell. Most people would have broken that promise, I think, but Maria had given her word, and no matter how dangerous it was for her to keep it, she refused to open her mouth. I must have run into her half a dozen times in those two years, but even when we talked about Sachs, she never let on that she knew more about his disappearance than I did. Last summer, when I finally learned how much she had been holding back from me, I got so angry that I wanted to kill her. But that was my problem, not Maria's, and I had no right to vent my frustration on her. A promise is a promise, after all, and even though her silence wound up causing a lot of damage, I don't think she was wrong to do what she did. If anyone should have spoken up, it was Sachs, He was the one responsible for what happened, and it was his secret that Maria was protecting. But Sachs said nothing. For two whole years, he kept himself hidden and never said a word.

We knew that he was alive, but as the months passed and no message came from him, not even that was certain anymore. Only bits and pieces remained, a few ghostlike facts. We knew that he had left Vermont, that he had not driven his own car, and that for one horrible minute Fanny had seen him in Brooklyn. Beyond that, everything was conjecture. Since he hadn't called to announce he was coming, we assumed that he had something urgent to tell her, but whatever that thing was, they never got around to talking about it. He just showed up one night out of the blue ('all distraught and crazy in the eyes,' as Fanny put it) and burst into the bedroom of their apartment. That led to the awful scene I mentioned earlier. If the room had been dark, it might have been less embarrassing for all of them, but several lights happened to be on, Fanny and Charles were naked on top of the covers, and Ben saw everything. It was clearly the last thing he expected to find. Before Fanny could say a word to him, he had already backed out of the room, stammering that he was sorry, that he hadn't known, that he hadn't meant to disturb her. She scrambled out of bed, but by the time she reached the front hall, the apartment door had banged shut and Sachs was racing down the stairs. She couldn't go outside with nothing on, so she rushed into the living room, opened the window, and called down to him in the street. Sachs stopped for a moment and waved up to her. 'My blessings on you both!' he shouted. Then he blew her a kiss, turned in the other direction, and ran off into the night.

Fanny telephoned us immediately after that. She figured he might be on his way to our place next, but her hunch proved wrong. Iris and I sat up half the night waiting for him, but Sachs never appeared. From then on, there were no more signs of his whereabouts. Fanny called the house in Vermont repeatedly, but no one ever answered. That was our last hope, and as the days went by, it seemed less and less likely that Sachs would return there. Panic set in; a contagion of morbid thoughts spread among us. Not knowing what else to do, Fanny rented a car that first weekend and drove up to the house herself. As she reported to me on the phone after she arrived, the evidence was puzzling. The front door had been left unlocked, the car was sitting in its usual place in the yard, and Ben's work was laid out on the desk in the studio: finished manuscript pages stacked in one pile, pens scattered beside it, a half-written page still in the typewriter. In other words, it looked as though he were about to come back any minute. If he had been planning to leave for any length of time, she said, the house would have been closed. The pipes would have been drained, the electricity would have been turned off, the refrigerator would have been emptied. 'And he would have taken his manuscript,' I added. 'Even if he had forgotten everything else, there's no way he would have left without that.'

The situation refused to add up. No matter how thoroughly we analyzed it, we were always left with the same conundrum. On the one hand, Sachs's departure had been unexpected. On the other hand, he had left of his own free will. If not for that fleeting encounter with Fanny in New York, we might have suspected foul play, but Sachs had made it down to the city unharmed. A bit frazzled, perhaps, but essentially unharmed. And yet, if nothing had happened to him, why hadn't he returned to Vermont? Why had he left behind his car, his clothes, his work? Iris and I talked it out with Fanny again and again, going over one possibility after another, but we never reached a satisfactory conclusion. There were too many blanks, too many variables, too many things we didn't know. After a month of beating it into the ground, I suggested that Fanny go to the police and report Ben as missing. She resisted the idea, however. She had no claims on him anymore, she said, which meant that she had no right to inter-fere. After what had happened in the apartment, he was free to do what he liked, and it wasn't up to her to drag him back. Charles (whom we had met by then and who turned out to be quite well off) was willing to hire a private detective at his own expense. 'Just so we know that Ben's all right,' he said. 'It's not a question of dragging him back, it's a question of knowing that he disappeared because he wanted to disappear.' Iris and I both thought that Charles's plan was sensible, but Fanny wouldn't allow him to go ahead with it. 'He gave us his blessings,' she said. 'That was the same thing as saying good-bye. I lived with him for twenty years, and I know how he thinks. He doesn't want us to look for him. I've already betrayed him once, and I'm not about to do it again. We have to leave him alone. He'll come back when he's ready to come back, and until then we have to wait. Believe me, it's the only thing to be done. We just have to sit tight and learn to live with it.'

Months passed. Then it was a year, and then it was two years, and the enigma remained unsolved. By the time Sachs showed up in Vermont last August, I was long past thinking we would ever find an answer. Iris and Charles both believed that he was dead, but my hopelessness didn't stem from anything as specific as that. I never had a strong feeling about whether Sachs was alive or dead – no sudden intuitions, no bursts of extrasensory knowledge, no mystical experiences – but I was more or less convinced that I would never see him again. I say 'more or less' because I wasn't sure of anything. In the first months after he disappeared, I went through a number of violent and contradictory responses, but these emotions gradually burned themselves out, and in the end terms such as *sadness* or *anger* or *grief* no longer seemed to apply. I had lost contact with him, and his absence felt less and less like a personal matter. Every time I tried to think about him, my imagination failed me. It was as if Sachs had become a hole in the universe. He was no longer just my missing friend, he was a symptom of my ignorance about all things, an emblem of the unknowable itself. This probably sounds vague, but I can't do any better than that. Iris told me that I was turning into a Buddhist, and I suppose that describes my position as accurately as anything else. Fanny was a Christian, Iris said, because she never abandoned her faith in Sachs's eventual return; she and Charles were atheists; and I was a Zen acolyte, a believer in the power of nothing. In all the years she had known me, she said, it was the first time I hadn't expressed an opinion.

Life changed, life went on. We learned, as Fanny had begged us, to live with it. She and Charles were together now, and in spite of ourselves, Iris and I were forced to admit that he was a decent fellow. Mid to late forties, an architect, formerly married, the father of two boys, intelligent, desperately in love with Fanny, beyond reproach. Little by little, we managed to form a friendship with him, and a new reality took hold for all of us. Last spring, when Fanny mentioned that she wasn't planning to go to Vermont for the summer (she just couldn't, she said, and probably never would again), it occurred to her that perhaps Iris and I would like to use the house. She wanted to give it to us for nothing, but we insisted on paying some kind of rent, and so we worked out an arrangement that would at least cover her costs – a pro-rated share of the taxes, the maintenance, and so on. That was how I happened to be present when Sachs turned up last summer. He arrived without warning, chugging into the yard one night in a battered blue Chevvy, spent the next couple of days here, and then vanished again. In between, he talked his head off. He talked so much, it almost scared me. But that was when I heard his story, and given how determined he was to tell it, I don't think he left anything out.

He went on working, he said. After Iris and I left with Sonia, he went on working for another three or four weeks. Our conversations about *Leviathan* had apparently been helpful, and he threw himself back into the manuscript that same morning, determined not to leave Vermont until he had finished a draft of the whole book. Everything seemed to go well. He made progress every day, and he felt happy with his monk's life, as happy as he had been in years. Then, early one evening in the middle of September, he decided to go out for a walk. The weather had turned by then, and the air was crisp, infused with the smells of fall. He put on his woolen hunting jacket and tramped up the hill beyond the house, heading north. He figured there was an hour of daylight left, which meant that he could walk for half an hour before he had to turn around and start back. Ordinarily, he would have spent that hour shooting baskets, but the change of seasons was in full swing now, and he wanted to have a look at what was happening in the woods: to see the red and yellow leaves, to watch the slant of the setting sun among the birches and maples, to wander in the glow of the pendant colors. So he set off on his little jaunt, with no more on his mind than what he was going to cook for dinner when he got home.

Once he entered the woods, however, he became distracted. Instead of looking at the leaves and migrating birds, he started thinking about his book. Passages he had written earlier that day came rushing back to him, and before he was conscious of what he was doing, he was already composing new sentences in his head, mapping out the work he wanted to do the next morning. He kept on walking, thrashing through the dead leaves and thorny underbrush, talking out loud to himself, chanting the words of his book, paying no attention to where he was. He could have gone on like that for hours, he said, but at a certain point he noticed that he was having trouble seeing. The sun had already set, and because of the thickness of the woods, night was fast coming on. He looked around him, hoping to get his bearings, but nothing was familiar, and he realized that he had never been in this place before. Feeling like an idiot, he turned around and started running in the direction he had come from. He had just a few minutes before everything disappeared, and he knew he would never make it. He had no flashlight, no matches, no food in his pockets. Sleeping outdoors promised to be an unpleasant experience, but he couldn't think of any alternative. He sat down on a tree stump and started to laugh. He found himself ridiculous, he said, a comic figure of the first rank. Then night fell in earnest, and he couldn't see a thing. He waited for a moon to appear, but the sky clouded over instead. He laughed again. He wasn't going to give the matter another thought, he decided. He was safe where he was, and freezing his ass off for one night wasn't going to kill him. So he did what he could to make himself comfortable. He stretched out on the ground, he covered himself haphazardly with some leaves and twigs, and tried to think about his book. Before long, he even managed to fall asleep.

He woke up at dawn, bone-cold and shivering, his clothes wet with dew. The situation didn't seem so funny anymore. He was in a foul temper, and his muscles ached. He was hungry and disheveled, and the only thing he wanted was to get out of there and find his way home. He took what he thought was the same path he had taken the previous evening, but after he had walked for close to an hour, he began to suspect that he was on the wrong path. He considered turning around and heading back to the place where he had started, but he wasn't sure he would be able to find it again – and even if he did, it was doubtful he would recognize it. The sky was gloomy that morning, with dense swarms of clouds blocking the sun. Sachs had never been much of a woodsman, and without a compass to orient his position, he couldn't tell if he was traveling east or west or north or south. On the other hand, it wasn't as though he were trapped in a primeval forest. The woods were bound to end sooner or later, and it hardly mattered which direction he followed, just as long as he walked in a straight line. Once he made it to an open road, he would knock on the door of the first house he saw. With any luck, the people inside would be able to tell him where he was.

It took a long time before any of that happened. Since he had no watch, he never knew exactly how long, but he guessed somewhere between three and four hours. He was thoroughly disgusted by then, and he cursed his stupidity over the last miles with a growing sense of rage. Once he came to the end of the woods, however, his dark mood lifted, and he stopped feeling sorry for himself. He was on a narrow dirt road, and even if he didn't know where he was, even if there wasn't a single house in sight, he could comfort himself with the thought that the worst of it was over. He walked for ten or fifteen more minutes, making bets with himself about how far he had strayed from home. If it was under five miles, he would spend fifty dollars on a present for Sonia. If it was over five but under ten, he would spend a hundred dollars. Over ten would be two hundred. Over fifteen would be three hundred, over twenty would be four hundred, and so on. As he was showering these imaginary gifts on his goddaughter (stuffed panda bears, dollhouses, ponies), he heard a car rumbling in the distance behind him. He stopped and waited for it to approach. It turned out to be a red pick-up truck, speeding along at a good clip. Figuring he had nothing to lose, Sachs stuck up his hand to get the driver's attention. The truck barreled past him, but before Sachs could turn around again, it slammed to a halt. He heard a clamor of flying pebbles, dust rose everywhere, and then a voice was calling out to him, asking if he needed a lift.

The driver was a young man in his early twenties. Sachs sized him up as a local kid, a road mender or plumber's assistant, maybe, and though he didn't feel much inclined to talk at first, the boy turned out to be so friendly and ingratiating that he soon fell into a conversation with him. There was a metal softball bat lying on the floor in front of Sachs's seat, and when the kid put his

149

foot on the accelerator to get the truck going again, the bat lurched up and hit Sachs in the ankle. That was the opener, so to speak, and once the kid had apologized for the inconvenience, he introduced himself as Dwight (Dwight McMartin, as Sachs later learned) and they started in on a discussion about softball. Dwight told him that he played on a team sponsored by the volunteer fire department in Newfane. The regular season had ended last week, and the first game of the playoffs was scheduled to be played that evening – 'if the weather holds,' he added several times, 'if the weather holds and the rain don't fall.' Dwight was the first baseman, the cleanup hitter, and number two in the league in homeruns, a bulky gulumph in the mold of Moose Skowron. Sachs said he'd try to make it down to the field to watch, and Dwight answered in all seriousness that it was bound to be worth it, that it was sure to be a terrific game. Sachs couldn't help smiling. He was rumpled and unshaven, there were brambles and leaf particles stuck to his clothes, and his nose was running like a spigot. He probably looked like a hobo, he thought, and yet Dwight didn't press him with personal questions. He didn't ask him why he had been walking on that deserted road, he didn't ask him where he lived, he didn't even bother to ask his name. He could have been a simpleton, Sachs realized, or maybe he was just a nice guy, but one way or the other, it was hard not to appreciate that discretion. All of a sudden, Sachs wished that he hadn't kept so much to himself over the past months. He should have gone out and mingled with his neighbors a bit more; he should have made an effort to learn something about the people around him. Almost as an ethical point, he told himself that he mustn't forget the softball game that night. It would do him some good, he thought, give him something to think about other than his book. If he had some people to talk to, maybe he wouldn't be so apt to get lost the next time he went walking in the woods.

When Dwight told him where they were, Sachs was appalled by how far he had drifted off course. He had evidently walked over the hill and down the other side, landing two towns to the east of where he lived. He had covered only ten miles on foot, but the return distance by car was well over thirty. For no particular reason, he decided to spill the whole business to Dwight. Out of gratitude, perhaps, or simply because he found it amusing now. Maybe the kid would tell it to his buddies on the softball team, and they'd all have a good laugh at his expense. Sachs didn't care. It was an exemplary tale, a classic moron joke, and he didn't mind being the butt of his own folly. The city slicker plays Daniel Boone in the Vermont woods, and look what happens to him, fellas. But once he began to talk about his misadventures, Dwight responded with unexpected compassion. The same thing had happened to him once, he told Sachs, and it hadn't been a bit of fun. He'd only been eleven or twelve at the time, and he'd been scared shitless, crouching behind a tree the whole night waiting for a bear to attack him. Sachs couldn't be sure, but he suspected that Dwight was inventing this story to make him feel a little less miserable. In any case, the kid didn't laugh at him. In fact, once he'd heard what Sachs had to say, he even offered to drive him home. He was running late as it was, he said, but a few more minutes wouldn't make any difference, and Christ, if he were in Sachs's shoes, he'd expect someone to do the same for him.

They were traveling along a paved road at that point, but Dwight said he knew a shortcut to Sachs's house. It meant turning around and backtracking for a couple of miles, but once he worked out the arithmetic in his head, he decided it made sense to change course. So he slammed on the brakes, did a U-turn in the middle of the road, and headed back in the other direction. The shortcut turned out to be the narrowest of dirt trails, a bumpy, one-lane sliver of ground that cut through a dark, tree-clogged patch of woods. Not many people knew about it, Dwight said, but if he wasn't mistaken it would lead them to a somewhat wider dirt road and that second road would spit them out on the county highway about four miles from Sachs's house. Dwight probably knew what he was talking about, but he never got a chance to demonstrate the correctness of his theory. Less than a mile after they started down the first dirt road, they ran into something unexpected. And before they could move around it, their journey came to an end.

It all happened very quickly. Sachs experienced it as a churning in the gut, a spinning in the head, a rush of fear in the veins. He was so exhausted, he told me, and so little time elapsed from beginning to end, that he could never quite absorb it as real – not even in retrospect, not even when he sat down to tell me about it two years later. One moment, they were tooling along through the woods, he said, and the next moment they had stopped. A man was standing up ahead of them on the road, leaning against the trunk of a white Toyota and smoking a cigarette. He looked to be in his late thirties, a tallish, slender man dressed in a flannel work shirt and loose Khaki pants. The only other thing Sachs noticed was that he had a beard – not unlike the one he used to wear himself, but darker. Thinking the man must be having car trouble, Dwight climbed out of the truck and walked toward him, asking if he needed help. Sachs couldn't hear the man's response, but the tone sounded angry, unnecessarily hostile somehow, and as he continued to watch them through the windshield, he was surprised when the man answered Dwight's next question with something even more vicious: fuck off, or get the fuck away from me, words to that effect. That was when the adrenaline started pumping through him, Sachs said, and he instinctively reached for the metal bat on the floor. Dwight was too good-natured to take the hint, however. He kept on walking toward the man, shrugging off the insult as if it didn't matter, repeating that he only wanted to help. The man backed away in agitation, and then he ran around to the front of the car, opened the door on the passenger's side, and reached for something in the glove compartment. When he straightened up and turned toward Dwight again, there was a gun in his hand. He fired it once. The big kid howled and clutched his stomach, and then the man fired again. The kid howled a second time and started staggering up the road, moaning and weeping in pain. The man turned to follow him with his eyes, and Sachs jumped out of the truck, holding the bat in his right hand. He didn't even think, he told me. He rushed up behind the man just as the third shot went off, got a good grip on the handle of the bat, and swung for all he was worth. He aimed for the man's head – hoping to split his skull in two, hoping to kill him, hoping to empty his brains all over the ground. The bat landed with horrific force, smashing into a spot just behind the man's right ear. Sachs heard the thud of impact, the cracking of cartilage and bone, and then the man dropped. He just fell down dead in the middle of the road, and everything went quiet.

Sachs ran over to Dwight, but when he bent down to examine the kid's body, he saw that the third shot had killed him. The bullet had gone straight into the back of his head, and his cranium was shattered. Sachs had lost his chance. It was all a matter of timing, and he had been too slow. If he had managed to get to the man a split-second earlier, that last shot would have missed, and instead of looking down at a corpse, he would have been bandaging Dwight's wounds, doing everything he could to save his life. A moment after he thought this thought, Sachs felt his own body start to tremble. He sat down on the road, put his head between his knees, and struggled not to throw up. Time passed. He felt the air blowing through his clothes; he heard a blue jay squawking in the woods; he shut his eyes. When he opened them again, he picked up a handful of loose dirt from the road and crushed it against his face. He put the dirt in his mouth and chewed it, letting the grit scrape against his teeth, feeling the pebbles against his tongue. He chewed until he couldn't stand it anymore, and then he bent over and spat the mess out, groaning like a sick, demented animal.

If Dwight had lived, he said, the whole story would have been different. The idea of running away never would have occurred to him, and once that first step had been eliminated, none of the things that followed from it would have happened. But standing out there alone in the woods, Sachs suddenly fell into a deep, unbridled panic. Two men were dead, and the idea of going to the state troopers seemed unimaginable to him. He had already served time in prison. He was a convicted felon, and without any witnesses to corroborate his story, no one was going to believe a word he said. It was all too bizarre, too implausible. He wasn't thinking too clearly, of course, but whatever thoughts he had were centered entirely on himself. He couldn't do anything for Dwight, but at least he could save his own skin, and in his panic the only solution that came to him was to get the hell away from there.

He knew the police would figure out that a third man had been present. It would be obvious that Dwight and the stranger hadn't killed each other, since a man with three bullets in his body would scarcely have the strength to bludgeon someone to death, and even if he did, he wouldn't be able to walk twenty feet down the road after he had done it, least of all with one of those bullets lodged in his skull. Sachs also knew that he was bound to leave some traces behind him. No matter how assiduously he cleaned up after himself, a competent forensic team would have no trouble unearthing something to work with: a footprint, a strand of hair, a microscopic fragment. But none of that would make any difference. As long as he managed to remove his fingerprints from the truck, as long as he remembered to take the bat with him, there wouldn't be anything to identify him as the missing man. That was the crucial point. He had to make sure that the missing man could have been anyone. Once he did that, he would be home free.

He spent several minutes wiping down the surfaces of the truck: the dashboard, the seat, the windows, the inside and outside door handles, everything he could think of. As soon as he was finished, he did it again, and then he did it once more for good measure. After collecting the bat from the ground, he opened the door of the stranger's car, saw that the key was still in the ignition, and climbed in behind the wheel. The engine kicked over on the first try. There were going to be tread marks, of course, and those marks would remove any doubt that a third man had been there, but Sachs was too frightened to leave on foot. That's what would have made the most sense: to walk away, to go home, to forget the whole nasty business. But his heart was pounding too fast for that, his thoughts were charging out of control, and deliberate actions of that sort were no longer possible. He craved speed. He craved the speed and noise of the car, and now that he was ready, all he wanted was to be gone, to be sitting in the car and driving as fast as he could. Only that would be able to match the tumult inside him. Only that would allow him to silence the roar of terror in his head.

He drove north on the Interstate for two and a half hours, following the Connecticut River until he reached the latitude of Barre. That was where hunger finally got the better of him. He was afraid he'd have trouble holding the food down, but he hadn't eaten in over twenty-four hours, and he knew he had to give it a try. He pulled off the Interstate at the next exit, drove along a two-lane road for fifteen or twenty minutes, and then stopped for lunch in a small town whose name he couldn't remember. Taking no chances, he ordered soft-boiled eggs and toast. After he was done, he went into the men's room and cleaned himself up, soaking his head in a sinkful of warm water and removing the twigs and dirt stains from his clothes. It made him feel much better. By the time he paid his bill and walked out of the restaurant, he understood that the next step was to turn around and go to New York. It wasn't going to be possible to keep the story to himself. That much was clear now, and once he realized he had to talk to someone, he knew that person had to be Fanny. In spite of everything that had happened in the past year, he suddenly ached to see her again.

As he walked toward the dead man's car, Sachs noticed that it had California license plates. He wasn't sure what to make of this discovery, but it surprised him just the same. How many other details had he missed? he wondered. Before returning to the Interstate and heading south, he turned off the main road and parked at the edge of what appeared to be a large forest preserve. It was a secluded spot, with no signs of anyone for miles around. Sachs opened all four doors of the car, got down on his hands and knees, and systematically combed the interior. Thorough as he was, the results of this search were disappointing. He found a few coins wedged under the front seat, some wadded-up balls of paper strewn about the floor (fast food wrappers, ticket stubs, crumpled cigarette packs), but nothing with a name on it, nothing that told him a single fact about the man he had killed. The glove compartment was similarly blank, containing nothing but the Toyota owner's manual, a box of thirty-eight caliber bullets, and an unopened carton of Camel Filters. That left the trunk, and when Sachs finally got around to opening it, the trunk proved to be a different matter.

There were three bags inside it. The largest one was filled with clothes, shaving equipment, and maps. At the very bottom, tucked away in a small white envelope, there was a passport. When he looked at the photograph on the first page, Sachs recognized the man from that morning – the same man minus the beard. The name given was Reed Dimaggio, middle initial N. Date of birth: November 12, 1950. Place of birth: Newark, New Jersey. The passport had been issued in San Francisco the previous July, and the back pages were empty, with no visa stamps or customs markings. Sachs wondered if it hadn't been forged. Given what had taken place in the woods that morning, it seemed almost certain that Dwight wasn't the first person Dimaggio had killed. And if he was a professional thug, there was a chance that he had been traveling with false documents. Still, the name was somehow too singular, too odd not to have been real. It must have belonged to someone, and for want of any other clues concerning the man's identity, Sachs decided to accept that someone as the man he had killed. Reed Dimaggio. Until something better came along, that was the name he would give him.

The next article was a steel suitcase, one of those shiny silver boxes that photographers sometimes carry their equipment in. The first bag had opened without a key, but this one was locked, and Sachs spent half an hour struggling to pry the hinges loose from their bolts. He hammered away at them with the jack and tire iron, and every time the box moved, he heard metallic objects rattling around inside it. He assumed they were weapons: knives, guns, and bullets, the tools of Dimaggio's trade. When the box finally relented, however, it yielded up a baffling collection of bric-a-brac, not at all what Sachs had been expecting. He found spools of electric wire, alarm clocks, screwdrivers, microchips, string, putty, and several rolls of black duct tape. One by one, he picked up each item and studied it, groping to fathom its purpose, but even after he had sifted through the entire contents of the box, he still couldn't guess what these things signified. It was only later that it hit him – long after he was back on the road. Driving down to New York that night, he suddenly understood that these were the materials for constructing a bomb.

The third piece of luggage was a bowling bag. There was nothing remarkable about it (a small leather pouch with red, white, and blue panels, a zipper, and a white plastic handle), but it frightened Sachs more than the other two, and he had instinctively saved it for last. Anything could have been hidden in there, he realized. Considering that it belonged to a madman, to a homicidal maniac, that *anything* became more and more monstrous for him to contemplate. By the time he had finished with the other two bags, Sachs had nearly lost the courage to open it. Rather than confront what his imagination had put in there, he had nearly talked himself into throwing it away. But he didn't. Just when he was on the point of lifting it out of the trunk and tossing it into the woods, he closed his eyes, hesitated, and then, with a single frantic tug, undid the zipper.

There was no head in the bag. There were no severed ears, no lopped-off fingers, no private parts. What there was was money. And not just a little money, but lots of it, more money than Sachs had ever seen in one place before. The bag was packed solid with it: thick bundles of one-hundred-dollar bills fastened with rubber bands, each bundle representing three, four, or five thousand dollars. When Sachs had finished counting them, he was reasonably sure that the total fell somewhere between one hundred sixty and one hundred sixty five thousand. His first response on discovering the cash was relief, gratitude that his fears had come to naught. Then, as he added it up for the first time, a sense of shock and giddiness. The next time he counted the bills, however, he found himself getting used to them. That was the strangest part of it, he told me: how quickly he digested the whole improbable occurrence. By the time he counted the money again, he had already begun to think of it as his own.

He kept the cigarettes, the softball bat, the passport, and the money. Everything else he threw away, scattering the contents of the suitcase and the metal strong-box deep inside the woods. A few minutes after that, he deposited the empty luggage in a dumpster at the edge of town. It was past four o'clock by then, and he had a long drive ahead of him. He stopped for another meal in Springfield, Massachusetts, smoking Dimaggio's Camels as he filled himself with extra coffee, and then made it down to Brooklyn a little after one in the morning. That was where he abandoned the car, leaving it on one of the cobbled streets near the Gowanus Canal, a no-man's-land of empty warehouses and packs of thin, roving dogs. He was careful to scrub the surfaces clean of fingerprints, but that was just an added precaution. The doors were unlocked, the key was in the ignition, and the car was sure to be stolen before the night was out.

He traveled the rest of the way on foot, carrying the bowling bag in one hand and the softball bat and cigarettes in the other. At the corner of Fifth Avenue and President Street, he slid the bat into a crowded trash receptacle, angling it in among the heaped-up newspapers and cracked melon rinds. That was the last piece of business he had to think about. There was still another mile to go, but in spite of his exhaustion, he trudged on toward his apartment with a growing sense of calm. Fanny would be there for him, he thought, and once he saw her, the worst of it would be finished.

That explains the confusion that followed. Not only was Sachs caught off balance when he entered the apartment, but he was in no condition to absorb the least new fact about anything. His brain was already overcharged, and he had gone home to Fanny precisely because he assumed there would be no surprises there, because it was the one place where he could count on being taken care of. Hence his bewilderment, his stunned reaction when he saw her rolling around naked on the bed with Charles. His certainty had dissolved into humiliation, and it was all he could do to mutter a few words of apology before rushing out of the apartment. Everything had happened at once, and while he managed to regain enough composure to shout his blessings from the street, that was no more than a bluff, a feeble, last-minute effort to save face. In point of fact, he felt as if the sky had fallen on his head. He felt as if his heart had been ripped out of him.

He ran down the block, running only to be gone, with no thought of what to do next. At the corner of Third Street and Seventh Avenue, he spotted a pay phone, and that gave him the idea to call me and ask for a place to spend the night. When he dialed my number, however, the line was busy. I must have been talking to Fanny at that moment (she called immediately after Sachs dashed away), but Sachs interpreted the busy signal to mean that Iris and I had taken our phone off the hook. That was a sensible conclusion, since it wasn't likely that either one of us would be talking to someone at two o'clock in the morning. Therefore, he didn't bother to try us again. When his quarter came back to him, he used it to call Maria instead. The ringing pulled her out of a deep sleep, but once she heard the desperation in his voice, she told him to come right over. Subways were scarce at that hour, and by the time he caught the train at Grand Army Plaza and traveled to her loft in Manhattan, she was already dressed and wide awake, sitting at the kitchen table and drinking her third cup of coffee.

It was the logical place for him to go. Even after his removal to the country, Sachs had stayed in touch with Maria, and when I finally talked to her about these things last fall, she showed me more than a dozen letters and postcards he had sent her from Vermont. There had been a number of phone conversations as well, she said, and in the six months he was out of town, she didn't think more than ten days had gone by without news from him of one sort or another. The point was that Sachs trusted her, and with Fanny suddenly gone from his life (and with my phone ostensibly off the hook), it was a natural step for him to turn to Maria. Since his accident the previous July, she was the only person he had unburdened himself to, the only person he had allowed into the inner sanctum of his thoughts. When all was said and done, she was probably closer to him at that moment than anyone else.

Still, it turned out to be a terrible mistake. Not because Maria wasn't willing to help him, not because she wasn't prepared to drop everything to see him through the crisis, but because she was in possession of the one fact powerful enough to turn an ugly misfortune into a full-scale tragedy. If Sachs hadn't gone to her, I'm certain that things would have been resolved rather quickly. He would have calmed down after a night's rest, and after that he would have contacted the police and told them the truth. With the help of a good lawyer, he would have walked away a free man. But a new element was added to the already unstable mixture of the past twenty-four hours, and it wound up producing a deadly compound, a beakerful of acid that hissed forth its dangers in a billowing profusion of smoke.

Even now, it's difficult for me to accept any of it. And I speak as someone who should know better, as someone who has thought long and hard about the issues at stake here. My whole adulthood has been spent writing stories, putting imaginary people into unexpected and often unlikely situations, but none of my characters has ever experienced anything as improbable as Sachs did that night at Maria Turner's house. If it still shocks me to report what happened, that is because the real is always ahead of what we can imagine. No matter how wild we think our inventions might be, they can never match the unpredictability of what the real world continually spews forth. This lesson seems inescapable to me now. *Anything can happen*. And one way or another, it always does.

The first hours they spent together were painful enough, and they both remembered them as a kind of tempest, an inward pummeling, a maelstrom of tears, silences, and choked-off words. Little by little, Sachs managed to get the story out. Maria held him in her arms through most of it, listening in rapt disbelief as he told her as much as he was able to tell. That was when she made her promise, when she gave him her word and swore to keep the killings to herself. Later on, she planned to talk him into going to the police, but for now her only concern was to protect him, to prove her loyalty. Sachs was falling apart, and once the words started coming out of his mouth, once he started listening to himself describe the things he had done, he was seized by revulsion. Maria tried to make him understand that he had acted in self-defense – that he wasn't responsible for the stranger's death – but Sachs refused to accept her argument. Like it or not, he had killed a man, and no amount of talk would ever obliterate that fact. But if he hadn't killed the stranger, Maria said, he would have been killed himself. Maybe so, Sachs answered, but in the long run that would have been preferable to the position he was in now. It would have been better to die, he said, better to have been shot and killed that morning than to have this memory with him for the rest of his life.

They kept on talking, weaving in and out of these tortured arguments, weighing the act and its consequences, reliving the hours Sachs had spent in the car, the scene with Fanny in Brooklyn, his night in the woods, going over the same ground three or four times, neither one of them able to sleep, and then, right in the middle of this conversation, everything stopped. Sachs opened the bowling bag to show Maria what he had found in the trunk of the car, and there was the passport lying on top of the money. He pulled it out and handed it to her, insisting that she take a look at it, intent on proving that the stranger had been a real person – a man with a name, an age, a place of birth. It made it all so concrete, he said. If the man had been anonymous, it might have been possible to think of him as a monster, to imagine that he had deserved to die, but the passport demythologized him, showed him to be a man like any other man. Here were his vital statistics, the delineation of an actual life. And here was his picture. Unbelievably, the man *was smiling* in the photograph. As Sachs told Maria when he put the document in her hand, he was convinced that smile would destroy him. No matter how far he traveled from the events of that morning, he would never manage to escape it.

So Maria opened the passport, already thinking of what she would say to Sachs, already casting about for some words that would reassure him, and glanced down at the picture inside. Then she took a second look, moving her eyes back and forth between the name and the photograph, and all of a sudden (as she put it to me last year) she felt as if her head were about to explode. Those were the precise words she used to describe what happened: 'I felt as if my head were about to explode.'

Sachs asked her if something was wrong. He had seen the change of expression in her face, and he didn't understand it.

'Jesus God,' she said.

'Are you okay?'

'This is a joke, right? It's all some kind of stupid gag, isn't it?'

'You're not making sense.'

'Reed Dimaggio. This is a picture of Reed Dimaggio.'

'That's what it says. I have no idea if that's his real name.'

'I know him.'

'You what?'

'I know him. He was married to my best friend. I was at their wedding. They named their little girl after me.'

'Reed Dimaggio.'

'There's only one Reed Dimaggio. And this is his picture. I'm looking at it right now.'

'That's not possible.'

'Do you think I'd make it up?'

'The man was a killer. He shot down a boy in cold blood.'

'I don't care. I knew him. He was married to my friend Lillian Stern. If it hadn't been for me, they never would have met.'

*

It was almost dawn then, but they went on talking for several more hours, staying up until nine or ten o'clock as Maria recounted the history of her friendship with Lillian Stern. Sachs, whose body had been crumbling with exhaustion, caught his second wind and refused to go to bed until she had finished. He heard about Maria and Lillian's early days in Massachusetts, about their move to New York after high school, about the long period when they lost contact with each other, about their unexpected reunion in the entryway of Lillian's apartment house. Maria went through the saga of the address book, she dug up the photographs she had taken of Lillian and spread them out on the floor for him, she told about their experiment in switching identities. This had led directly to Lillian's meeting with Dimaggio, she explained, and to the whirlwind romance that followed. Maria herself never got to know him very well, and except for the fact that she liked him, she couldn't say much about who he was. Only a few random details had stuck in her mind. She remembered that he had fought in Vietnam, but whether he had been drafted into the Army or had enlisted wasn't clear anymore. He must have been discharged some time in the early seventies, however, since she knew for a fact that he had gone to college on the GI bill, and when Lillian met him in 1976, he had already finished his BA and was about to go off to Berkeley as a graduate student in American history. All in all, she had met him only five or six times, and several of those encounters had taken place right at the beginning, just when he and Lillian were falling in love. Lillian went out to California with him the following month, and after that Maria saw him on only two other occasions: at the wedding in 1977, and after their daughter was born in 1981. The marriage ended in 1984. Lillian talked to Maria several times during the period of the breakup, but since then their contacts had been fitful, with wider and wider intervals between each call.

She had never seen any cruelty in Dimaggio, she said, nothing to suggest that he would have been capable of hurting anyone – let alone shooting down a stranger in cold blood. The man wasn't a criminal. He was a student, an intellectual, a teacher, and he and Lillian had lived a rather dull life in Berkeley. He taught classes as a graduate assistant at the university and worked on his doctorate; she studied acting, held different part-time jobs, and performed in local theater productions and student films. Lillian's savings helped get them through the first couple of years, but after that money was tight, and more often than not it was a struggle to make ends meet. Hardly the life of a criminal, Maria said.

Nor was it the life she imagined her friend would choose for herself. After those wild years in New York, it seemed strange that Lillian would have settled down with someone like Dimaggio. But she had already been thinking about leaving New York, and the circumstances of their meeting were so extra-ordinary (so 'rapturous' as Maria put it), that the idea of running off with him must have been irresistible – not so much a choice as a matter of destiny. It's true that Berkeley wasn't Hollywood, but neither was Dimaggio some cringing little bookworm with wire-rimmed spectacles and a caved-in chest. He was a strong, good-looking young man, and physical attraction couldn't have been a problem. Just as important, he was smarter than anyone she had ever met: he talked better and knew more than anyone else, and he had all kinds of impressive opinions about everything. Lillian, who hadn't read more than two or three books in her life, must have been overpowered by him. As Maria saw it, she probably imagined that Dimaggio would transform her, that just knowing him would lift her out of her mediocrity and help her to make something of herself. Becoming a movie star was only a childish dream anyway. She might have had the looks for it, she might even have had enough talent – but, as Maria explained to Sachs, Lillian was far too lazy to pull it off, too impulsive to bear down and concentrate, too lacking in ambition. When she asked Maria for advice, Maria told her flat out to forget the movies and stick with Dimaggio. If he was willing to marry her, then she should jump at the chance. And that's exactly what Lillian did.

As far as Maria could tell, it seemed to be a successful marriage.

Lillian never complained about it in any case, and though Maria began to have some doubts after she visited California in 1981 (finding Dimaggio morose and overbearing, devoid of any sense of humor), she attributed it to the early flutters of parenthood and kept her thoughts to herself. Two and half years later, when Lillian called to announce their impending separation, Maria was caught by surprise. Lillian claimed that Dimaggio was seeing another woman, but then in the next breath she mentioned something about her past 'catching up with her.' Maria had always assumed that Lillian had told Dimaggio about her life in New York, but it seems that she had never gotten around to it, and once they moved to California, she decided it would be better for both of them if he didn't know. One evening, while she and Dimaggio were eating dinner in a San Francisco restaurant, a former client of hers happened to sit down at the next table. The man was drunk, and after Lillian refused to acknowledge his stares and smiles and obnoxious winks, he stood up and made some loud, insulting remarks, spilling her secret right there in front of her husband. According to what she told Maria, Dimaggio went into rage when they returned home. He pushed her to the ground, he kicked her, he threw pots and pans against the wall, he yelled 'whore' at the top of his voice. If the baby hadn't woken up, she said, there was a chance he would have killed her. The next day, however, when she talked to Maria again, Lillian never even referred to this incident. This time, her story was that Dimaggio 'had gone weird on her,' that he was hanging out with 'a bunch of idiot radicals' and had turned into a 'creep.' So she had finally gotten fed up and kicked him out of the house. That made three different stories, Maria said, a typical example of how Lillian confronted the truth. One of the stories might have been real. It was even possible that all of them were real – but then again, it was just as possible that all of them were false. You could never tell with Lillian, she explained to Sachs. For all she knew, Lillian might have been unfaithful to Dimaggio, and he had walked out on her. It might have been that simple. And then again, it might not.

They were never officially divorced. Dimaggio, who finished his degree in 1982, had been teaching at a small private college in Oakland for the past couple of years. After the final rupture with Lillian (fall 1984), he moved to a one-room efficiency flat in the center of Berkeley. For the next nine months, he came to the house every Saturday to pick up little Maria and spend the day with her. He always arrived punctually at ten in the morning, and he always brought her back by eight at night. Then, after close to a year of this routine, he failed to show up. There was never any excuse, never any word of explanation. Lillian called his apartment several times over the next two days, but no one answered. On Monday, she tried to reach him at work, and when no one picked up the phone in his office, she redialed and asked for the secretary of the history department. It was only then that she learned that Dimaggio had quit his position at the college. Just last week, the secretary said, on the day he handed in his final grades for the semester. He had told the chairman that he'd been hired for a tenure-track job at Cornell, but when Lillian called the history department at Cornell, no one there had heard of him. After that, she never saw Dimaggio again. For the next two years, it was as if he had vanished from the face of the earth. He didn't write, he didn't call, he didn't make a single attempt to contact his daughter. Until he materialized in the Vermont woods on the day of his death, the story of those two years was a complete blank.

In the meantime, Lillian and Maria continued to talk on the phone. After Dimaggio had been missing for a month, Maria suggested that Lillian pack a suitcase and come with little Maria to New York. She even offered to pay the fare, but considering how broke Lillian was just then, they both decided the money would be better spent on paying bills. So Maria wired Lillian a loan of three thousand dollars (every penny she could afford), and the trip was shelved for some future date. Two years later, it still hadn't happened. Maria kept imagining that she would go out to California to spend a couple of weeks with Lillian, but there never seemed to be a good time, and it was all she could do to keep up with her work. After the first year, they began calling each other less. At one point, Maria sent another fifteen hundred dollars, but it had been four months since their last conversation, and she suspected that Lillian was in rather poor shape. It was a terrible way to treat a friend, she said, suddenly giving in to a fresh round of tears. She didn't even know what Lillian was doing anymore, and now that this wretched thing had happened, she saw how selfish she had been, she realized how badly she had let her down.

Fifteen minutes later, Sachs was stretched out on the sofa in Maria's studio, drifting off to sleep. He could give in to his exhaustion because he had already worked out a plan, because he was no longer in doubt about what to do next. Once Maria had told him about Dimaggio and Lillian Stern, he understood that the nightmare coincidence was in fact a solution, an opportunity in the shape of a miracle. The essential thing was to accept the uncanniness of the event – not to deny it, but to embrace it, to breathe it into himself as a sustaining force. Where all had been dark for him, he now saw a beautiful, awesome clarity. He would go to California and give Lillian Stern the money he had found in Dimaggio's car. Not just the money – but the money as a token of everything he had to give, his entire soul. The alchemy of retribution demanded it, and once he had performed this act, perhaps there would be some peace for him, perhaps he would have some excuse to go on living. Dimaggio had taken a life; he had taken Dimaggio's life. Now it was his turn, now his life had to be taken from him. That was the inner law, and unless he found the courage to obliterate himself, the circle of damnation would never be closed. No matter how long he lived, his life would never belong to him again. By handing the money over to Lillian Stern, he would be putting himself in her hands. That would be his penance: to use his life in order to give life to someone else; to confess; to risk everything on an insane dream of mercy and forgiveness.

He never talked about any of these things to Maria. He was afraid that she wouldn't understand him, and he dreaded the thought of confusing her, of causing her any further alarm. Still, he put off leaving as long as he could. His body required rest, and since Maria was in no hurry to get rid of him, he wound up staying with her for three more days. In all that time, he never set foot outside her loft. Maria bought new clothes for him; she shopped for groceries and cooked him meals; she supplied him with newspapers every morning and afternoon. Beyond reading the papers and watching the television news, he did almost nothing. He slept. He stared out the window. He thought about the immensity of fear.

On the second day, there was a small article in *The New York Times* that reported the discovery of the two bodies in Vermont. That was how Sachs learned that Dwight's last name had been McMartin, but the piece was too sketchy to offer any details about the investigation that was apparently underway. In the *New York Post* that afternoon, there was a second story that emphasized how baffled the local authorities were by the case. But nothing about a third man, nothing about a white Toyota abandoned in Brooklyn, nothing about any evidence that would establish a link between Dimaggio and McMartin. The headline announced: *Mystery in the Northern Woods*. That night on the national news, one of the networks picked up the story, but other than a short, tasteless interview with McMartin's parents (the mother weeping in front of the camera, the father stone-faced and rigid) and a shot of Lillian Stern's house ('Mrs Dimaggio refused to talk to reporters') there were no significant developments. A police spokesman came on and said that paraffin tests proved that Dimaggio had fired the gun that killed McMartin, but Dimaggio's own death was still unexplained. A third man had clearly been involved, he added, but they still had no idea who he was or where he had gone. For all intents and purposes, the case was an enigma.

The whole time Sachs spent with Maria, she kept calling Lillian's number in Berkeley. At first, there was no answer. Then, when she tried again an hour later, she was greeted by a busy signal. After several more attempts, she called the operator and asked if there was trouble on the line. No, she was informed, the phone had been taken off the hook. Once the report was shown on television the next evening, the busy signal became understandable. Lillian was protecting herself from reporters, and for the rest of Sach's stay in New York, Maria was unable to get through to her. In the long run, perhaps that was just as well. No matter how urgently she wanted to talk to her friend, Maria would have been hard-pressed to tell her what she knew: that Dimaggio's killer was a friend of hers, that he was standing next to her at that very moment. Things were awful enough without having to grope for the words to explain all that. On the other hand, it might have been useful to Sachs if Maria had managed to talk to Lillian before he left. The way would have been smoothed for him, so to speak, and his first hours in California would have been considerably less difficult. But how could Maria have known that? Sachs said nothing to her about his plan, and beyond the brief note of thanks he put on the kitchen table when she was out shopping for dinner on the third day, he didn't even say good-bye to her. It embarrassed him to behave like that, but he knew she wouldn't let him go without some explanation, and the last thing he wanted was to tell her lies. So once she had gone out to do the shopping, he gathered his belongings together and went downstairs to the street. His luggage consisted of the bowling bag and a plastic sack (into which he had dumped his shaving equipment, his toothbrush, and the few articles of clothing that Maria had found for him). From there he walked over to West Broadway, waved down a cab, and asked the driver to take him to Kennedy Airport. Two hours later, he boarded a plane for San Francisco.

She lived in a small, pink stucco house in the Berkeley flats, a poor neighborhood of cluttered lawns and peeling façades and sidewalks sprouting with weeds. Sachs pulled up in his rented Plymouth a little past ten in the morning, but no one answered the door when he rang. This was the first time he had been in

Berkeley, but rather than go off to explore the town and come back later, he parked himself on the front steps and waited for Lillian Stern to appear. The air throbbed with an uncommon sweetness. As he paged through his copy of the *San Francisco Chronicle*, he smelled the jacaranda bushes, the honeysuckle, the eucalyptus trees, the shock of California in its eternal bloom. It didn't matter to him how long he had to sit there. Talking to this woman had become the sole task of his life now, and until that happened, it was as though time had stopped for him, as though nothing could exist but the suspense of waiting. Ten minutes or ten hours, he told himself: as long as she turned up, it wasn't going to make any difference.

There was a piece in that morning's *Chronicle* about Dimaggio, and it proved to be longer and fuller than anything Sachs had read in New York. According to local sources, Dimaggio had been involved with a left-wing ecology group, a small band of men and women committed to shutting down the operations of nuclear power plants, logging companies, and other 'despoilers of the earth.' The article speculated that Dimaggio might have been on a mission for this group at the time of his death, an accusation strenuously denied by the chairman of the Berkeley chapter of Children of the Planet, who stated that his organization was ideologically opposed to all forms of violent protest. The reporter then went on to suggest that Dimaggio could have been acting on his own initiative, a renegade member of the Children who had disagreed with the group on questions of tactics. None of this was substantiated, but it hit Sachs hard to learn that Dimaggio had been no ordinary criminal. He had been something altogether different: a crazed idealist, a believer in a cause, a person who had dreamed of changing the world. That didn't eliminate the fact that he had killed an innocent boy, but it somehow made it worse. He and Sachs had stood for the same things. In another time and another place, they might even have been friends.

Sachs spent an hour with the paper, then tossed it aside and stared out at the street. Dozens of cars drove past the house, but the only pedestrians were the very old or the very young: little children with their mothers, an ancient black man inching along with a cane, a white-haired Asian woman with an aluminum walker. At one o'clock, Sachs temporarily abandoned his post to look for something to eat, but he returned within twenty minutes and consumed his fast food lunch on the steps. He was counting on her to come by five thirty or six o'clock, hoping that she was off at work somewhere, doing her job as she always did, continuing to go through the paces of her normal routine. But that was only a guess. He didn't know that she had a job, and even if she did have one, it was by no means certain that she was still in town. If the woman had disappeared, his plan would be worthless, and yet the only way to find out was to go on sitting where he was. He suffered through the early evening hours in a tumult of anticipation, watching the clouds darken overhead as dusk turned into night. Five o'clock became six o'clock, six o'clock became seven o'clock, and from then on it was all he could do not to feel singed by disappointment. He went out for more food at seven thirty, but again he returned to the house, and again he went on waiting. She could have been at a restaurant, he told himself, or visiting friends, or doing any number of other things that would explain her absence. And if and when she did return, it was essential that he be there. Unless he talked to her before she entered the house, he might lose his chance forever.

Even so, when she finally did turn up, Sachs was caught by surprise. It was a few minutes past midnight, and because he was no longer expecting her by then, he had allowed his vigilance to slacken. He had leaned his shoulder against the cast-iron railing, his eyes had shut, and he was just on the point of dozing off when the sound of an idling car engine roused him back to alertness. He opened his eyes and saw the car standing in a parking space directly across the street. An instant later, the engine was silent and the headlights were turned off. Still unsure whether it was Lillian Stern, Sachs climbed to his feet and watched from his position on the steps – heart pounding, the blood singing in his brain.

171

She came toward him with a sleeping child in her arms, scarcely bothering to glance at the house as she crossed the street. Sachs heard her whisper something into her daughter's ear, but he couldn't make out what it was. He realized that he was no more than a shadow, an invisible figure hidden in the darkness, and the moment he opened his mouth to speak, the woman would be frightened half to death. He hesitated for several seconds. Then, still unable to see her face, he plunged in at last, breaking the silence when she was halfway up the front walk.

'Lillian Stern?' he said. The moment he heard his own words, he knew his voice had betrayed him. He had wanted the question to carry a certain warmth and friendliness, but it came out awkwardly, sounding tense and belligerent, as if he were planning to do her harm.

He heard a quick, shuddering gasp escape from the woman's throat. She stopped short, adjusted the child in her arms, and then answered in a low voice that seethed with anger and frustration: 'Get the fuck away from my house, mister. I'm not talking to anyone.'

'I just want a word with you,' Sachs said, beginning to descend the stairs. He waved his open hands back and forth in a gesture of negation, as if to prove he had come in peace. 'I've been waiting here since ten o'clock this morning. I've got to talk to you. It's very important.'

'No reporters. I'm not talking to any reporters.'

'I'm not a reporter. I'm a friend. You don't have to say a word to me if you don't want to. I'm only asking you to listen.'

'I don't believe you. You're just another one of those filthy pricks.'

'No, you're wrong. I'm a friend. I'm a friend of Maria Turner's. She's the one who gave me your address.'

'Maria?' the woman said. There was a sudden, unmistakable softening in her voice. 'You know Maria?'

'I know her very well. If you don't believe me, you can go inside and call her. I'll wait out here until you're finished.'

He had reached the bottom of the stairs, and once again the

172

woman was walking toward him, as if freed to move now that Maria's name had been mentioned. They were standing on the flagstone path within two feet of each other, and for the first time since her arrival, Sachs was able to make out her features. He saw the same extraordinary face he had seen in the photographs at Maria's house, the same dark eyes, the same neck, the same short hair, the same full lips. He was nearly a foot taller than she was, and as he looked down at her with the little girl's head resting against her shoulder, he realized that in spite of the pictures, he hadn't expected her to be so beautiful.

'Who the hell are you?' she said.

'My name is Benjamin Sachs.'

'And what do you want from me, Benjamin Sachs? What are you doing here in front of my house in the middle of the night?'

'Maria's tried to get in touch. She called you for days, and when she couldn't get through, I decided to come out here instead.'

'All the way from New York?'

'There wasn't any other choice.'

'And why would you want to do that?'

'Because I have something important to tell you.'

'I don't like the way that sounds. The last thing I need is more bad news.'

'This isn't bad news. Strange news, maybe, even incredible news, but it's definitely not bad. As far as you're concerned, it's very good. Astounding, in fact. Your whole life's about to take a turn for the better.'

'You're awfully sure of yourself, aren't you?'

'Only because I know what I'm talking about.'

'And this can't wait until morning?'

'No. I've got to talk to you now. Just give me half an hour, and then I'll leave you alone. I promise.'

Without saying another word, Lillian Stern removed a set of keys from her coat pocket, walked up the steps, and opened the door to the house. Sachs followed her across the threshold and entered the darkened hallway. Nothing was taking place as he had imagined it would, and even after the light went on, even after he watched her carry her daughter upstairs to bed, he wondered how he was going to find the courage to talk to her, to tell her what he had come three thousand miles to tell.

He heard her close the door of her daughter's bedroom, but instead of coming downstairs, she went into another room and used the phone. He distinctly heard her dial a number, but then, just as she spoke Maria's name, the door slammed shut and the ensuing conversation was lost to him. Lillian's voice filtered down through the ceiling as a wordless rumble, an erratic hum of sighs and pauses and muffled bursts. Desperate as he was to know what she was saying, his ears weren't sharp enough, and he abandoned the effort after one or two minutes. The longer the conversation continued, the more nervous he became. Not knowing what else to do, he left his spot at the bottom of the stairs and began wandering in and out of the ground-floor rooms. There were just three of them, and each one was in woeful disarray. Dirty dishes were piled high in the kitchen sink; the living room was a chaos of scattered pillows, overturned chairs, and brimming ashtrays; the dining room table had collapsed. One by one, Sachs switched on the lights and then switched them off. It was a mean place, he discovered, a house of unhappiness and troubled thoughts, and it stunned him just to look at it.

The phone conversation lasted another fifteen or twenty minutes. By the time he heard Lillian hang up, Sachs was in the hall again, waiting for her at the bottom of the stairs. She came down looking grim-faced and sullen, and from the faint trembling he detected in her lower lip, he gathered that she had been crying. The coat she had been wearing earlier was gone, and her dress had been replaced by a pair of black jeans and a white T-shirt. Her feet were bare, he noted, and her toenails were painted a vivid red. Even though he was looking straight at her the whole time, she refused to return his glance as she descended the stairs. When she reached the bottom, he moved aside to let her pass, and it was only then, when she was halfway to the kitchen, that she stopped and turned to him, addressing him from over her left shoulder.

'Maria says hello,' she said. 'She also says that she doesn't understand what you're doing here.'

Without waiting for a response, she continued on into the kitchen. Sachs couldn't tell if she wanted him to follow her or stay where he was, but he decided to go in anyway. She flicked on the overhead light, groaned softly to herself when she saw the state of the room, and then turned her back on him and opened a cupboard. She took out a bottle of Johnnie Walker, found an empty glass in another cupboard, and poured herself a drink. It would have been impossible not to see the hostility buried in that gesture. She neither offered him a drink nor asked him to sit down, and all of a sudden Sachs realized that he was in danger of losing control of the situation. It had been his show, after all, and now here he was with her, inexplicably reeling and tongue-tied, unsure of how to begin.

She took a sip of her drink and eyed him from across the room. 'Maria says she doesn't understand what you're doing here,' she repeated. Her voice was husky and without expression, and yet the very flatness of it conveyed scorn, a scorn verging on contempt.

'No,' Sachs said, 'I don't imagine she does.'

'If you have something to tell me, you'd better tell it to me now. And then I want you on your way. Do you understand that? On your way and out of here.'

'I'm not going to cause any trouble.'

'There's nothing to stop me from calling the police, you know. All I have to do is pick up the phone, and your life goes straight down the toilet. I mean, what fucking planet were you born on anyway? You shoot my husband, and then you come out here and expect me to be nice to you?'

'I didn't shoot him. I've never held a gun in my life.'

'I don't care what you did. It's got nothing to do with me.'

'Of course it does. It has everything to do with you. It has everything to do with both of us.'

'You want me to forgive you, don't you? That's why you came. To fall on your knees and beg my forgiveness. Well, I'm not interested. It's not my job to forgive people. That's not my line of work.'

'Your little girl's father is dead, and you're telling me you don't care?'

'I'm telling you it's none of your business.'

'Didn't Maria mention the money?'

'The money?'

'She told you, didn't she?'

'I don't know what you're talking about.'

'I have money for you. That's why I'm here. To give you the money.'

'I don't want your money. I don't want a goddamned thing from you. I just want you to get out.'

'You're turning me down before you've heard what I have to say.'

'Because I don't trust you. You're after something, and I don't know what it is. No one gives away money for nothing.'

'You don't know me, Lillian. You don't have the slightest idea of what I'm about.'

'I've learned enough. I've learned enough to know that I don't like you.'

'I didn't come here to be liked. I came here to help you, that's all, and what you think of me is unimportant.'

'You're crazy, do you know that? You talk just like a crazy man.'

'The only crazy thing would be for you to deny what's happened. I've taken something from you, and now I'm here to give you something back. It's that simple. I didn't choose you. Circumstances gave you to me, and now I've got to make good on my end of the bargain.'

'You're beginning to sound like Reed. A fast-talking son-of-a-bitch, all puffed up with your stupid arguments and theories. But it won't wash, professor. There is no bargain. It's all in your head, and I don't owe you a thing.'

'That's just it. You don't. I'm the one who owes you.'

'Bullshit.'

'If my reasons don't interest you, then don't think about my reasons. But take the money. If not for yourself, then at least for your little girl. I'm not asking you for anything. I just want you to have it.'

'And then what?'

'Then nothing.'

'I'll be in your debt, won't I? That's what you'll want me to think. Once I take your money, you'll feel that you own me.'

'Own you?' Sachs said, suddenly giving in to his exasperation. 'Own you? I don't even *like* you. From the way you've acted with me tonight, the less I have to do with you the better.'

At that moment, without the least hint of what was coming, Lillian started to smile. It was a spontaneous interruption, a wholly involuntary response to the war of nerves that had been building between them. Even though it lasted no more than a second or two, Sachs was encouraged. Something had been communicated, he felt, some little connection had been established, and even though he couldn't say what that thing was, he sensed that the mood had shifted.

He didn't waste any time after that. Seizing on the opportunity that had just presented itself, he told her to stay where she was, left the room, and then walked outside to fetch the money from the car. There was no point in trying to explain himself to her. The moment had come to offer proof, to eliminate the abstractions and let the money talk for itself. That was the only way to make her believe him: to let her touch it, to let her see it with her own eyes.

But nothing was simple anymore. Now that he had unlocked the trunk of the car and was looking at the bag again, he hesitated to follow his impulse. All along, he had seen himself giving the money to her in one go: walking into her house, handing over the bag, and then walking out. It was supposed to have been a quick, dream-like gesture, an action that would take no time at all. He would swoop down like an angel of mercy and shower her with wealth, and before she realized that he was there, he would vanish. Now that he had talked to her, however, now that he had stood face to face with her in the kitchen, he saw how absurd that fairy tale was. Her animosity had frightened him and demoralized him, and he had no way to predict what would happen next. If he gave her the money all at once, he would lose whatever advantage he still had over her. Anything would be possible then, any number of grotesque reversals could follow from that error. She might humiliate him by refusing to accept it, for example. Or, even worse, she might take the money and then turn around and call the police. She had already threatened to do that, and given the depth of her anger and suspicion, he wouldn't have put it past her to betray him.

Instead of carrying the bag into the house, he counted out fifty one-hundred-dollar bills, shoved the money into his two jacket pockets, then zipped up the bag again and slammed the trunk shut. He had no idea what he was doing anymore. It was an act of pure improvisation, a blind leap into the unknown. When he turned toward the house again, he saw Lillian standing in the doorway, a small, illuminated figure with her hands on her hips, watching intently as he went about his business in the quiet street. He crossed the lawn knowing that her eyes were on him, suddenly exhilarated by his own uncertainty, by the madness of whatever terrible thing was about to happen.

When he reached the top of the steps, she moved aside to let him in and then closed the door behind him. He didn't wait for an invitation this time. Entering the kitchen before she did, he walked over the table, pulled out one of the rickety wooden chairs, and sat down. A moment later, Lillian sat down opposite him. There were no more smiles, no more flashes of curiosity in her eyes. She had turned her face into a mask, and as he looked across at her, searching for a signal, for some clue that would help him to begin, he felt as though he were studying a wall. There was no way to get through to her, no way to penetrate what she was thinking. Neither one of them spoke. Each was waiting for the other to start, and the longer her silence went on, the more obstinately she seemed to resist him. At a certain point, understanding that he was about to choke, that a scream was beginning to gather in his lungs, Sachs lifted his right arm and calmly swept everything in front of him onto the floor. Dirty dishes, coffee cups, ashtrays, and silverware landed with a ferocious clatter, breaking and skidding across the green linoleum. He looked straight into her eyes, but she refused to respond, continuing to sit there as though nothing had happened. It was a sublime moment, he felt, a moment for the ages, and as they went on looking at each other, he almost began to tremble with happiness, with a wild happiness that came surging up from his fear. Then, not missing a beat, he pulled the two bundles of cash from his pockets, slapped them onto the table, and pushed them toward her.

'This is for you,' he said. 'It's yours if you want it.'

She glanced down at the money for a split second but made no move to touch it. 'Hundred-dollar bills,' she said. 'Or are those just the ones on top?'

'It's hundreds all the way through. Five thousand dollars' worth.'

'Five thousand dollars isn't nothing. Even rich people wouldn't sneeze at five thousand dollars. But it's not exactly the kind of money that changes anyone's life.'

'This is only the beginning. What you might call a down payment.'

'I see. And what kind of balance are you talking about?'

'A thousand dollars a day. A thousand dollars a day for as long as it lasts.'

'And how long is that?'

'A long time. Long enough for you to pay off your debts and quit your job. Long enough to move away from here. Long enough to buy yourself a new car and a new wardrobe. And once you've done all that, you'll still have more than you know what to do with.'

'And what are you supposed to be, my fairy godmother?'

'Just a man paying off a debt, that's all.'

'And what if I told you I didn't like the arrangement? What if I said I'd rather have the money all at once?'

'That was the original plan, but things changed after I got here. We're on to Plan B now.'

'I thought you were trying to be nice to me.'

'I am. But I want you to be nice to me, too. If we do it this way, there's a better chance of keeping things in balance.'

'You're saying you don't trust me, is that it?'

'Your attitude makes me a little nervous. I'm sure you can understand that.'

'And what happens while you're giving me these daily installments? Do you show up every morning at an appointed hour, hand over the money, and then split, or are you thinking about staying for breakfast, too?'

'I told you before: I don't want anything from you. You get the money free and clear, and you don't owe me a thing.'

'Yeah, well, just so we've got it straight, wiseguy. I don't know what Maria told you about me, but my pussy's not for sale. Not for any amount of money. Do you understand that? Nobody forces me into bed. I fuck who I want to fuck, and fairy godmother keeps her wand to herself. Am I making myself clear?'

'You're telling me I'm not in your plans. And I've just finished telling you you're not in mine. I don't see how it could be any clearer than that.'

'Good. Now give me some time to think about all this. I'm dead tired, and I've got to go to sleep.'

'You don't have to think. You know the answer already.'

'Maybe I do, maybe I don't. But I'm not going to talk about it anymore tonight. It's been a rough day, and I'm about to fall over. But just to show you how nice I can be, I'm going to let you sleep on the couch in the living room. For Maria's sake – just this once. It's the middle of the night, and you'll never find a motel if you start looking now.'

'You don't have to do that.'

'I don't have to do anything, but that doesn't mean I can't do it. If you want to stay, then stay. If you don't, then don't. But you'd better decide now, because I'm going up to bed.'

'Thank you, I appreciate it.'

'Don't thank me, thank Maria. The living room's a mess. If something's in your way, just shove it onto the floor. You've already shown me you know how to do that.'

'I don't usually go in for such primitive forms of communication.'

'As long as you don't do any more communicating with me tonight, I don't care what happens down here. But upstairs is off limits. Capeesh? There's a gun in my bedside table, and if anyone comes prowling around, I know how to use it.'

'That would be like killing the goose who laid the golden egg.'

'No it wouldn't. You might be the goose, but the eggs are somewhere else. All snug in the trunk of your car, remember? Even if the goose got killed, I'd still have all the eggs I needed.'

'So we're back to making threats, are we?'

'I don't believe in threats. I'm just asking you to be nice to me, that's all. To be very nice. And not to get any funny ideas into your head about who I am. If you don't, then we might be able to do business together. I'm not making any promises, but if you don't screw up, I might even learn to stop hating you.'

He was woken the next morning by a warm breath fluttering against his cheek. When he opened his eyes, he found himself looking into the face of a child, a little girl frozen in concentration, exhaling tremulously through her mouth. She was on her knees beside the sofa, and her head was so close to his that their lips were almost touching. From the dimness of the light filtering through her hair, Sachs gathered that it was only six-thirty or seven o'clock. He had been asleep for less than four hours, and in those first moments after he opened his yes, he felt too groggy to move, too leaden to stir a muscle. He wanted to close his eyes again, but the little girl was watching him too intently, and so he went on staring into her face, gradually coming to the realization that this was Lillian Stern's daughter.

'Good morning,' she said at last, responding to his smile as an invitation to talk. 'I thought you'd never wake up.'

'Have you been sitting here long?'

'About a hundred years, I think. I came downstairs to look for my doll, and then I saw you sleeping on the couch. You're a very long man, did you know that?'

'Yes, I know that. I'm what you call a beanpole.'

'Mr Beanpole,' the girl said thoughtfully. 'That's a good name.'

'And I'll bet that your name is Maria, isn't it?'

'To some people it is, but I like to call myself Rapunzel. It's much prettier, don't you think?'

'Much prettier. And how old are you, Miss Rapunzel?'

'Five and three-quarters.'

'Ah, five and three-quarters. An excellent age.'

'I'll be six in December. My birthday is the day after Christmas.'

'That means you get presents two days in a row. You must be a clever girl to have worked out a system like that.'

'Some people have all the luck. That's what Mommy says.'

'If you're five and three-quarters, then you've probably started school, haven't you?'

'Kindergarten. I'm in Mrs Weir's class. Room one-oh-four. The kids call her Mrs Weird.'

'Does she look like a witch?'

'Not really. I don't think she's old enough to be a witch. But she does have an awfully long nose.'

'And shouldn't you be getting ready to go to kindergarten now? You don't want to be late.'

'Not today, silly. There's no school on Saturday.'

'Of course. I'm such a dingbat sometimes, I don't even know what day it is.'

He was awake by then, awake enough to feel the urge to stand up. He asked the girl if she was interested in eating breakfast, and when she answered that she was starving, he promptly rolled off the couch and put on his shoes, pleased to have this little job in front of him. They took turns using the downstairs bathroom, and once Sachs had emptied his bladder and splashed some water on his face, he moved on into the kitchen to begin. The first thing he saw there was the five thousand dollars – still sitting on the table, in the same spot where he had put it the night before. It

182

puzzled him that Lillian hadn't taken it upstairs with her. Was there a hidden meaning to this, he wondered, or was it simply the result of negligence on her part? Fortunately, Maria was still in the bathroom then, and by the time she joined him in the kitchen, he had already removed the cash from the table and stored it on a shelf in one of the cupboards.

The breakfast got off to a shaky start. The milk in the refrigerator had turned sour (which eliminated the possibility of cereal), and since the stock of eggs seemed to have been exhausted as well, he was unable to make French toast or an omelet (her second and third choices). He managed to find a package of sliced whole wheat bread, however, and once he had discarded the top four pieces (which were covered with a fuzzy, bluish mold), they settled on a meal of toast and strawberry jam. While the bread was warming in the toaster, Sachs unearthed a snow-encrusted can of frozen orange juice from the back of the freezer, mixed it up in a plastic pitcher (which first had to be washed), and served it along with the food. No true coffee was on hand, but after a thorough search of the cupboards, he finally discovered a jar of decaffeinated instant. As he drank down the bitter concoction, he made funny faces and clutched at his throat. Maria laughed at the performance, which inspired him to stagger around the room and emit a series of dreadful, gagging noises. 'Poison,' he whispered, as he sank slowly to the floor, 'the scoundrels have poisoned me.' This made her laugh even harder, but once the stunt was over and he sat down in his chair again, her amusement quickly faded, and he noticed a troubled look in her eyes.

'I was only pretending,' he said.

'I know,' she said. 'It's just that I don't like people to die.'

He understood his mistake then, but it was too late to undo the damage. 'I'm not going to die,' he said.

'Yes you will. Everybody has to die.'

'I mean not today. And not tomorrow either. I'm going to be around for a long time to come.'

'Is that why you slept on the sofa? Because you're going to live with us now?'

'I don't think so. But I'm here to be your friend. And your mother's friend, too.'

'Are you Mommy's new man?'

'No, I'm just her friend. If she lets me, I'm going to help her out.'

'That's good. She needs somebody to help her out. They're putting Daddy in the ground today, and she's very sad.'

'Is that what she told you?'

'No, but I saw her crying. That's how I know she's sad.'

'Is that where you're going today? To watch them put your daddy in the ground?'

'No, they won't let us. Grandma and Grandpa said we couldn't.'

'And where do your Grandma and Grandpa live? Here in California?'

'I don't think so. It's somewhere far away. You have to take a plane to get there.'

'Somewhere back East, maybe.'

'It's called Maplewood. I don't know where it is.'

'Maplewood, New Jersey?'

'I don't know. It's very far away. Whenever Daddy talked about it, he said it was the end of the world.'

'It makes you sad when you think about your father, doesn't it?'

'I can't help it. Mommy said he didn't love us anymore, but I don't care, I wish he would come back.'

'I'm sure he wanted to.'

'That's what I think. But he wasn't able to, that's all. He had an accident, and instead of coming back to us, he had to go to heaven.'

She was so small, Sachs thought, and yet she handled herself with almost frightening composure, her fierce little eyes boring steadily into him as she spoke – unflinching, without the slightest tremor of confusion. It astonished him that she could mimic the ways of adults so well, that she could appear so self-possessed when in fact she knew nothing, knew absolutely nothing at all.

He pitied her for her courage, for the sham heroism of her bright and earnest face, and he wished he could take back everything he had said and turn her into a child again, something other than this pathetic, miniaturized grown-up with her missing teeth and the yellow-ribboned barrette dangling from her curly hair.

As they polished off the last fragments of their toast, Sachs saw by the kitchen clock that it was only a few minutes past seven thirty. He asked Maria how long she thought her mother would go on sleeping, and when she said it could be another two or three hours, an idea suddenly occurred to him. Let's plan a surprise for her, he said. If we get busy now, we might be able to clean the whole downstairs before she wakes up. Wouldn't that be nice? She'll come down here and find everything all neat and sparkling. That's bound to make her feel better, don't you think? The little girl thought so. More than that, she seemed excited by the prospect, as if she were relieved that someone had finally stepped in to take charge of the situation. But we must be quiet, Sachs said, putting his finger to his lips. As quiet as elves.

So the two of them set to work, moving about the kitchen in brisk and silent harmony as the table was cleared, the broken crockery was swept up from the floor, and the sink was filled with warm suds. In order to keep the clamor to a minimum, they scraped the dishes with their bare fingers, smearing their hands with garbage as they dumped uneaten food and crushed cigarettes into a paper bag. It was foul work, and they registered their disgust by sticking out their tongues and pretending to vomit. Still, Maria more than kept up her end, and once the kitchen was in passable shape, she marched out to the living room with undiminished enthusiasm, eager to push on with the next task. It was getting close to nine o'clock by then, and sunlight was pouring in through the front windows, illuminating slender trails of dust in the air. As they surveyed the mess before them, discussing how they should best attack it, a look of apprehension swept across Maria's face. Without saying a word, she lifted her arm and pointed to one of the windows. Sachs turned, and an instant later he saw it too: a man standing on the lawn and looking up at the house. He was wearing a checkered tie and a brown corduroy jacket, a youngish man with prematurely thinning hair who looked as though he were debating whether to walk up the steps and ring the bell. Sachs patted Maria on the head and told her to go back to the kitchen and pour herself another glass of juice. She seemed as if she were about to balk, but then, not wanting to disappoint him, she nodded her head and reluctantly did as she was told. Sachs then picked his way through the living room to the front door, pulled it open as softly as he could, and stepped outside.

'Is there something I can do for you?' he said.

'Tom Mueller,' the man said. '*San Francisco Chronicle*. I wonder if I could have a word with Mrs Dimaggio.'

'Sorry. She's not giving any interviews.'

'I don't want an interview, I just want to talk to her. My paper is interested in hearing her side of the story. We're willing to pay for an exclusive article.'

'Sorry, no dice. Mrs Dimaggio isn't talking to anyone.'

'Don't you think the lady should have a chance to turn me down herself?'

'No, I don't think so.'

'And who are you, Mrs Dimaggio's press agent?'

'A friend of the family.'

'I see. And you're the one who does her talking for her.'

'That's right. I'm here to protect her from guys like you. Now that we've settled that question, I think it's time for you to leave.'

'And how would you suggest that I get in touch with her?'

'You could write her a letter. That's how it's generally done.'

'A good idea. I'll write her a letter, and then you can throw it away before she reads it.'

'Life is filled with disappointments, Mr Mueller. And now if you don't mind, I think it's time for you to be on your way. I'm sure you don't want me to call the police. But you are standing on Mrs Dimaggio's property, you know.'

'Yeah, I know. Thanks a lot, pal. You've been a tremendous help.'

'Don't feel too bad. This too shall pass. In another week's time, there won't be a person in San Francisco who can remember what this story was about. If someone mentions Dimaggio to them, the only person they'll think of is Joe.'

That ended the conversation, but even after Mueller had left the yard, Sachs went on standing in front of the door, determined not to move until he had seen the man drive away. The reporter crossed the street, climbed into his car, and started the engine. As a farewell gesture, he raised the middle finger of his right hand as he drove by the house, but Sachs shrugged off the obscenity, understanding that it was unimportant, that it merely proved how well he had handled the confrontation. As he turned to go back inside, he couldn't help smiling at the man's anger. He didn't feel like a press agent so much as a town marshal, and when all was said and done, it wasn't an entirely unpleasant feeling.

The moment he entered the house again, he looked up and saw Lillian standing at the top of the stairs. She was dressed in a white terrycloth robe, looking puffy-eyed and tousled, struggling to shake the sleep out of her system.

'I suppose I should thank you for that,' she said, running a hand through her short hair.

'Thank me for what?' Sachs said, feigning ignorance.

'For getting rid of that guy. You were very smooth about it. I was impressed.'

'That? Aw shucks. T'weren't nothin', ma'am. Just doin' my job, that's all. Just doin' my job.'

She smiled briefly at his dumb hick's twang. 'If that's the job you want, then you can have it. You're a lot better at it than I am.'

'I told you I'm not all bad,' he said, speaking in his normal voice again. 'If you give me a chance, I might even turn out to be useful.'

Before Lillian could answer this last remark, Maria came running into the hallway. Lillian shifted her eyes away from Sachs and said, 'Hi, baby. You were up early weren't you?'

'You'll never guess what we've been doing,' the little girl said. 'You won't believe your eyes, Mommy.'

'I'll be down in a few minutes. I have to take a shower first and then put on some clothes. Remember, we're going to Billie and Dot's house today, and we don't want to be late.'

She disappeared upstairs again, and in the thirty or forty minutes it took her to get ready, Sachs and Maria resumed their assault on the living room. They rescued pillows and cushions from the floor, tossed out newspapers and coffee-soaked magazines, vacuumed up cigarette ashes from the interstices of the woolen rug. The more areas they were able to clear (progressively giving themselves more space to move in), the faster they were able to work, until, at the very end, they began to resemble two speeded-up characters in an old film.

It would have been hard for Lillian not to notice the difference, but once she came downstairs, she responded with less enthusiasm than Sachs had thought she would – if only for Maria's sake. 'Nice,' she said, pausing briefly on the threshold and nodding her head, 'very nice. I should remember to sleep late more often.' She smiled, she made her small show of gratitude, and then, scarcely bothering to glance around her, she strode on into the kitchen to look for something to eat.

Sachs felt minimally assuaged by the kiss she planted on her daughter's forehead, but once Maria had been shooed upstairs to change her clothes, he didn't know what to do with himself anymore. Lillian paid only the scantest attention to him, moving about the kitchen in her own private world, and so he clung to his spot in the doorway, standing there in silence as she dug out a bag of real coffee from the freezer (which he had managed to overlook) and placed a kettle of water on the stove to boil. She was dressed in casual clothes – dark slacks, white turtleneck, flat shoes – but she had put on lipstick and eye-shadow, and there was an unmistakable smell of perfume in the air. Again, Sachs had no idea how to interpret what was going on. Her behavior was unfathomable to him – one moment friendly, one moment closed off, one moment alert, one moment distracted – and the more he tried to make sense of it, the less he understood.

Eventually, she invited him in for a cup of coffee, but even then she barely spoke, continuing to act as if she wasn't sure whether she wanted him to be there or to vanish. For want of anything else to say, he started talking about the five thousand dollars he'd found on the table that morning, opening up the cupboard and pointing to where he had stored the cash. It didn't seem to make much of an impression on her. 'Oh,' she said, nodding at the sight of the money, and then she turned and gazed out the window into the backyard, drinking her coffee in silence. Undaunted, Sachs put down his cup and announced that he was going to give her that day's installment. Without waiting for an answer, he went outside to his car and collected the money from the bowling bag in the trunk. When he returned to the kitchen three or four minutes later, she was still standing in the same position, staring out the window with one hand on her hip, following some secret train of thought. He walked right up to her, flapped the thousand dollars in her face, and asked her where he should put it. Wherever you like, she said. Her passivity was beginning to unnerve him, and so rather than place the money on the counter, Sachs went over to the refrigerator, opened the top door, and tossed the bills into the freezer. This produced the desired result. She turned on him with a puzzled look on her face and asked him why he had done that. Instead of answering her, he walked back to the cupboard, removed the original five thousand dollars from the shelf, and put that bundle in the freezer as well. Then, patting the freezer door, he turned to her and said: 'Frozen assets. Since you won't tell me if you want the money or not, we'll just put your future on ice. Not bad, huh? We'll bury your nest egg in the snow, and when spring comes and the ground starts to thaw, you'll look in here and discover that you're rich.'

A vague smile began to form at the corners of her mouth, signaling that she had weakened, that he had managed to draw her into the game. She took another sip of coffee, buying herself a little time as she prepared her comeback. 'It doesn't sound like such a good investment to me,' she finally said. 'If the money just sits there, it won't collect any interest, will it?'

'I'm afraid not. There's no interest until you start to get interested. After that, the sky's the limit.'

'I haven't said I'm not interested.'

'True. But you haven't said you are, either.'

'As long as I don't say no, it could be I'm saying yes.'

'Or it could be you aren't saying anything. That's why we shouldn't talk about it anymore. Until you know what you want to do, we'll keep our mouths shut, okay? We'll just pretend it isn't happening.'

'That's fine with me.'

'Good. In other words, the less said the better.'

'We won't say a word. And one day I'll open my eyes, and you won't be there anymore.'

'Exactly. The genie will crawl back into his bottle, and you'll never have to think about him again.'

His strategy seemed to have worked, but other than causing a general change in the mood, it was difficult to know what this conversation had accomplished. When Maria came bouncing into the kitchen a few moments later, decked out in a pink-and-white jumper and patent-leather shoes, he discovered that it had accomplished a great deal. Breathless and excited, she asked her mother if Sachs was going with them to Billie and Dot's house. Lillian said no, he wasn't, and Sachs was about to take that as his cue to drive off and look for a motel when Lillian added that he was nevertheless welcome to stay, that since she and Maria would be gone until late that night, there was no rush for him to leave the house. He could shower and shave if he wanted to, she said, and as long as he shut the door firmly behind him and made sure it was locked, it didn't matter when he left. Sachs hardly knew how to respond to this offer. Before he could think of anything to say, Lillian had coaxed Maria into the downstairs bathroom to brush her hair, and by the time they came out again, it was somehow a foregone conclusion that they would be going before he did. All this struck Sachs as remarkable, a turnaround that defied understanding. But there it was, and the last thing he wanted to do was object. Less than five minutes later, Lillian and Maria were walking out the front door, and less than a minute after that, they were gone, driving down the street in their dusty blue Honda and vanishing into the bright, midmorning sun.

He spent close to an hour in the upstairs bathroom – first soaking in the tub, then shaving in front of the mirror. It was altogether odd to be there, he found, lying naked in the water as he stared up at Lillian's things: the endless jars of creams and lotions, the lipstick containers and eye-liner bottles, the soaps and nail polishes and perfumes. There was a forced intimacy to it that both excited him and repulsed him. He had been allowed into her secret realm, the place where she enacted her most private rituals, and yet even here, sitting in the heart of her kingdom, he was no closer to her than he had been before. He could sniff and delve and touch all he liked. He could wash his hair with her shampoo, he could shave his beard with her razor, he could brush his teeth with her toothbrush – and yet the fact that she had let him do those things only proved how little they meant to her.

Still, the bath relaxed him, made him feel almost drowsy, and for several minutes he wandered in and out of the upstairs rooms, absent-mindedly drying his hair with a towel. There were three small bedrooms on the second floor. One of them was Maria's, another belonged to Lillian, and the third, scarcely bigger than a large closet, had once evidently served as Dimaggio's study or office. It was furnished with a desk and bookcase, but so much junk had been squeezed into its narrow confines (cardboard boxes, piles of old clothes and toys, a black-and-white television set) that Sachs did no more than poke his head in there before shutting the door again. He went into Maria's room next, browsing among her dolls and books, the nursery school photos on the wall, the board games and stuffed animals. Disordered as the room was, it turned out to be in better shape than Lillian's. That was the capital of mess, the headquarters of catastrophe. He took note of the unmade bed, the clumps of discarded clothes and underwear, the portable television crowned with two lipstick-stained coffee cups, the books and magazines scattered on the floor. Sachs scanned a few of the titles at his feet (an illustrated guide to Oriental massage, a study of reincarnation, a couple of paperback detective novels, a biography of Louise Brooks) and wondered if any conclusions could be drawn from this assortment. Then, almost in a trance, he began to pull open the drawers of the bureau and look through Lillian's clothes, examining her panties and bras, her stockings and slips, holding each article in his hand for a moment before moving on to the next one. After doing the same with the things in the closet, he turned his attention to the bedside tables, suddenly remembering the threat she had made the night before. After looking on both sides of the bed, however, he concluded that she had been lying. There was no gun anywhere to be found.

Lillian had disconnected the phone, and the instant he plugged it back into the wall, it started to ring. The sound made him jump, but rather than lift the receiver off the hook, he sat down on the bed and waited for the caller to give up. The phone rang another eighteen or twenty times. As soon as it stopped, Sachs grabbed the receiver and dialed Maria Turner's number in New York. Now that she had talked to Lillian, he couldn't put it off any longer. It wasn't just a matter of clearing the air between them, it was a matter of clearing his own conscience. If nothing else, he owed her an explanation, an apology for having run out on her in the way he did.

He knew that she would be angry, but he wasn't prepared for the barrage of insults that followed. The moment she heard his voice, she started calling him names: idiot, bastard, double-crosser. He had never heard her talk like that before – not to anyone, not under any circumstances – and her fury became so large, so monumental, that several minutes passed before she allowed him to speak. Sachs was mortified. As he sat there listening to her, he finally understood what he had been too stupid to recognize in New York. Maria had fallen for him, and beyond all the obvious reasons for her attack (the suddenness of his departure, the affront of his ingratitude), she was talking to him like a jilted lover, like a woman who had been spurned for someone else. To make matters worse, she imagined that that someone else had once been her closest friend. Sachs struggled to disabuse her of this notion. He had gone to California for his own private reasons, he said, Lillian meant nothing to him, this wasn't what she thought it was, and so on – but he made a clumsy job of it, and Maria accused him of lying. The conversation was in danger of turning ugly, but Sachs somehow managed to resist answering her, and in the end Maria's pride won out over her anger, which meant that she no longer had the will to keep insulting him. She started to laugh at him instead, or perhaps laugh at herself, and then, without any perceptible transition, the laughter changed to tears, a fit of awful sobbing that made him feel every bit as wretched as she did. It took some time before the storm passed, but after that they were able to talk. Not that the talk led them anywhere, but at least the rancor was gone. Maria wanted him to call Fanny – just to let her know that he was alive – but Sachs wouldn't do it. Contacting her would be risky, he said. Once they started to talk, he was bound to tell her about Dimaggio, and he didn't want to implicate her in any of his troubles. The less she knew, the safer she would be, and why drag her into it when it wasn't necessary? Because it was the right thing to do, Maria said. Sachs went through his argument all over again, and for the next half hour they continued to talk in circles, with neither one of them able to convince the other. There was no right and wrong anymore, only opinions and theories and inter-pretations, a swamp of conflicting words. For all the difference it made, they could just as well have kept those words to them-selves.

'It's no use,' Maria finally said. 'I'm not getting through to you, am I?'

'I hear you,' Sachs answered. 'It's just that I don't agree with what you're saying.'

'You're only going to make things worse for yourself, Ben. The longer you keep it to yourself, the harder it's going to be when you have to talk.'

'I'm never going to have to talk.'

'You can't know that. They might find you, and then you won't have any choice.'

'They're never going to find me. The only way that could happen is if someone tips them off, and you wouldn't do that to me. At least I don't think you would. I can trust you that far, can't I?'

'You can trust me. But I'm not the only person who knows. Lillian's in on it now, too, and I'm not sure she's as good at keeping promises as I am.'

'She wouldn't talk. It wouldn't make sense for her to talk. She'd stand to lose too much.'

'Don't count on sense when you're dealing with Lillian. She doesn't think the way you do. She doesn't play by your rules. If you haven't figured that out yet, you're only asking for trouble.'

'Trouble's all I've got anyway. A little more won't hurt me.'

'Clear out now, Ben. I don't care where you go or what you do, but get into your car and drive away from that house. Right now, before Lillian comes back.'

'I can't do that. I've already started this thing, and I have to see it through to the end. There's no other way. This is my chance, and I can't blow it by being scared.'

'You'll be in over your head.'

'That's where I am now. The whole point of this is to get out from under.'

'There are simpler ways.'

'Not for me there aren't.'

There was a long pause on the other end, an intake of breath, another pause. When Maria spoke again, her voice was trembling. 'I'm trying to decide if I should pity you or just open my mouth and scream.'

'You don't have to do either one.'

'No, I don't suppose I do. I can forget all about you, can't I? There's always that option.'

'You can do whatever you want, Maria.'

'Right. And if you want to go off the deep end, that's your business. But just remember that I told you so. Okay? Just remember that I tried to talk to you like a friend.'

He was badly shaken after they hung up. Maria's last words had been a kind of farewell, a declaration that she was no longer with him. It didn't matter what had led to the disagreement: whether it had been provoked by jealousy or honest concern or a combination of the two. The result was that he wouldn't be able to turn to her anymore. Even if she hadn't meant for him to think that, even if she would welcome hearing from him again, the conversation had left behind too many clouds, too many uncertainties. How could he look to her for support when the very act of talking to him would cause her pain? He hadn't intended to go that far, but now that the words had been spoken, he understood that he had lost his best ally, the one person he could have counted on for help. He had been in California for just over a day, and already his bridges were burning behind him.

He could have repaired the damage by calling her back, but he didn't do it. Instead, he returned to the bathroom and put on his clothes, brushed his hair with Lillian's brush, and spent the next eight and a half hours cleaning the house. Every now and then he would pause for a snack, scavenging the refrigerator and kitchen cupboards for something edible (canned soup, liverwurst, cocktail nuts), but other than that he stuck with it, working without interruption until past nine o'clock. His goal was to make the house spotless, to turn it into a model of domestic order and tranquility. There was nothing he could do about the tattered furniture, of course, or the cracked ceilings in the bedrooms, or the rusted enamel in the sinks, but at least he could make the place clean. Tackling one room at a time, he scrubbed and dusted and scoured and rearranged, progressing methodically from the back to the front, from the first floor to the second, from large messes to small. He washed out toilets, he reorganized the silverware, he folded and put away clothes, he collected Lego pieces, miniature tea-set utensils, the amputated limbs of plastic dolls. Last of all, he repaired the legs of the dining-room table, fastening them back into position with an assortment of nails and screws he found at the bottom of a kitchen drawer. The only room he didn't touch was Dimaggio's study. He was reluctant to open the door again, but even if he had wanted to go in there, he wouldn't have known what to do with all the debris. Time was running short by then, and he wouldn't have been able to finish the job.

He knew that he should be going. Lillian had made it clear that she wanted him out of the house before she returned, but instead of driving off to look for a motel, he went back to the living room, slid out of his shoes, and lay down on the sofa. He only wanted to rest for a few minutes. He was tired from the work he had done, and there didn't seem to be any harm in lingering. By ten o'clock, however, he still hadn't made a move for the front door. He knew that crossing Lillian could be dangerous, but the thought of going out into the night filled him with dread. The house felt safe to him, safer than anywhere else, and even if he had no right to take this liberty, he suspected that it might not be such a bad thing for her to walk in and find him there. She would be shocked, perhaps, but at the same time an important point would be established, the one point that needed to be made above all others. She would see that he meant for there to be no getting rid of him, that he was already an inescapable fact of her life. Depending on how she responded, he would be able to judge whether she understood that or not.

His plan was to pretend to be asleep when she arrived. But Lillian came home late, long past the hour she had mentioned that morning, and by then Sachs's eyes had closed on him and he was sleeping in earnest. It was an unpardonable lapse – sprawled out on the sofa with the lights burning all around him – but in the end it didn't seem to matter. The noise of a slamming door jolted him awake at one thirty, and the first thing he saw was Lillian standing in the entranceway with Maria in her arms. Their eyes met, and for the briefest moment a smile flashed across her lips. Then, without saying a word to him, she marched up the stairs with her daughter. He assumed she would come down again after she put Maria to bed, but as with so many other assumptions he made in that house, he was wrong. He heard Lillian go into the upstairs bathroom and brush her teeth, and then, after a time, he followed the sound of her footsteps as she went into her bedroom and turned on the television. The volume was low, and the only thing he could make out was a blur of mumbling voices, a thump of music vibrating in the walls. He sat on the sofa, fully conscious now, expecting her to come down any minute and talk to him. He waited ten minutes, then twenty minutes, then half an hour, and at last the television went off. He waited another twenty minutes after that, and when she still hadn't come down by then, he understood that she had no intention of talking to him, that she had already gone to sleep for the night. It was a triumph of sorts, he felt, but now that it was over, he wasn't quite sure what to make of his victory. He turned off the lamps in the living room, stretched out on the sofa again, and then lay in the darkness with his eyes open, listening to the silence of the house.

After that, there was no more talk of moving to a motel. The living room sofa became Sachs's bed, and he started sleeping there every night. They all took this for granted, and the fact that he now belonged to the household was never so much as even mentioned. It was a natural development, a phenomenon as little worth discussing as a tree or a stone or a particle of dust in the air. That was precisely what Sachs had hoped for, and yet his role among them was never clearly defined. Everything had been set up according to some secret, unspoken understanding, and he instinctively knew that it would be a mistake to confront Lillian with questions about what she wanted of him. He had to figure it out on his own, to find a spot for himself on the strength of the smallest hints and gestures, the most inscrutable remarks and evasions. It wasn't that he was afraid of what might happen if he did the wrong thing (although he never doubted that the situation could turn on him, that she could back up her threat and call the police), but rather that he wanted his conduct to be exemplary. That was the reason he had come to California in the first place: to reinvent his life, to embody an ideal of goodness that would put him in an altogether different relation with himself. But Lillian was the instrument he had chosen, and it was only through her that this transformation could be achieved. He had thought of it as a journey, as a long voyage into the darkness of his soul, but now that he was on his way, he couldn't be sure if he was traveling in the right direction or not.

It might not have been so hard on him if Lillian had been someone else, but the strain of sleeping under the same roof with her every night kept him permanently off balance. After just two days, it appalled him to discover how desperately he wanted to touch her. The problem wasn't her beauty, he realized, but the fact that her beauty was the only part of herself she allowed him to know. If she had been less intransigent, less unwilling to engage him in a directly personal way, he would have had something else to think about, and the spell of desire might have been broken. As it was, she refused to reveal herself to him, which meant that she never became more than an object, never more than the sum of her physical self. And that physical self carried a tremendous power within it: it dazzled and assaulted, it quickened the pulse, it demolished every lofty resolve. This wasn't the kind of struggle Sachs had prepared himself for. It didn't fit into the scheme he had worked out so carefully in his head. His body had been added to the equation now, and what had once seemed simple was turned into a morass of feverish strategies and clandestine motives.

He kept all this hidden from her. Under the circumstances, his only recourse was to match her indifference with an unflappable calm, to pretend that he was perfectly happy with the way things stood between them. He affected a lighthearted manner when he was with her; he was nonchalant, friendly, accommodating; he smiled often; he never complained. Since he knew that she was already on her guard, that she already suspected him of the feelings he was now guilty of, it was particularly important that she never see him looking at her in the way he wanted to look at her. A single glance could ruin him, especially with a woman as experienced as Lillian. She had spent her whole life being stared at by men, and she would be highly sensitive to his looks, to the smallest hint of meaning in his eyes. This produced an almost unbearable tension in him whenever she was around, but he hung on bravely and never abandoned hope. He asked nothing from her, expected nothing from her, and prayed that he would eventually wear her down. That was the only weapon at his disposal, and he brought it out at every opportunity, humiliating himself before her with such purpose, such passionate self-denial, that his very weakness became a form of strength.

For the first twelve or fifteen days, she scarcely said a word to him. He had no idea what she did during her long and frequent absences from the house, and though he would have given almost anything to find out, he never dared to ask. Discretion was more important than knowledge, he felt, and rather than run the risk of offending her, he kept his curiosity to himself and waited to see what would happen. On most mornings, she would leave the house by nine or ten o'clock. Sometimes, she would return in the evening, and at other times she would stay out late, not returning until well past midnight. Sometimes, she would go out in the morning, return to the house in the evening to change her clothes, and then vanish for the rest of the night. On two or three occasions, she did not return until the following morning, at which point she would walk into the house, change her clothes, and then promptly leave again. Sachs assumed that she spent those late nights in the company of men – perhaps one man, perhaps different men – but it was impossible to know where she went during the day. It seemed likely that she had a job of some kind, but that was only a guess. For all he knew, she could have spent her time driving around in her car, or going to the movies, or standing by the water and looking at the waves.

In spite of these mysterious comings and goings, Lillian never failed to tell him when he could expect her to turn up again. This was more for Maria's sake than for his, and even if the hours she gave were only approximate ('I won't be back until late,' 'See you tomorrow morning'), it helped him to structure his own time and keep the household from falling into confusion. With Lillian gone so often, the job of looking after Maria fell almost entirely to Sachs. That was the strangest twist of all, he found, for however curt and standoffish she might have been when they were together, the fact that Lillian showed no hesitation in letting him care for her daughter proved that she already trusted him, perhaps more than she even realized herself. Sachs tried to take heart from this anomaly. He never doubted that on one level she was taking advantage of him – palming off her responsibilities on a willing dupe – but on another level the message seemed quite clear: she felt safe with him, she knew that he wasn't there to hurt her.

Maria became his companion, his consolation prize, his indelible reward. He cooked breakfast for her every morning, he walked her to school, he picked her up in the afternoon, he brushed her hair, he gave her baths, he tucked her in at night. These were pleasures he couldn't have anticipated, and as his place in her routine became more firmly entrenched, the affection between them only deepened. In the past, Lillian had relied on a woman who lived down the block to look after Maria, but amiable as Mrs Santiago was, she had a large family of her own and rarely paid much attention to Maria except when one of her children was picking on her. Two days after Sachs moved in, Maria solemnly announced that she was never going to Mrs Santiago's house again. She preferred the way he took care of her, she said, and if it didn't bother him too much, she would just as soon spend her time with him. Sachs told her he would enjoy that. They were walking down the street just then, on their way home from school, and a moment after he gave that answer, he felt her tiny hand grab hold of his thumb. They walked on in silence for half a minute, and then Maria stopped and said: 'Besides, Mrs Santiago has her own children, and you don't have any little girls or boys, do you?' Sachs had already told her that he didn't, but he shook his head to show her that her reasoning was correct. 'It's not fair that someone has too many and another person is all alone, is it?' she continued. Again, Sachs shook his head and didn't interrupt. 'I think this is good,' she said. 'You'll have me now, and Mrs Santiago will have her own children, and everyone will be happy.'

On the first Monday, he rented a mailbox at the Berkeley post office to give himself an address, returned the Plymouth to the local branch of the car agency, and bought a nine-year-old Buick Skylark for less than a thousand dollars. On Tuesday and Wednesday, he opened eleven different savings accounts at various banks around town. He was wary of depositing all the money in one place, and starting multiple accounts seemed more prudent than walking in somewhere with a bundle of over a hundred and fifty thousand dollars in cash. Besides, he would call less attention to himself when he made his daily withdrawals for Lillian. His business would be kept in permanent rotation, and that would prevent any of the tellers or bank managers from getting to know him too well. At first, he figured he would visit each bank every eleven days, but when he discovered that withdrawals of one thousand dollars required a special signature from the manager, he started going to two different banks every morning and using the automatic cash machines, which disbursed a maximum of five hundred dollars per transaction. That amounted to weekly withdrawals of just five hundred dollars from each bank, a piddling sum by any standard. It was an efficient arrangement, and in the end he much preferred slipping his plastic card into the slot and pushing buttons than having to talk to a living person.

The first few days were hard on him, however. He suspected that the money he had found in Dimaggio's car was stolen – which could have meant that the serial numbers on the bills had been circulated by computer to banks around the country. But faced with a choice between running that risk or keeping the money in the house, he had decided to run the risk. It was too early to know if Lillian could be trusted, and leaving the money under her nose would hardly be an intelligent way to find out. At each bank he went to, he kept expecting the manager to glance down at the money, excuse himself from the conversation, and return to the office with a policeman in tow. But nothing like that ever happened. The men and women who opened his accounts were exceedingly courteous. They counted his money with swift, robotlike skill; they smiled, shook his hand, and told him how happy they were to have him as a customer. As a bonus for coming in with initial deposits of over ten thousand dollars, he received five toaster-ovens, four clock radios, a portable television set, and an American flag.

By the beginning of the second week, his days had fallen into a regular pattern. After taking Maria to school, he would walk back to the house, clean up the breakfast dishes, and then drive off to the two banks on his list. Once he had completed his withdrawals (with an occasional visit to a third bank to take out money for himself), he would go to one of the espresso bars along Telegraph Avenue, settle into a quiet corner, and spend an hour drinking cappuccinos as he read through the *San Francisco Chronicle* and *The New York Times*. As it turned out, surprisingly little was reported about the case in either paper. The *Times* had stopped talking about Dimaggio's death even before Sachs's departure from New York, and except for a short follow-up interview with a captain from the Vermont State Police, nothing further was published. As for the *Chronicle*, they seemed to be tiring of the business as well. After a flurry of articles about the ecology movement and the Children of the Planet (all of them written by Tom Mueller), Dimaggio's name was no longer mentioned. Sachs was comforted by this, but in spite of the diminishing pressure, he never went so far as to suppose it couldn't tighten again. All during his stay in California, he continued to study the papers every morning. It became his private religion, his form of daily prayer. Scan the newspapers and hold your breath. Make sure they weren't after you. Make sure you could go on living another twenty-four hours.

The rest of the morning and early afternoon were devoted to practical tasks. Like any other American housewife, he shopped for food, he cleaned, he took dirty clothes to the laundromat, he worried about buying the right brand of peanut butter for school lunches. On days when he had some time to spare, he would stop in at the local toy store before picking up Maria. He showed up at school with dolls and hair ribbons, with storybooks and crayons, with yoyos, bubble gum, and stick-on earrings. He didn't do this to bribe her. It was a simple outpouring of affection, and the better he got to know her, the more seriously he took the job of making her happy. Sachs had never spent much time with children, and it startled him to discover how much effort was involved in taking care of them. It required an enormous inner adjustment, but once he settled into the rhythm of Maria's demands, he began to welcome them, to relish the effort for its own sake. Even when she was gone, she kept him occupied. It was a remedy against loneliness, he found, a way to relieve the burden of always having to think about himself.

Every day, he put another thousand dollars in the freezer. The bills were stored in a plastic bag to protect them from moisture, and each time Sachs added a new allotment, he would check to see if any of the money had been removed. As it happened, not a single bill was ever touched. Two weeks passed, and the sum kept growing by increments of a thousand dollars a day. Sachs had no idea what to make of this detachment, this strange disregard for what he had given her. Did it mean that she wanted no part of it, that she was refusing to accept his terms? Or was she telling him that the money was unimportant, that it had nothing to do with her decision to allow him to live in her house? Both interpretations made sense, and therefore they cancelled each other out, leaving him with no way to understand what was happening in Lillian's mind, no way to decipher the facts that confronted him.

Not even his growing closeness to Maria seemed to affect her. It provoked no fits of jealousy, no smiles of encouragement, no response that he could measure. She would walk into the house while he and the little girl were curled up on the sofa reading a book, or crouched on the floor drawing pictures, or arranging a tea party for a roomful of dolls, and all Lillian would do was say hello, give her daughter a perfunctory kiss on the cheek, and then go off to her bedroom, where she would change her clothes and get ready to leave again. She was nothing more than a specter, a beautiful apparition who floated in and out of the house at irregular intervals and left no traces behind her. Sachs felt that she must have known what she was doing, that there must have been a reason for this enigmatic behavior, but none of the reasons he could think of ever satisfied him. At most, he concluded that she was putting him to a test, titillating him with this game of peekaboo to see how long he could stand it. She wanted to know if he would crack, she wanted to know if his will was as strong as hers.

Then, with no apparent cause, everything suddenly changed. Late one afternoon in the middle of the third week, Lillian walked into the house carrying a bag of groceries and announced that she was taking charge of dinner that night. She was in high spirits, full of jokes and fast, amusing patter, and the difference in her was so great, so bewildering, that the only explanation Sachs could think of was that she was on drugs. Until then, the three of them had never sat down to a meal together, but Lillian seemed not to notice what an extraordinary breakthrough this dinner represented. She pushed Sachs out of the kitchen and worked steadily for the next two hours, preparing what turned out to be a delicious concoction of vegetables and lamb. Sachs was impressed, but given everything that had preceded this performance, he wasn't quite prepared to accept it at face value. It could have been a trap, he felt, a ruse to trick him into letting down his guard, and while he wanted nothing more than to go along with her, to join in with the flow of Lillian's gaiety, he couldn't bring himself to do it. He was stiff and awkward, at a loss for words, and the blithe manner he had worked so hard to affect with her suddenly abandoned him. Lillian and Maria did most of the talking, and after a while he was scarcely more than an observer, a dour presence lurking around the edges of the party. He hated himself for acting like that, and when he refused a second glass of wine that Lillian was about to pour for him, he began to think of himself with disgust, as an out-and-out dunce. 'Don't worry,' she said as she poured the wine into his glass anyway. 'I'm not going to bite you.' 'I know that,' Sachs answered. 'It's just that I thought – ' Before he could complete the sentence, Lillian interrupted him. 'Don't think so much,' she said. 'Just take the wine and enjoy it. It's good for you.'

The next day, however, it was as though none of this had happened. Lillian left the house early, did not return until the following morning, and for the rest of that week continued to make herself as scarce as possible. Sachs grew numb with confusion. Even his doubts were now subject to doubt, and little by little he could feel himself buckling under the weight of the whole terrible adventure. Perhaps he should have listened to Maria Turner, he thought. Perhaps he had no business being there and should pack his bags and get out. For several hours one night, he even toyed with the idea of turning himself in to the police. At least the agony would be over then. Instead of throwing away the money on a person who didn't want it, perhaps he should use it to hire a lawyer, perhaps he should start thinking about how to keep himself out of jail.

Then, less than an hour after thinking these thoughts, everything turned upside-down again. It was somewhere between twelve and one o'clock in the morning, and Sachs was drifting off to sleep on the living room sofa. Footsteps began to stir on the second floor. He figured that Maria was on her way to the toilet, but just as he started to drift off again, he heard the sound of someone coming down the stairs. Before he could throw off the blanket and stand up, the living room lamp was turned on, and his makeshift bed was inundated with light. He automatically covered his eyes, and when he forced them open a second later, he saw Lillian sitting in the armchair directly opposite the sofa, dressed in her terrycloth robe. 'We have to talk,' she said. He studied her face in silence as she pulled out a cigarette from the pocket of her robe and lit it with a match. The bright confidence and flagrant posing of the past weeks were gone, and even her voice sounded hesitant to him now, more vulnerable than it had ever been before. She put the matches down on the coffee table between them. Sachs followed the movement of her hand, then glanced down at the writing on the matchbook cover, momentarily distracted by the lurid green letters emblazoned against the pink background. It turned out to be an advertisement for telephone sex, and just then, in one of those unbidden flashes of insight, it occurred to him that nothing was meaningless, that everything in the world was connected to everything else.

'I've decided that I don't want you to think of me as a monster anymore,' Lillian said. Those were the words that started it, and in the next two hours she told him more about herself than in all the previous weeks combined, talking to him in a way that gradually eroded the resentments he had been harboring against her. It wasn't that she came out and apologized for anything, nor was it that he jumped to believe what she said, but little by little, in spite of his wariness and suspicion, he understood that she was no better off than he was, that he had made her just as miserable as she had made him.

It took a while, however. At first, he assumed it was all an act, yet another ploy to keep his nerves on edge. In the whirl of nonsense that stormed through him, he even managed to convince himself that she knew he was planning to run away – as if she could read his mind, as if she had entered his brain and heard him thinking those thoughts. She hadn't come downstairs to make peace with him. She had done it to soften him up, to make sure he wouldn't decamp before he had given her all the money. He was on the point of delirium by then, and if Lillian hadn't mentioned the money herself, he never would have known how badly he had misjudged her. That was the moment when the conversation turned. She started talking about the money, and what she said bore so little resemblance to what he had imagined she would say, he suddenly felt ashamed of himself, ashamed enough to start listening to her in earnest.

'You've given me close to thirty thousand dollars,' she said. 'It keeps coming in, more and more of it every day, and the more money there is, the more scared of it I feel. I don't know how long you're planning to keep this up, but thirty thousand dollars is enough. It's more than enough, and I think we should stop before things get out of hand.'

'We can't stop,' Sachs found himself saying to her. 'We've only just started.'

'I'm not sure I can take it anymore.'

'You can take it. You're the toughest person I've ever seen, Lillian. As long as you don't worry, you can take it just fine.'

'I'm not tough. I'm not tough, and I'm not good, and once you get to know me, you'll wish you'd never set foot in this house.'

'The money isn't about goodness. It's about justice, and if justice means anything, it has to be the same for everyone, whether they're good or not.'

She began to cry then, staring straight ahead at him and letting the tears run down her cheeks – without touching them, as if she didn't want to acknowledge that they were there. It was a proud sort of crying, Sachs felt, at once a baring of distress and a refusal to submit to it, and he respected her for holding onto herself as tightly as she did. As long as she ignored them, as long as she didn't wipe them away, those tears would never humiliate her.

Lillian did most of the talking after that, chain-smoking her way through a long monologue of regrets and self-recriminations. Much of it was difficult for Sachs to follow, but he didn't dare to interrupt, fearing that a wrong word or badly timed question might bring her to a halt. She rambled on for a while about a man named Frank, then talked about another man named Terry, and then, a moment later, she was going over the last years of her marriage to Dimaggio. That led to something about the police (who had apparently questioned her after Dimaggio's body was discovered), but before she had finished with that, she was telling him about her plan to move, to leave California and start over again somewhere else. She had pretty much decided to do it, she said, but then he turned up on her doorstep, and the whole thing fell apart. She couldn't think straight anymore, she didn't know if she was coming or going. He expected her to continue with that a bit longer, but then she digressed onto the topic of work, talking almost boastfully about how she had managed to fend for herself without Dimaggio. She had a license as a trained masseuse, she told him, she did some modeling for department-store catalogues, and all in all she'd kept her head above water. But then, very abruptly, she waved off the subject as if it were of no importance and started crying again.

'Everything will work out,' Sachs said. 'You'll see. All the bad things are behind you now. You just haven't realized it yet.'

It was the correct thing to say, and it ended the conversation on a positive note. Nothing had been resolved, but Lillian seemed comforted by his remark, touched by his encouragement. When she gave him a quick hug of thanks before going up to bed, he resisted the temptation to squeeze any harder than he should have. Nevertheless, it was an exquisite moment for him, a moment of true and undeniable contact. He felt her naked body under the robe, he kissed her gently on the cheek, and understood that they were back at the beginning now, that everything that had come before this moment had been erased.

The next morning, Lillian left the house when she always did, disappearing while Sachs and Maria were on their way to school. But this time there was a note in the kitchen when he returned, a brief message that seemed to support his wildest, most improbable hopes. 'Thanks for last night,' it said. 'XXX.' He liked it that she had used kiss marks instead of signing her name. Even if they had been put there with the most innocent intentions – as a reflex, as a variant on the standard salutation – the triple-X hinted at other things as well. It was the same code for sex he had seen on the matchbook cover the night before, and it excited him to imagine that she had done it on purpose, that she had substituted those marks for her name in order to plant that association in his mind.

On the strength of this note, he went ahead and did something he knew he shouldn't have done. Even as he was doing it, he understood that it was wrong, that he was beginning to lose his head, but he no longer had it in him to stop. After he finished his morning rounds, he looked up the address of the massage studio where Lillian told him she worked. It was somewhere out on Shattuck Avenue in North Berkeley, and without even bothering to call for an appointment, he climbed into his car and drove over. He wanted to surprise her, to walk in unannounced and say hello – very casually, as if they were old friends. If she happened to be free at that moment, he would ask for a massage. That would give him a legitimate excuse to be touched by her again, and even as he savored the feel of her hands along his skin, he could still his conscience with the thought that he was helping her to earn her living. I've never been massaged by a professional, he would say to her, and I just wanted to know what it felt like. He found the place without difficulty, but when he walked inside and asked the woman at the front desk for Lillian Stern, he was given a curt, glacial response. 'Lillian Stern quit on me last spring,' the woman said, 'and she hasn't shown her face in here since.'

It was the last thing he had expected, and he walked out of there feeling betrayed, scorched by the lie she had told him. Lillian didn't come home that night, and he was almost glad to be left to himself, to be spared the awkwardness of having to see her. There was nothing he could say, after all. If he mentioned where he had been that afternoon, his secret would be exposed, and that would destroy whatever chance he still had with her. In the long run, perhaps he was lucky to have been through this now rather than later. He would have to be more careful with his feelings, he told himself. No more impulsive gestures. No more flights of enthusiasm. It was a lesson he had needed to learn, and he hoped he wouldn't forget it.

But he did. And not just in due course, but the very next day. Again, it was after dark. Again, he had already put Maria to bed, and again he was camped out on the living room sofa – still awake this time, reading one of Lillian's books about reincarnation. It appalled him that she could be interested in such claptrap, and he read on with a kind of vindictive sarcasm, studying each page as though it were a testament to her stupidity, to the breathtaking shallowness of her mind. She was ignorant, he told himself, a brainless muddle of fads and half-baked notions, and how could he expect a person like that to understand him, to absorb the tenth part of what he was doing? But then, just as he was about to put down the book and turn out the light, Lillian walked through the front door, her face flushed with drink, wearing the tightest, smallest black dress he had ever seen, and he couldn't help but smile when he saw her. She was that ravishing. She was that beautiful to look at, and now that she was standing in the room with him, he couldn't turn his eyes away from her.

'Hi, kiddo,' she said. 'Did you miss me?'

'Nonstop,' he said. 'From the minute I last saw you until now.' He delivered the line with enough bravura to make it sound like a joke, a bit of facetious banter, but the truth was that he meant it.

'Good. Because I missed you, too.'

She stopped in front of the coffee table, let out a short laugh, and then spun around in a full circle, arms spread like a fashion model, pivoting deftly on her toes. 'How do you like my dress?' she asked. 'Six hundred dollars on sale. A hell of a bargain, don't you think?'

'It was worth every penny. And just the right size, too. If it was any smaller, the imagination would be out of business. You'd hardly be wearing it when you put it on.'

'That's the look. Simple and seductive.'

'I'm not so sure about simple. The other thing, yes, but definitely not simple.'

'But not vulgar.'

'No, not at all. It's too well-made for that.'

'Good. Someone told me it was vulgar, and I wanted to get your opinion before I took it off.'

'You mean the fashion show is over?'

'All over. It's getting late, and you can't expect an old broad like me to stand on her feet all night.'

'Too bad. Just when I was beginning to enjoy it.'

'You're kind of thick sometimes, aren't you?'

'Probably. I'm often good at complicated things. But simple things tend to confuse me.'

'Like taking off a dress, I suppose. If you drag it out much longer, I'm going to have to take it off myself. And that wouldn't be so good, would it?'

'No, not so good. Especially since it doesn't look very hard. No buttons or snaps to fiddle with, no zippers to snag. Just pull from the bottom and slide it off.'

'Or start from the top and work your way down. The choice is yours, Mr Sachs.'

A moment later, she was sitting beside him on the sofa, and a few moments after that the dress was on the floor. Lillian went at him with a mixture of fury and playfulness, attacking his body in short, breathless surges, and at no point did he do anything to stop her. Sachs knew that she was drunk, but even if it was all an accident, even if it was only booze and boredom that had pushed her into his arms, he was willing to settle for it. There might never be another chance, he told himself, and after four weeks of waiting for precisely this one thing to happen, it would have been unimaginable to turn her down.

They made love on the sofa, and then they made love in Lillian's bed upstairs, and even after the effects of the alcohol had worn off, she remained as ardent as she had been in the first few moments, offering herself to him with an abandon and a concentration that nullified any lingering doubts he might have had. She swept him away, she emptied him out, she dismantled him. And the remarkable thing was that early the next morning, when they woke up and found each other in bed, they went at it again, and this time, with the pale light spreading into the corners of the small room, she said that she loved him, and Sachs, who was looking straight into her eyes at that moment, saw nothing in those eyes to make him disbelieve her.

It was impossible to know what had happened, and he never found the courage to ask. He simply went with it, floating along on a wave of inexplicable happiness, wanting nothing else but to be exactly where he was. Overnight, he and Lillian had become a couple. She stayed home with him during the day now, sharing the chores of the household, taking on her responsibilities as

Maria's mother again, and every time she looked at him, it was as though she were repeating what she had told him that first morning in bed. A week passed, and the less likely it seemed that she would recant, the more he came to accept what was happening. For several days in a row, he took Lillian out on buying sprees – showering her with dresses and shoes, with silk underwear, with ruby earrings and a strand of pearls. They binged on good restaurants and expensive wines, they talked, they made plans, they fucked until the cows came home. It was too good to be true, perhaps, but by then he was no longer able to think about what was good or what was true. When it came right down to it, he was no longer able to think about anything.

There's no telling how long it could have gone on. If it had just been the two of them, they might have made something of this sexual explosion, this bizarre and wholly implausible romance. In spite of its demonic implications, it's possible that Sachs and Lillian could have settled down somewhere and had a real life together. But other realities impinged on them, and less than two weeks after this new life began, it was already being called into question. They had fallen in love, perhaps, but they had also upset the balance of the household, and little Maria wasn't the least bit happy with the change. Her mother had been given back to her, but she had lost something as well, and from her point of view this loss must have felt like the crumbling of a world. For nearly a month, she and Sachs had lived together in a kind of paradise. She had been the sole object of his affections, and he had coddled her and doted on her in ways that no one else had ever done. Now, without a single word of warning, he had abandoned her. He had moved into her mother's bed, and rather than stay at home and keep her company, he left her with baby-sitters and went out every night. She resented all this. She resented her mother for coming between them, and she resented Sachs for letting her down, and by the time she had put up with it for three or four days, the normally obliging and affectionate Maria had turned into a horror, a tiny engine of sulks and tantrums and angry tears.

On the second Sunday, Sachs proposed a family outing to the Rose Garden in the Berkeley Hills. For once, Maria seemed to be in good spirits, and after Lillian fetched an old quilt from the upstairs closet, the three of them climbed into the Buick and drove to the other end of town. Everything went well for the first hour. Sachs and Lillian lay on the quilt, Maria played on the swings, and the sun burned off the last of the morning fog. Even when Maria banged her head on the jungle gym a little while later, there didn't seem to be any cause for alarm. She came running to them in tears, just as any other child would have done, and Lillian hugged her and soothed her, kissing the red mark on her temple with particular care and tenderness. It was good medicine, Sachs felt, the time-honored treatment, but in this case it had little or no effect. Maria went on crying, refusing to be consoled by her mother, and even though the injury was no more than a scratch, she complained about it vehemently, sobbing so hard that she nearly began to choke. Undaunted, Lillian hugged her again, but this time Maria recoiled from her, accusing her mother of squeezing her too hard. Sachs could see the hurt in Lillian's eyes when this happened, and then, when Maria pushed Lillian away from her, a flash of anger as well. Out of nowhere, they seemed to be on the verge of a full-blown crisis. An ice cream vendor had set up a stand about fifty feet from their quilt, and Sachs, thinking it might be a useful diversion, offered to buy Maria a cone. It will make you feel better, he said, smiling as sympathetically as he could, and then he ran off to the multicolored umbrella parked on the footpath just below them. It turned out that there were sixteen different flavors to choose from. Not knowing which one to pick, he settled on a combination of pistachio and tutti frutti. If nothing else, he thought, the sounds of the words might amuse her. But they didn't. Even though her tears had slackened by the time he returned, Maria eyed the scoops of green ice cream suspiciously, and when he handed the cone to her and she took her first tentative bite, all hell broke loose again. She made a terrible face, spat out the ice cream as though it were poison, and pronounced it 'disgusting.' This led to another fit of sobbing, and then, as her fury mounted, she took the cone in her right hand and hurled it at Sachs. It hit him squarely in the stomach, splattering all over his shirt. As he glanced down at the damage, Lillian rushed over to where Maria was standing and slapped her across the face.

'You brat!' she screamed at the little girl. 'You miserable, ungrateful brat! I'll kill you, do you understand! I'll kill you right here in front of all these people!' And then, before Maria had time to put up her hands and protect her face, Lillian slapped her again.

'Stop it,' Sachs said. His voice was hard, aghast with anger, and for a moment he was tempted to push Lillian to the ground. 'Don't you dare lay a hand on that child, do you hear me?'

'Butt out, mister,' she said, every bit as angry as he was. 'She's my kid, and I'll do what I damn please with her.'

'No hitting. I won't allow it.'

'If she deserves to be hit, I'll hit her. And no one interferes. Not even you, smartass.'

It got worse before it got better. Sachs and Lillian ranted at each other for the next ten minutes, and if they hadn't been in a public place, arguing in front of several dozen onlookers, God knows how far it might have gone. As it was, they eventually got a grip on themselves and reined in their tempers. Each one apologized to the other, they kissed and made up, and no more was said about it for the rest of the afternoon. The three of them went to the movies, then out to a Chinese restaurant for dinner, and by the time they returned home and Maria was put to bed, the incident had been all but forgotten. Or so they thought. In point of fact, that was the first sign of doom, and from the moment Lillian slapped Maria across the face until the moment Sachs left Berkeley five weeks later, nothing was ever the same for them again.

5

On January 16, 1988, a bomb went off in front of the court house in Turnbull, Ohio, blowing up a small, scale-model replica of the Statue of Liberty. Most people assumed it was a teenage prank, an act of petty vandalism without political motives, but because a national symbol had been destroyed, the incident was reported briefly by the wire services the next day. Six days after that, another Statue of Liberty was blown up in Danburg, Pennsylvania. The circumstances were almost identical: a small explosion in the middle of the night, no injuries, nothing damaged except the statue itself. Still, it was impossible to know if the same person was involved in both bombings or if the second blast was an imitation of the first – a so-called copy-cat crime. No one seemed to care much at that point, but one prominent conservative senator issued a statement condemning 'these deplorable acts' and urged the culprits to stop their shenanigans at once. 'It's not funny,' he said. 'Not only have you destroyed property, but you've desecrated a national icon. Americans love their statue, and they don't take kindly to this brand of horseplay.'

All in all, there are some one hundred and thirty scale-model replicas of the Statue of Liberty standing in public places across America. They can be found in city parks, in front of town halls, on the tops of buildings. Unlike the flag, which tends to divide people as much as it brings them together, the statue is a symbol that causes no controversy. If many Americans are proud of their flag, there are many others who feel ashamed of it, and for every person who regards it as a holy object, there is another who would like to spit on it, or burn it, or drag it through the mud. The Statue of Liberty is immune from these conflicts. For the past hundred years, it has transcended politics and ideology, standing at the threshold of our country as an emblem of all that is good within us. It represents hope rather than reality, faith rather than facts, and one would be hard-pressed to find a single person willing to denounce the things it stands for: democracy, freedom, equality under the law. It is the best of what America has to offer the world, and however pained one might be by America's failure to live up to those ideals, the ideals themselves are not in question. They have given comfort to millions. They have instilled the hope in all of us that we might one day live in a better world.

Eleven days after the Pennsylvania incident, another statue was destroyed on a village green in central Massachusetts. This time there was a message, a prepared statement phoned into the offices of the *Springfield Republican* the next morning. 'Wake up, America,' the caller said. 'It's time to start practicing what you preach. If you don't want any more statues blown up, prove to me that you're not a hypocrite. Do something for your people besides building them bombs. Otherwise, my bombs will keep going off. Signed: The Phantom of Liberty.'

Over the next eighteen months, nine more statues were destroyed in various parts of the country. Everyone will remember this, and there's no need for me to give an exhaustive account of the Phantom's activities. In some towns, twenty-four-hour guards were posted around the statues, manned by volunteer groups from the American Legion, the Elks Club, the high school football team, and other local organizations. But not every community was so vigilant, and the Phantom continued to elude detection. Each time he struck, there would be a pause before the next explosion, a long enough period to make people wonder if that was the end of it. Then, out of the blue, he would turn up somewhere a thousand miles away, and another bomb would go off. Many people were outraged, of course, but there were others who found themselves in sympathy with the Phantom's objectives. They were in the minority, but America is a large place, and their numbers were by no means small. To them, the Phantom eventually became a kind of underground folk hero. The messages had a lot to do with it, I think, the statements he phoned into newspapers and radio stations the morning after each explosion. They were necessarily short, but they seemed to get better as time went on: more concise, more poetic, more original in the way they expressed his disappointment in the country. 'Each person is alone,' one of them began, 'and therefore we have nowhere to turn but to each other.' Or: 'Democracy is not given. It must be fought for every day, or else we run the risk of losing it. The only weapon at our disposal is the Law.' Or: 'Neglect the children, and we destroy ourselves. We exist in the present only to the degree that we put our faith in the future.' Unlike the typical terrorist pronouncement with its inflated rhetoric and belligerent demands, the Phantom's statements did not ask for the impossible. He simply wanted America to look after itself and mend its ways. In that sense, there was something almost Biblical about his exhortations, and after a while he began to sound less like a political revolutionary than some anguished, soft-spoken prophet. At bottom, he was merely articulating what many people already felt, and in some circles at least, there were those who actually spoke out in support of what he was doing. His bombs hadn't hurt anyone, they argued, and if these two-bit explosions forced people to rethink their positions about life, then maybe it wasn't such a bad idea after all.

To be perfectly honest, I didn't follow this story very closely. There were more important things happening in the world just then, and whenever the Phantom of Liberty caught my attention, I shrugged him off as a crank, as one more transient figure in the annals of American madness. Even if I had been more interested, however, I don't think I ever could have guessed that he and Sachs were the same person. It was too far removed from what I was capable of imagining, too alien to anything that seemed possible, and I don't see how it ever would have occurred to me to make the connection. On the other hand (and I know this will sound odd), if the Phantom made me think about anyone, it was Sachs. Ben had been missing for four months when the first bombings were reported, and mention of the Statue of Liberty immediately brought him to mind. That was natural enough, I suppose – considering the novel he had written, considering the circumstances of his fall two years earlier – and from then on the association stuck. Every time I read about the Phantom, I would think about Ben. Memories of our friendship would come rushing back to me, and all of a sudden I would begin to ache, trembling at the thought of how much I missed him.

But that was as far as it went. The Phantom was a sign of my friend's absence, a catalyst for personal pain, but more than a year went by before I took notice of the Phantom himself. That was in the spring of 1989, and it happened when I switched on my television set and saw the students of the Chinese democracy movement unveil their clumsy imitation of the Statue of Liberty in Tienanmen Square. I realized then that I had underestimated the power of the symbol. It stood for an idea that belonged to everyone, to everyone in the world, and the Phantom had played a crucial part in resurrecting its meaning. I had been wrong to dismiss him. He had caused a disturbance somewhere deep inside the earth, and the waves were now beginning to rise to the surface, touching every part of the ground at once. Something had happened, something new was in the air, and there were days that spring when I walked through the city and almost imagined that I could feel the sidewalks vibrating under my feet.

I had started a new novel at the beginning of the year, and by the time Iris and I left New York for Vermont last summer, I was buried in my story, scarcely able to think about anything else. I settled into Sachs's old studio on June twenty-fifth, and not even that potentially eerie situation could disrupt my rhythm. There is a point at which a book begins to take over your life, when the world you have imagined becomes more important to you than the real world, and it barely crossed my mind that I was sitting in the same chair that Sachs used to sit in, that I was writing at the same table he used to write at, that I was breathing the same air he had once breathed. If anything, it was a source of pleasure to me. I enjoyed having my friend close to me again, and I sensed that if

218

he had known I was occupying his old space, he would have been glad. Sachs was a welcoming ghost, and he'd left behind no threats or evil spirits in his shack. He wanted me to be there, I felt, and even though I had gradually come around to Iris's opinion (that he was dead, that he would never come back), it was as if we still understood each other, as if nothing between us had changed.

In early August, Iris left for Minnesota to take part in the wedding of a childhood friend. Sonia went with her, and with David still off at summer camp until the end of the month, I hunkered down here alone and pushed on with my book. After a couple of days, I found myself slipping into the same patterns that set in whenever Iris and I are apart: too much work; too little food; restless, insomniac nights. With Iris in bed with me I always sleep, but the instant she goes away I dread just closing my eyes. Each night becomes a little harder than the night before, and in no time at all I'm up with the lamp on until one, two, or three o'clock in the morning. None of this is important, but because I was having these same troubles during Iris's absence last summer, I happened to be awake when Sachs made his sudden, unexpected appearance in Vermont. It was nearly two o'clock, and I was lying in bed upstairs reading a trashy thriller, a murder mystery that some guest had left behind years before, when I heard the sound of a car chugging up the dirt road. I lifted my eyes from the book, waiting for the car to move on past the house, but then, unmistakably, the engine slowed, the headlights swept their beams across my window, and the car turned, scraping against the hawthorn bushes as it came to a halt in the yard. I pulled on a pair of pants and rushed downstairs, arriving in the kitchen just seconds after the engine was turned off. There was no time to think. I went straight for the utensils on the counter, grabbed the longest knife I could find, and then stood there in the darkness, waiting for whoever it was to walk in. I figured it was a burglar or a maniac, and for the space of the next ten or twenty seconds, I was as scared as I've ever been in my life.

The light went on before I could attack him. It was an automatic gesture – stepping into the kitchen and turning on the light – and the instant after my ambush was foiled, I realized that Sachs was the person who had done it. There was the smallest interval between these two perceptions, however, and in that time I gave myself up for dead. He took three or four steps into the room and then froze. That was when he saw me standing in the corner – the knife still poised in the air, my body still ready to pounce.

'Jesus God,' he said. 'It's you.'

I tried to say something, but no words came out of my mouth.

'I saw the light,' Sachs said, still staring at me in disbelief. 'I thought it was probably Fanny.'

'No,' I said. 'It's not Fanny.'

'No, it doesn't look that way.'

'But it's not you either. It can't be you, can it? You're dead. Everyone knows that now. You're lying in a ditch somewhere at the edge of a road, rotting under a mound of leaves.'

It took some time to recover from the shock, but not long, not as long as I would have thought. He was looking well, I found, as clear-eyed and fit as I had ever seen him, and except for the gray that had spread through his hair now, he was essentially the same person he had always been. That must have reassured me. This was no specter who had returned – it was the old Sachs, as vibrant and full of words as ever. Fifteen minutes after he walked into the house, I was already used to him again, I was already willing to accept that he was alive.

He hadn't expected to run into me, he said, and before we sat down and began to talk, he apologized several times for having looked so stunned. Under the circumstances, I doubted that any apologies were necessary. 'It was the knife,' I said. 'If I'd walked in here and found someone about to stab me, I think I would have looked stunned, too.'

'It's not that I'm unhappy to see you. I just wasn't counting on it, that's all.'

'You don't have to be happy. After all this time, there's no reason why you should be.'

'I don't blame you for feeling burned.'

'I don't. At least I didn't until now. I admit that I was pretty angry at first, but that went away after a few months.'

'And then?'

'Then I began to feel scared for you. I suppose I've been scared ever since.'

'And what about Fanny? Has she been scared, too?'

'Fanny's braver than I am. She's never stopped thinking you were alive.'

Sachs smiled, visibly pleased by what I had said. Until that moment, I hadn't been sure if he was planning to stay or go, but now, suddenly, he pulled out a chair from the kitchen table and sat down, acting as though he had just come to an important decision. 'What are you smoking these days?' he said, looking up at me with the smile still on his face.

'Schimmelpennincks. The same thing I've always smoked.'

'Good. Let's have a couple of your little cigars, and then maybe a bottle of something to drink.'

'You must be tired.'

'Of course I'm tired. I've just driven four hundred miles, and it's two o'clock in the morning. But you want me to talk to you, don't you?'

'It can wait until tomorrow.'

'There's a chance I'll lose my nerve by tomorrow.'

'And you're ready to talk now?'

'Yes, I'm ready to talk. Until I came in here and saw you holding that knife, I wasn't going to say a word. That was always the plan: to say nothing, to keep it all to myself. But I think I've changed my mind now. It's not that I can't live with it, but it suddenly occurs to me that someone should know. Just in case something happens to me.'

'Why should anything happen to you?'

'Because I'm in a dangerous spot, that's why, and my luck could run out.'

'But why tell me?'

'Because you're my best friend, and I know you can keep a

secret.' He paused for a moment and looked straight into my eyes. 'You can keep a secret, can't you?'

'I think so. To tell you the truth, I'm not sure I've ever heard one. I'm not sure I've ever had one to keep.'

That was how it started: with these enigmatic remarks and hints of impending disaster. I found a bottle of bourbon in the pantry, collected two clean glasses from the drainboard, and then led Sachs across the yard to the studio. That was where I kept my cigars, and for the next five hours he smoked and drank, struggling against exhaustion as he spilled out his story to me. We were both sitting in armchairs, facing each other across my cluttered work table, and in all that time neither one of us moved. Candles burned all around us, flickering and sputtering as the room filled with his voice. He talked and I listened, and bit by bit I learned everything I have told so far.

Even before he began, I knew that something extraordinary must have happened to him. Otherwise, he wouldn't have kept himself hidden for so long; he wouldn't have gone to so much trouble to make us believe he was dead. That much was clear, and now that Sachs had returned, I was ready to accept the most far-flung and outrageous disclosures, to listen to a story I never could have dreamed of myself. It wasn't that I was expecting him to tell *this particular story*, but I knew that it would be something like it, and when Sachs finally began (leaning back in his chair and saying, 'You've heard of the Phantom of Liberty, I suppose?') I scarcely even blinked. 'So that's what you've been up to,' I said, interrupting him before he could go any further. 'You're the funny little man who's been blowing up all those statues. A nice line of work if you can get it, but who on earth picked you as the conscience of the world? The last time I saw you, you were writing a novel.'

It took him the rest of the night to answer that question. Even then there were gaps, holes in the account I haven't been able to fill in. Roughly speaking, the idea seems to have come to him in stages, beginning with the slap he witnessed that Sunday afternoon in Berkeley and ending with the disintegration of his affair with Lillian. In between, there was a gradual surrender to Dimaggio, a growing obsession with the life of the man he had killed.

'I finally found the courage to go into his room,' Sachs said. 'That's what started it, I think, that was the first step toward some kind of legitimate action. Until then, I hadn't even opened the door. Too scared, I suppose, too afraid of what I might find if I started looking. But Lillian was gone again, and Maria was off at school, and there I was sitting alone in the house, slowly beginning to lose my mind. Predictably enough, most of Dimaggio's belongings had been cleared out of the room. Nothing personal was left – no letters or documents, no diaries or telephone numbers, no clues about his life with Lillian. But I did stumble across some books. Three or four volumes of Marx, a biography of Bakunin, a pamphlet by Trotsky on race relations in America, that sort of thing. And then, sitting in a black binder in the bottom drawer of his desk, I found a copy of his dissertation. That was the key. If I hadn't found that, I don't think any of the other things would have happened.

'It was a study of Alexander Berkman – a reappraisal of his life and works in four hundred fifty-odd pages. I'm sure you've run across the name. Berkman was the anarchist who shot Henry Clay Frick – the man whose house is now a museum on Fifth Avenue. That was during the Homestead Steel Strike in 1892, when Frick called in an army of Pinkertons and had them open fire on the workers. Berkman was twenty at the time, a young Jewish radical who'd emigrated from Russia just a few years before, and he traveled down to Pennsylvania and went after Frick with a gun, hoping to eliminate this symbol of capitalist oppression. Frick survived the attack, and Berkman was thrown into the state penitentiary for fourteen years. After his release, he wrote *Prison Memoirs of an Anarchist* and continued to involve himself in political work, mostly with Emma Goldman. He was the editor of *Mother Earth*, helped found a libertarian school, gave speeches, agitated for causes like the Lawrence textile strike, and so on. When America entered the First World War, he was put in jail again, this time for speaking out against conscription. Two years later, not long after he was released, he and Emma Goldman were deported to Russia. At the farewell dinner before they left, news came that Frick had died that same evening. Berkman's only comment was: "Deported by God." An exquisite statement, no? In Russia, it didn't take long for him to become disillusioned. The Bolsheviks had betrayed the Revolution, he felt; one kind of despotism had replaced another, and after the Kronstadt rebellion was crushed in 1921, he decided to emigrate from Russia for the second time. He eventually settled in the South of France, where he lived out the last ten years of his life. He wrote the *ABC of Communist Anarchism*, kept body and soul together by doing translations, editing, and ghost-writing, but still needed help from friends in order to survive. By 1936, he was too sick to go on, and rather than continue to ask for handouts, he picked up a gun and shot himself through the head.

'It was a good dissertation. A bit clumsy and didactic at times, but well-researched and passionate, a thorough and intelligent job. It was hard not to respect Dimaggio for it, to see that he'd been a man with a real mind. Considering what I knew about his later activities, the dissertation was obviously something more than just an academic exercise. It was a step in his inner development, a way of coming to grips with his own ideas about political change. He didn't come right out and say it, but I could tell that he supported Berkman, that he believed there was a moral justification for certain forms of political violence. Terrorism had its place in the struggle, so to speak. If used correctly, it could be an effective tool for dramatizing the issues at stake, for enlightening the public about the nature of institutional power.

'I couldn't help myself after that. I started to think about Dimaggio all the time, to compare myself to him, to question how we'd come to be together on that road in Vermont. I sensed a kind of cosmic attraction, the pull of some inexorable force. Lillian wouldn't tell me much about him, but I knew he'd been a soldier in Vietnam and that the war had turned him inside-out, that he'd left the army with a new understanding of America, of politics, of his own life. It fascinated me to think that I'd gone to prison because of that war – and that fighting in it had brought him around to more or less the same position as mine. We'd both become writers, we both knew that fundamental changes were needed – but whereas I started to lose my way, to dither around with half-assed articles and literary pretentions, Dimaggio kept developing, kept moving forward, and in the end he was brave enough to put his ideas to the test. It's not that I think blowing up logging camps is a good idea, but I envied him for having the balls to act. I'd never lifted a finger for anything. I'd sat around grumbling and complaining for the past fifteen years, but for all my self-righteous opinions and embattled stances, I'd never put myself on the line. I was a hypocrite and Dimaggio wasn't, and when I thought about myself in comparison to him, I began to feel ashamed.

'My first thought was to write something about him. Something similar to what he had written about Berkman – only better, deeper, a genuine examination of his soul. I planned it as an elegy, a memorial in the shape of a book. If I could do this for him, I thought, then maybe I could start to redeem myself, then maybe something good could start to come out of his death. I would have to talk to a lot of people, of course, go around the country gathering information, setting up interviews with as many people as I could find: his parents and relatives, his army buddies, the people he went to school with, professional colleagues, old girlfriends, members of Children of the Planet, hundreds of different people. It would be an enormous project, a book that would take me years to finish. But that was the point somehow. As long as I was devoting myself to Dimaggio, I would be keeping him alive. I would give him my life, so to speak, and in exchange he would give my life back to me. I'm not asking you to understand this. I barely understood it myself. But I was groping, you see, thrashing out blindly for something to cling to, and for a little while this felt solid, a better solution than anything else.

'I never got anywhere with it. I sat down a few times to take notes, but I couldn't concentrate, I couldn't organize my thoughts. I don't know what the problem was. Maybe I still had too much hope that things would work out with Lillian. Maybe I didn't believe it would be possible for me to write again. God knows what was stopping me, but every time I picked up a pen and tried to start, I would break out in a cold sweat, my head would spin, and I'd feel as though I was about to fall. Just like the time I fell off the fire escape. It was the same panic, the same feeling of helplessness, the same rush toward oblivion.

'Then something strange happened. I was walking down Telegraph Avenue one morning to get my car when I spotted someone I knew from New York. Cal Stewart, a magazine editor I'd written a couple of articles for back in the early eighties. It was the first time since coming to California that I'd seen anyone I knew, and the thought that he might recognize me stopped me dead in my tracks. If one person knew where I was, I'd be finished, I'd be absolutely destroyed. I ducked into the first doorway I came to, just to get myself off the street. It turned out to be a used bookstore, a big place with high ceilings and six or seven rooms. I went all the way to the back and hid out behind a row of tall shelves, my heart thumping, trying to pull myself together. There was a mountain of books in front of me, millions of words piled on top of each other, a whole universe of discarded literature – books that people no longer wanted, that had been sold, that had outlived their usefulness. I didn't realize it at first, but I happened to be standing in the American fiction section, and right there at eye level, the first thing I saw when I started to look at the titles, was a copy of *The New Colossus*, my own little contribution to this graveyard. It was an astonishing coincidence, a thing that hit me so hard I felt it had to be an omen.

'Don't ask me why I bought it. I had no intention of reading the book, but once I saw it there on the shelf, I knew I had to have it. The physical object, the thing itself. It cost only five dollars for the original hardcover edition, complete with dust jacket and purple end papers. And there was my picture on the back flap: the portrait of the artist as a young moron. Fanny took that photo, I remember. I was twenty-six or twenty-seven at the time, with my beard and long hair, and I'm staring into the lens with an unbelievably earnest, soulful expression in my eyes. You've seen that picture, you know the one I'm talking about. When I opened up the book and saw it in the store that day, I almost burst out laughing.

'Once the coast was clear, I left the store and drove back to Lillian's house. I knew I couldn't stay in Berkeley anymore. Seeing Cal Stewart had scared the hell out of me, and I suddenly understood how precarious my position was, how vulnerable I had made myself. When I got home with the book, I put it on the coffee table in the living room and sat down on the sofa. I had no ideas anymore. I had to leave, but at the same time I couldn't leave, I couldn't bring myself to walk out on Lillian. I had just about lost her, but I wasn't willing to let go, I couldn't face the thought of never seeing her again. So I sat there on the sofa, staring at the cover of my novel, feeling like someone who's just run into a brick wall. I hadn't done anything with the book about Dimaggio; I'd thrown away more than a third of the money; I'd botched every hope for myself. Out of pure wretchedness, I kept my eyes fixed on the cover of the book. For a long time I don't think I even saw it, but then, little by little, something began to happen. It must have taken close to an hour, but once the idea took hold of me, I couldn't stop thinking about it. The Statue of Liberty, remember? That strange, distorted drawing of the Statue of Liberty. That was where it started, and once I realized where I was going, the rest followed, the whole cockeyed plan fell into place.

'I closed out a few of my bank accounts that afternoon and then took care of the others the next morning. I needed cash to do what I had to do, which meant reversing all the commitments I had made – taking the rest of the money for myself instead of giving it to Lillian. It bothered me to have broken my word, but not as much as I would have thought. I had already given her sixty-five thousand dollars, and even if it wasn't all there was, it was a lot of money, a lot more than she had been expecting me to give her.

227

The ninety-one thousand I still had would take me a long way, but it wasn't as if I was going to blow it on myself. The purpose I had contrived for that money was just as meaningful as my original plan. More meaningful, in fact. Not only would I be using it to carry out Dimaggio's work, but I would be using it to express my own convictions, to take a stand for what I believed in, to make the kind of difference I had never been able to make before. All of a sudden, my life seemed to make sense to me. Not just the past few months, but my whole life, all the way back to the beginning. It was a miraculous confluence, a startling conjunction of motives and ambitions. I had found the unifying principle, and this one idea would bring all the broken pieces of myself together. For the first time in my life, I would be whole.

'I can't begin to convey the power of my happiness to you. I felt free again, utterly liberated by my decision. It wasn't that I wanted to leave Lillian and Maria, but there were more important things to take care of now, and once I understood that, all the bitterness and suffering of the past month just melted out of my heart. I was no longer bewitched. I felt inspired, invigorated, cleansed. Almost like a man who had found religion. Like a man who had heard the call. The unfinished business of my life suddenly ceased to matter. I was ready to march out into the wilderness and spread the word, ready to begin all over again.

'Looking back on it now, I see how pointless it was to have pinned my hopes on Lillian. Going out there was a crazy thing to do, an act of desperation. It might have worked if I hadn't fallen in love with her, but once that happened, the venture was doomed to fail. I had put her in an impossible bind, and she didn't know how to cope with it. She wanted the money, and she didn't want it. It made her greedy, and her greed humiliated her. She wanted me to love her, and she hated herself for loving me back. I don't blame her for putting me through hell anymore. She's a wild person, Lillian. Not just beautiful, you understand, but incandescent. Fearless, out of control, ready for anything – and she never had a chance to be who she was with me.

'In the end, the remarkable thing wasn't that I left, but that I managed to stay as long as I did. The circumstances were so peculiar, so dangerous and unsettling, that I think they began to excite her. That's what sucked her in: not me, but the excitement of my being there, the darkness I represented. The situation was fraught with all sorts of romantic possibilities, and after a while she couldn't resist them anymore, she let herself go a lot farther than she ever intended to. Not unlike the weird and implausible way she had met Dimaggio. That had led to marriage. In my case, it led to a honeymoon, those two dazzling weeks when nothing could go wrong for us. It doesn't matter what happened after that. We couldn't have sustained it, and sooner or later she would have started running around again, she would have slipped back into her old life. But while it lasted, I don't think there's any question that she was in love with me. Whenever I begin to doubt it, I have only to remember the proof. She could have turned me in to the police, and she didn't. Even after I told her the money had run out. Even after I was gone. If nothing else, that proves that I meant something to her. It proves that everything that happened to me in Berkeley really happened.

'But no regrets. Not anymore at least. It's all behind me – over and done with, ancient history. The hard part was having to leave the little girl. I didn't think it would affect me, but I missed her for a long time, much more than I ever missed Lillian. Whenever I happened to be driving west, I'd start to think about going all the way to California – just to look her up and pay her a visit. But I never did. I was afraid of what might happen if I saw Lillian again, so I kept myself clear of California, and I haven't set foot in the state since the morning I left. Eighteen, nineteen months ago. By now, Maria's probably forgotten who I am. At one time, before things fell apart with Lillian, I used to think I'd wind up adopting her, that she would actually become my daughter. It would have been good for her, I think, good for both of us, but it's too late to dream about that now. I don't suppose I was ever meant to be a father. It didn't work with Fanny, and it didn't work with Lillian. Little seeds. Little eggs and seeds. You get just so many chances, and then life takes hold of you, and then you're off on your own forever. I've become who I am now, and there's no going back. This is it, Peter. For as long as I make it last, this is it.'

He was beginning to ramble. The sun was already up by then, and a thousand birds were singing in the trees: larks, finches, warblers, the morning chorus at full strength. Sachs had been talking for so many hours, he scarcely knew what he was saying anymore. As the light streamed through the windows, I could see that his eyes were about to close on him. We can go on talking later, I said. If you don't lie down and get some sleep, you're probably going to black out, and I'm not sure I'm strong enough to carry you over to the house.

I put him in one of the empty bedrooms on the second floor, pulled down the shades, and then tiptoed back to my own room. I doubted that I would be able to sleep. There were too many things to digest, too many images churning in my mind, but the moment my head touched the pillow, I began to lose consciousness. I felt as if I'd been clubbed, as if my skull had been crushed by a stone. Some stories are too terrible, perhaps, and the only way to let them into you is to escape, to turn your back on them and steal off into the darkness.

I woke up at three in the afternoon. Sachs slept on for another two or two and a half hours, and in the interval I puttered around the yard, staying out of the house so as not to disturb him. Sleep had done nothing for me. I was still too numb to think, and if I managed to keep myself busy during those hours, it was only by planning out the menu for dinner that night. I struggled over every decision, weighing each pro and con as if the fate of the world depended on it: whether to cook the chicken in the oven or on the grill, whether to serve rice or potatoes, whether there was enough wine left in the cupboard. It's odd how vividly all this comes back to me now. Sachs had just told me how he had killed a man, how he had spent the past two years roaming the country as a fugitive, and all I could think about was what to prepare for dinner. It was as if I needed to pretend that life still consisted of such mundane particulars. But that was only because I knew it didn't.

We stayed up late again that night, talking through dinner and on into the early hours of the morning. We were outside this time, sitting in the same Adirondack chairs we had sat in on so many other nights over the years: two disembodied voices in the dark, invisible to each other, seeing nothing except when one of us struck a match and our faces flared up briefly from the shadows. I remember the glowing ends of cigars, the fireflies pulsing in the bushes, an enormous sky of stars overhead – the same things I remember from so many other nights in the past. That helped to keep me calm, I think, but even more than the setting there was Sachs himself. The long sleep had refreshed him, and right from the start he was in full command of the conversation. There was no uncertainty in his voice, nothing to make me feel I couldn't trust him. That was the night he told me about the Phantom of Liberty, and at no point did he sound like a man confessing to a crime. He was proud of what he had done, unshakeably at peace with himself, and he talked with the assurance of an artist who knows he has just created his most important work.

It was a long, incredible tale, a saga of journeys and disguises, of lulls and frenzies and last-minute escapes. Until I heard it from Sachs, I never would have guessed how much work went into each explosion: the weeks of planning and preparation, the elaborate, roundabout methods for amassing the materials to construct the bombs, the meticulous alibis and deceptions, the distances that had to be covered. Once he had selected the town, he had to find a way to spend some time there without arousing suspicion. The first step was to concoct an identity and a cover story, and since he was never the same person twice, his powers of invention were constantly put to the test. He always had a different name, as bland and nondescript as he could make it (Ed Smith, Al Goodwin, Jack White, Bill Foster), and from one operation to the next, he did what he could to produce minor alterations in his physical appearance (beardless one time, bearded another, dark-haired in one place, light-haired in the next, wearing glasses or not wearing glasses, dressed in a suit or dressed in work clothes – a set number of variables that he would mix into different combinations for each town). The fundamental challenge, however, was to come up with a reason for being there, a plausible excuse to spend several days in a community where no one knew him. Once he posed as a college professor, a sociologist doing research for a book on small-town American life and values. Another time, he pretended to be on a sentimental journey, an adopted child looking for information about his biological parents. Another time he was a businessman hoping to invest in local commercial property. Another time he was a widower, a man who had lost his wife and children in an auto accident and was thinking about settling in a new town. Then, almost perversely, once the Phantom had made a name for himself, he showed up in a small Nebraska city as a newspaper reporter, at work on a feature article about the attitudes and opinions of people who lived in places with their own replicas of the Statue of Liberty. What did they think about the bombings? he asked them. And what did the statue mean to them? It was a nerve-shattering experience, he said, but worth every minute.

Early on, he decided that openness was the most useful strategy, the best way to avoid creating the wrong impression. Rather than skulk around and keep himself hidden, he chatted people up, he charmed them, he got them to think of him as an okay kind of guy. This friendliness came naturally to Sachs, and it gave him the breathing room he needed. Once people knew why he was there, they wouldn't be alarmed to see him strolling through town, and if he happened to pass the site of the statue several times during the course of his walks, no one would pay any attention. Likewise with the tours he made after dark, driving through the shut-up town at two in the morning to familiarize himself with the traffic patterns, to calculate the odds of anyone being in the vicinity when he planted the bomb. He was thinking of moving there, after all, and who could blame him if he wanted to get a feel for the place after the sun went down? He realized that it was a flimsy excuse, but these nocturnal outings were unavoidable, a necessary precaution, for not only did he have to save his own skin, he had to make sure that no one was ever hurt. A bum sleeping at the base of the pedestal, two teenagers necking on the grass, a man out walking his dog in the middle of the night – it would only take a single fragment of flying stone or metal to kill someone, and then the entire cause would be ruined. That was Sachs's greatest fear, and he went to enormous lengths to guard against accidents. The bombs he built were small, much smaller than he would have liked, and even though it increased the risks, he never set the timer to go off more than twenty minutes after he had taped the explosives to the crown of the statue. There was nothing to say that someone couldn't pass by in those twenty minutes, but given the hour, and given the nature of those towns, the chances were slim.

Along with everything else, Sachs gave vast amounts of technical information that night, a crash course in the mechanics of bomb-building. I confess that most of it went straight through me. I have no knack for mechanical things, and my ignorance made it difficult for me to follow what he said. I understood the occasional word, terms like *alarm clock*, *gunpowder*, *fuse*, but the rest was incomprehensible to me, a foreign language I couldn't penetrate. Still, judging from the way he talked, I gathered that a great deal of ingenuity was involved. He didn't rely on any pre-established formulas, and with the added burden of having to cover his tracks, he took great pains to use only the most homespun materials, to put together his explosives from odds and ends that could be found in any hardware store. It must have been an arduous process, traveling somewhere just to buy a clock, then driving fifty miles down the road to buy a spool of wire, then going somewhere else to buy a package of tape. No purchase was ever larger than twenty dollars, and he was careful to avoid using anything but cash – in every store, in every restaurant, in every broken-down motel. In and out; hello and good-bye. Then he would be gone, as if his body had melted into thin air. It was hard work, but after a year and a half, he hadn't left a single trace behind him.

He had a cheap apartment on the South Side of Chicago, which he rented under the name of Alexander Berkman, but that was a refuge more than a home, a place to pause between travels, and he spent no more than a third of his time there. Just thinking about this life made me uncomfortable. The constant movement, the pressure of always pretending to be someone else, the loneliness – but Sachs shrugged off my qualms as if they were of no importance. He was too preoccupied, he said, too absorbed by what he was doing to think about such things. If he had created any problem for himself, it was only how to cope with success. With the Phantom's reputation steadily increasing, it had become more and more difficult to find any statues to attack. Most of them were guarded now, and whereas in the beginning it had taken him anywhere from one to three weeks to accomplish his missions, the average time had grown to nearly two and a half months. Earlier that summer, he had been forced to abandon a project at the last minute, and several others had been postponed – put off until winter, when the cold temperatures would no doubt slacken the determination of the all-night guards. But still, for every obstacle that arose, there was a compensating benefit, another sign that proved how far his influence had spread. In the past few months, the Phantom of Liberty had been the subject of editorials and sermons. He had been discussed on call-in radio shows, caricatured in political cartoons, excoriated as a menace to society, extolled as a man of the people. Phantom of Liberty T-shirts and buttons were on sale in novelty shops, jokes had begun to circulate, and just last month two strippers in Chicago had presented an act in which the Statue of Liberty was gradually disrobed and then seduced by the Phantom. He was making a mark, he said, a much greater mark than he had ever thought possible. As long as he could keep it up, he was willing to face any inconvenience, to gut his way through any hardship. It was the kind of thing a fanatic would say, I later realized, an admission that he didn't need a life of his own anymore, but he spoke with such happiness, such enthusiasm and lack of doubt, that I scarcely understood the implication of those words at the time.

There was more to be said. All sorts of questions had accumulated in my mind, but dawn had come by then, and I was too exhausted to go on. I wanted to ask him about the money (how much was left, what he was going to do when it ran out); I wanted to know more about his breakup with Lillian Stern; I wanted to ask him about Maria Turner, about Fanny, about the manuscript of *Leviathan* (which he hadn't even bothered to look at). There were a hundred loose threads, and I figured I had a right to know everything, that he had an obligation to answer all my questions. But I didn't push him to continue. We would talk about those things over breakfast, I told myself, but now it was time for bed.

When I woke up later that morning, Sachs's car was gone. I assumed he had driven to the store and would be coming back any minute, but after waiting over an hour for him to return, I began to lose hope. I didn't want to believe that he had left without saying good-bye, and yet I knew that anything was possible. He had run out on others before, and why should I think he would act any differently with me? First Fanny, then Maria Turner, then Lillian Stern. Perhaps I was only the latest in a long line of silent departures, another person he had crossed off his list.

At twelve thirty, I went over to the studio to sit down with my book. I didn't know what else to do, and rather than go on waiting outside, feeling more and more ridiculous as I stood there listening for the sound of Sachs's car, I thought it might help to distract myself with some work. That was when I found his letter. He had placed it on top of my manuscript, and I saw it the moment I sat down at my desk.

'I'm sorry to sneak out on you like this,' it began, 'but I think we've covered almost everything. If I stayed around any longer, it would only cause trouble. You'd try to talk me out of what I'm doing (because you're my friend, because you'd see that as your responsibility to me as a friend), and I don't want to fight with you, I don't have the stomach for arguments now. Whatever you might think of me, I'm grateful to you for listening. The story needed to be told, and better to you than to anyone else. If and when the time comes, you'll know how to tell it to others, you'll make them understand what this business is all about. Your books prove that, and when everything is said and done, you're the only person I can count on. You've gone so much farther than I ever did, Peter. I admire you for your innocence, for the way you've stuck to this one thing for your whole life. My problem was that I could never believe in it. I always wanted something else, but I never knew what it was. Now I know. After all the horrible things that happened, I've finally found something to believe in. That's all that matters to me anymore. Sticking with this one thing. Please don't blame me for it – and above all, don't feel sorry for me. I'm fine. I've never been better. I'm going to keep on giving them hell for as long as I can. The next time you read about the Phantom of Liberty, I hope it gives you a good laugh. Onward and upward, old man. I'll see you in the funny papers. Ben.'

I must have read through this note twenty or thirty times. There was nothing else to do, and it took me at least that long to absorb the shock of his departure. The first few readings left me feeling hurt, angry at him for absconding when my back was turned. But then, very slowly, as I went through the letter again, I grudgingly began to admit to myself that Sachs had been right. The next conversation would have been more difficult than the others. It was true that I had been planning to confront him, that I had made up my mind to do what I could to talk him out of continuing. He had sensed that, I suppose, and rather than allow any bitterness to develop between us, he had left. I couldn't really blame him for it. He had wanted our friendship to survive, and since he knew this visit could be the last time we ever saw each other, he hadn't wanted it to end badly. That was the purpose of the note. It had brought things to an end without ending them. It had been his way of telling me that he couldn't say good-bye.

*

He lived for another ten months, but I never heard from him again. The Phantom of Liberty struck twice during that period – once in Virginia and once in Utah – but I didn't laugh. Now that I knew the story, I couldn't feel anything but sadness, an immeasurable grief. The world went through extraordinary changes in those ten months. The Berlin Wall was torn down, Havel became president of Czechoslovakia, the Cold War suddenly stopped. But Sachs was still out there, a solitary speck in the American night, hurtling toward his destruction in a stolen car. Wherever he was, I was with him now. I had given him my word to say nothing, and the longer I kept his secret, the less I belonged to myself. God knows where my stubbornness came from, but I never breathed a hint to anyone. Not to Iris, not to Fanny and Charles, not to a living soul. I had taken on the burden of that silence for him, and in the end it nearly crushed me.

I saw Maria Turner in early September, a few days after Iris and I returned to New York. It was a relief to be able to talk to someone about Sachs, but even with her I held back as much as I could. I didn't even mention that I had seen him – only that he had called and that we had talked on the phone for an hour. It was a grim little dance I danced with Maria that day. I accused her of misguided loyalty, of betraying Sachs by keeping her promise to him, while all along that was precisely what I was doing myself. We had both been let in on the secret, but I knew more than she did, and I wasn't about to share the particulars with her. It was enough for her to know that I knew what she knew. She talked quite willingly after that, realizing how futile it would have been to con me. That much was out in the open now, and I wound up hearing more about her relations with Sachs than Sachs ever told me himself. Among other things, that was the day I first saw the photographs she had taken of him, the so-called 'Thursdays with Ben.' Even more importantly, I also learned that Maria had seen Lillian Stern in Berkeley the year before – about six months after Sachs had left. According to what Lillian had told her, Ben had been back to visit twice. That contradicted what he had told me, but when I pointed out the discrepancy to Maria, she only shrugged. 'Lillian's not the only person who lies,' she said. 'You know that as well as I do. After what those two did to each other, all bets are off.'

'I'm not saying that Ben couldn't lie,' I answered. 'I just don't understand why he would.'

'It seems that he made certain threats. Maybe he was too embarrassed to tell you about them.'

'Threats?'

'Lillian said that he threatened to kidnap her daughter.'

'And why on earth would he do that?'

'Apparently, he didn't like the way she was raising Maria. He said that she was a bad influence on her, that the kid deserved a chance to grow up in healthy surroundings. He took the high moral ground, and it turned into a nasty scene.'

'That doesn't sound like Ben.'

'Maybe not, but Lillian was scared enough to do something about it. After Ben's second visit, she put Maria on a plane and sent her to her mother's house back East. The little girl's been living there ever since.'

'Maybe Lillian had her own reasons for wanting to get rid of her.'

'Anything is possible. I'm just telling you what she told me.'

'What about the money he gave her? Did she ever spend it?'

'No. At least not on herself. She told me that she put it in a trust fund for Maria.'

'I wonder if Ben ever told her where it came from. I'm not too clear on that point, and it might have made a difference.'

'I'm not sure. But a more interesting question is to ask where Dimaggio got the money in the first place. It was a phenomenal amount of cash for him to be carrying around.'

'Ben thought it was stolen. At least at first. Then he thought it might have been given to Dimaggio by some political organization. If not the Children of the Planet, then someone else. Terrorists, for example. The PLO, the IRA, any one of a dozen groups. He figured that Dimaggio might have been connected to people like that.'

'Lillian has her own opinion about what Dimaggio was up to.'

'I'm sure she does.'

'Yeah, well, it's kind of interesting once you start to think about it. In her view, Dimaggio was working as an undercover agent for the government. The CIA, the FBI, one of those cloak-and-dagger gangs. She thinks it started when he was a soldier in Vietnam. That they signed him up over there and paid his way through college and graduate school. To give him the right credentials.'

'You mean he was a plant? An *agent provocateur*?'

'That's what Lillian thinks.'

'It sounds pretty farfetched to me.'

'Of course it does. But that doesn't mean it isn't true.'

'Does she have proof, or is she just making a wild guess?'

'I don't know, I didn't ask her. We didn't really talk about it much.'

'Why don't you ask her now?'

'We're not exactly on speaking terms anymore.'

'Oh?'

'It was a pretty rocky visit, and I haven't been in touch with her since last year.'

'You had a falling out.'

'Yeah, something like that.'

'About Ben, I suppose. You're still stuck on him, aren't you? It must have been hard listening to your friend tell you how he'd fallen in love with her.'

Maria suddenly turned her head away from me, and I knew I was right. But she was too proud to admit anything, and a moment later she had composed herself sufficiently to look back in my direction. She flashed me a tough, ironic smile. 'You're the only man I've ever loved, Chiquita,' she said. 'But then you went off and got married on me, didn't you? When a girl's heart is broken, she's gotta do what she's gotta do.'

I managed to talk her into giving me Lillian's address and telephone number. A new book of mine was coming out in October, and my publisher had arranged for me to give readings in a number of cities around the country. San Francisco was the last stop on the tour, and it wouldn't have made sense to go there without trying to meet Lillian. I had no idea if she knew where Sachs was or not (and even if she did, it wasn't certain she would tell me), but I figured we would have a lot to talk about anyway. If nothing else, I wanted to set eyes on her myself, to be able to form my own opinion of who she was. Everything I knew about her had come from either Sachs or Maria, and she was too important a figure for me to rely on their accounts. I called the day after I got her number from Maria. She wasn't in, but I left a message on her machine, and much to my surprise, she called back the next afternoon. It was a brief but friendly conversation. She knew who I was, she said. Ben had talked to her about me, and he had even given her one of my novels, which she confessed she hadn't had time to read. I didn't dare to ask her any questions on the phone. It was enough to have made contact with her, and so I got right to the point, asking her if she would be willing to see me when I was in the Bay Area at the end of October. She hesitated for a moment, but when I told her how much I was counting on it, she gave in. Call me after you check into your hotel, she said, and we'll have a drink together somewhere. It was that simple. She had an interesting voice, I thought, somewhat throaty and deep, and I liked the sound of it. If she had ever made it as an actress, it was the kind of voice that people would have remembered.

The promise of that meeting kept me going for the next month and a half. When the earthquake hit San Francisco in early October, my first thought was to wonder if my visit would have to be canceled. I'm ashamed of my heartlessness now, but at the time I scarcely even noticed it. Collapsed highways, burning buildings, crushed and mangled bodies – these disasters meant nothing to me except insofar as they could prevent me from talking to Lillian Stern. Fortunately, the theater where I had been booked to do the reading escaped without damage, and the trip went off as planned. After checking into the hotel, I went straight to my room and called the house in Berkeley. A woman with an unfamiliar voice answered the phone. When I asked to speak to

Lillian Stern, she told me that Lillian was gone, that she'd left for Chicago three days after the earthquake. When was she coming back? I asked. The woman didn't know. You mean to say the earthquake frightened her that much? I said. Oh no, the woman said, Lillian had been planning to leave before it happened. She had run the ad to sublet her house in early September. What about a forwarding address? I asked. She didn't have one, the woman said, she paid her rent directly to the landlord. Well, I said, struggling to overcome my disappointment, if you ever hear from her, I'd appreciate it if you let me know. Before hanging up, I gave her my number in New York. Call me collect, I said, any time day or night.

I understood then how thoroughly Lillian had tricked me. She had known she would be gone before I ever got there – which meant that she had never had any intention of keeping our appointment. I cursed myself for my gullibility, for the time and hope I had squandered. Just to make sure, I checked with Chicago information, but there was no listing for Lillian Stern. When I called Maria Turner in New York and asked her for Lillian's mother's address, she told me she'd been out of touch with Mrs Stern for years and had no idea where she lived. The trail had suddenly gone cold. Lillian was just as lost to me now as Sachs was, and I couldn't even imagine how to begin looking for her. If there was any consolation in her disappearance, it came from the word *Chicago*. There had to have been a reason why she didn't want to talk to me, and I prayed it was because she was trying to protect Sachs. If that were so, then maybe they were on better terms than I had been led to believe. Or maybe the situation had improved after his visit to Vermont. What if he had driven out to California and talked her into running off with him? He had told me that he kept an apartment in Chicago, and Lillian had told her tenant that she was moving to Chicago. Was it a coincidence, or had one or both of them been lying? I couldn't even guess, but for Sachs's sake I hoped they were together now, living some mad outlaw existence as he crisscrossed the country, furtively plotting his next move. The Phantom of Liberty and his moll. If nothing else, he wouldn't have been alone then, and I preferred to imagine him with her than alone, preferred to imagine any life other than the one he had described to me. If Lillian was as fearless as he had said she was, then maybe she was with him, maybe she was wild enough to have done it.

I learned nothing more after that. Eight months passed, and when Iris and I returned to Vermont at the end of June, I had all but given up on the notion of finding him. Of the hundreds of possible outcomes I imagined, the one that seemed most plausible was that he would never surface again. I had no idea how long the bombings would last, no inkling of when the end would come. And even if there was an end, it seemed doubtful that I would ever know about it – which meant that the story would go on and on, secreting its poison inside me forever. The struggle was to accept that, to coexist with the forces of my own uncertainty. Desperate as I was for a resolution, I had to understand that it might never come. You can hold your breath for just so long, after all. Sooner or later, a moment comes when you have to start breathing again – even if the air is tainted, even if you know it will eventually kill you.

The article in the *Times* caught me with my guard down. I had grown so accustomed to my ignorance by then that I no longer expected anything to change. Someone had died on that road in Wisconsin, but even though I knew it could have been Sachs, I wasn't prepared to believe it. It took the arrival of the FBI men to convince me, and even then I clung to my doubts until the last possible moment – when they mentioned the telephone number that had been found in the dead man's pocket. After that, a single image burned itself into my mind, and it has stayed with me ever since: my poor friend bursting into pieces when the bomb went off, my poor friend's body scattering in the wind.

That was two months ago. I sat down and started this book the next morning, and since then I have worked in a state of continual panic – struggling to finish before I ran out of time, never knowing if I would be able to reach the end. Just as I predicted, the men from the FBI have kept themselves busy on my account.

They've talked to my mother in Florida, to my sister in Connecticut, to my friends in New York, and all summer long people have been calling to tell me about these visits, worried that I must be in some kind of trouble. I'm not in trouble yet, but I fully expect to be in the near future. Once my friends Worthy and Harris discover how much I've held back from them, they're bound to be irritated. There's nothing I can do about that now. I realize there are penalties for withholding information from the FBI, but under the circumstances I don't see how I could have acted any differently. I owed it to Sachs to keep my mouth shut, and I owed it to him to write this book. He was brave enough to entrust me with his story, and I don't think I could have lived with myself if I had let him down.

I wrote a short, preliminary draft in the first month, sticking only to the barest essentials. When the case was still unsolved at that point, I went back to the beginning and started filling in the gaps, expanding each chapter to more than twice its original length. My plan was to go through the manuscript as many times as necessary, to add new material with each successive draft, and to keep at it until I felt there was nothing left to say. Theoretically, the process could have continued for months, perhaps even for years – but only if I was lucky. As it is, these past eight weeks are all I will ever have. Three-quarters of the way into the second draft (in the middle of the fourth chapter), I was forced to stop writing. That was yesterday, and I'm still trying to come to grips with how suddenly it happened. The book is over now because the case is over. If I put in this final page, it is only to record how they found the answer, to note the last little surprise, the ultimate twist that concludes the story.

Harris was the one who cracked it. He was the older of the two agents, the talkative one who had asked me questions about my books. As it happened, he eventually went to a store and bought some of them, just as he had promised to do when he visited with his partner in July. I don't know whether he was planning to read them or was simply acting on a hunch, but the copies he bought turned out to have been signed with my name. He must have remembered what I told him about the curious autographs that had been cropping up in my books, and so he called here about ten days ago to ask me if I had ever been in that particular store, located in a small town just outside of Albany. I told him no, I hadn't, I'd never even set foot in that town, and then he thanked me for my help and hung up. I told the truth only because I saw no purpose in lying. His question had nothing to do with Sachs, and if he wanted to look for the person who had been forging my signature, what possible harm could come of that? I thought he was doing me a favor, but in point of fact I had just handed him the key to the case. He turned the books over to the FBI lab the next morning, and after a thorough search for fingerprints, they came up with a number of clean sets. One of them belonged to Sachs. Ben's name must have been known to them already, and since Harris was a crafty fellow, he wouldn't have missed the connection. One thing led to another, and by the time he showed up here yesterday, he had already fit the pieces together. Sachs was the man who had blown himself up in Wisconsin. Sachs was the man who had killed Reed Dimaggio. Sachs was the Phantom of Liberty.

He came here alone, unencumbered by the silent, scowling Worthy. Iris and the children were off swimming in the pond, and it was just me again, standing in front of the house as I watched him climb out of his car. Harris was in good spirits, more jovial than the last time, and he greeted me as though we were old familiars, colleagues in the quest to solve life's mysteries. He had news, he said, and he thought it might interest me. They'd identified the person who'd been signing my books, and it turned out to have been a friend of mine. A man named Benjamin Sachs. Now why would a friend want to do a thing like that?

I stared down at the ground, fighting back tears as Harris waited for an answer. 'Because he missed me,' I finally said. 'He went away on a long trip and forgot to buy postcards. It was his way of staying in touch.'

'Ah,' Harris said, 'a real practical joker. Maybe you can tell me something more about him.'

'Yes, there's a lot I can tell you. Now that he's dead, it doesn't matter anymore, does it?'

Then I pointed to the studio, and without saying another word I led Harris across the yard in the hot afternoon sun. We walked up the stairs together, and once we were inside, I handed him the pages of this book.

ff

Faber and Faber – a home for writers

Faber and Faber is one of the great independent publishing houses in London. We were established in 1929 by Geoffrey Faber and our first editor was T. S. Eliot. We are proud to publish prize-winning fiction and non-fiction, as well as an unrivalled list of modern poets and playwrights. Among our list of writers we have five Booker Prize winners and eleven Nobel Laureates, and we continue to seek out the most exciting and innovative writers at work today.

www.faber.co.uk – a home for readers

The Faber website is a place where you will find all the latest news on our writers and events. You can listen to podcasts, preview new books, read specially commissioned articles and access reading guides, as well as entering competitions and enjoying a whole range of offers and exclusives. You can also browse the list of Faber Finds, an exciting new project where reader recommendations are helping to bring a wealth of lost classics back into print using the latest on-demand technology.